CRIMSON MELODIES

CRIMSON MELODIES

LESLIE O'SULLIVAN

CITY OWL
PRESS

CRIMSON MELODIES
Rockin' Fairy Tales, Book 4

Cover Design by MiblArt. All stock photos licensed appropriately.

Edited by Lisa Green.

For information on subsidiary rights, please contact the publisher at info@cityowlpress.com.

Print Edition ISBN: 978-1-64898-361-0

Digital Edition ISBN: 978-1-64898-362-7

Printed in the United States of America

PRAISE FOR LESLIE O'SULLIVAN

"As full of heart and soul as the music it describes, Crimson Melodies drew me in with a fresh take on a classic tale, masterfully combining celebrity and monster romance vibes to give me everything I wanted and more!" — S.C. Grayson, author of *Beauty and the Blade*

"Submerging readers into a fantastical world, *Wild Azure Waves* is a love story swimming with music, mysticism, and magic." — *InD'tale*

"*Pink Guitars and Falling Stars* is a fast paced and very engaging read, with a constantly evolving main character and a colorful cast. The adventure wraps up nicely, and ends with a hint of what is next in the Rockin' Fairy Tales series. This is a great read if you are looking for an action-packed modern fairy tale with aspiring rock stars who fall from the sky." — *Paranormal Romance Guild*

"*Gilded Butterfly* is a unique and magical mashup of fairy tales, Shakespeare, and lore, unlike anything I've read before. At its heart, is a beautiful story about family, the destructive power of chasing fame and money, and the healing power of love. The twists, turns, and magic sprinkled throughout create an engaging story that brings a new kind of fairy tale to modern Hollywood." — *Megan Van Dyke, author of Second Star to the Left*

"*Pink Guitars and Falling Stars* is an interesting take on the story of Rapunzel...O'Sullivan has definitely nailed the initial animosity between Justin and Zeli. As they become closer, the relationship jumps off the page and morphs beautifully. There are awesome love scenes with a lot of description which pull the reader right in and keep a tight grip... A fascinating remix of a popular fairy tale with some very sexy differences. One to add to the e-reader and to be read list!" — *InD'tale*

"With wickedly clever wordplay, fresh and lovable characters, and an utterly unique take on a classic fairytale, *Pink Guitars and Falling Stars* is one of the swooniest romances I've ever read. You'll be cheering for B.A.S.E. jumper Justin to help Zeli escape her tower in the heart of Hollywood's twisted music industry and fall equally hard for their chosen family on the Boulevard. A romantic, heart-in-your-throat read!" — *Sarah Skilton, author of Fame Adjacent*

"Leslie O'Sullivan's narrative style in *Gilded Butterfly* celebrates truth, love, and heritage, and reads as pure poetry from the opening line until the end." — *InD'tale*

"*Pink Guitars and Falling Stars* reads like glitter and stardust, like a song of the heart set free and realizing every dream." —*Fairrryprose*

Pink Guitars and Falling Stars is a winner of a 2023 Gold Author Shout Reader Ready Awards "Top Pick."

Hot Set is a 2023 Holt Medallion Winner for Mid-Length Contemporary

To Cameron and Elizabeth, the IRL Claudio and Hero

ROCKIN' FAIRY TALES

BY LESLIE O'SULLIVAN

Pink Guitars and Falling Stars

Gilded Butterfly

Wild Azure Waves

Crimson Melodies

Emerald Spire

"I do love nothing in the world so well as you – is not that strange?"

-Benedick, Much Ado About Nothing, William Shakespeare

1

THE BOYS ARE BACK

ONCE I STEP INSIDE THE HOTEL CALIWOOD, I'LL HAVE TO ADMIT she's gone. My irrepressible, garage sale couture, brilliant, sharp-tongued lyricist and singing partner will not be waiting. She won't be waiting anywhere for me. Beatrice is no longer mine.

Was she ever?

God knows I was completely hers.

Fumes from the departing tour bus that's been our home for the better part of a year, gag me solidly in the present. The bus wrap with *Ben and the Boulevard Bunch's* logo will be peeled off tomorrow as our mobile digs are repurposed for the next band eager to hit the road. I'm blindsided with an urge to chase the bus and proclaim, "*The tour must go on.*"

It's all glamour and roadies until you find your ass home and off the Caliwood, Inc. record company's per diem dime. A bankroll we cranked into overtime partying too hard and long in Vegas after our final stop of the tour yesterday. We were scheduled to pull an all-nighter drive home, hitting our neon clad stretch of Hollywood Boulevard in the early morning, but our tour manager couldn't gather everyone's drunken asses onto the bus until this afternoon. Everyone being my band bros, Claude, D.G., and the two horn players and keyboardist we'd added to jazz up the tour. In the band's defense, the performance high from a sold-out crowd for a tour finale impairs one's power of good decision making.

Alfie, our bass guitarist, the keeper of the link between the melody and rhythm of the band's sound, thwarted my temptation to disappear into the oily shadows of Vegas and embrace a state of oblivion. He lovingly strong-armed me into the bus somewhere between round three and full shit-face status of our post-show champagne and whiskey fest. My personal saint knew a semblance of mental clarity would be required for me to hit the ground running today and finish the already overdue songs for our upcoming album.

I squeeze my eyes shut, a catalyst for calm. If I wasn't facing a blazing deadline to hit the studio in less than a month to record *Ben and the Boulevard Bunch's* next album, I'd have fought Alfie off and let Vegas swallow me whole. Anything to prevent the syrup of dread seeping through my veins at the thought of returning to the apartment I shared with the woman who was the damned love of my life until I royally detonated our relationship.

The combo of hangover brain and closed eyes hit me with a wave of vertigo. I flail for anything to support me. The stack of D.G.'s drum cases accommodates my sway. Luckily, I don't knock his precious babies to the asphalt.

My album deadline is a finger snap away. I've got a full roster of songs and not a single lyric. *B.B.*, before Beatrice, I was shit at lyrics, but with the help of a mountain of poetry books, I cobbled together passable phrases. *A.B.*, after Beatrice, every line I attempt to write is utter crap. The rhymes––empty and flat, cadences––pathetic, basically a reflection of who I've become.

The peeling sticker for *B 'n B + 3*, on D.G.'s drum case insta-grows a lump the size of a chinchilla in my throat.

B 'n B + 3.

It's a glaring reminder of my band's rebrand during that magical stretch when Beatrice wrote and performed with us. *Beatrice and Benedict Plus Three* chokes off the last of my wind.

Beatrice and Benedict

Even our damn names sound perfect together. The friction, the fire we conjured making music, and making love burned the world into beautiful glowing embers, until they reduced us to ash.

Benedict without Beatrice

A clingy pocket of L.A. heat permeates the late September evening. I lean my damp forehead against the stucco wall of Hotel Caliwood, feeling its texture press into my skin. The mixed bag of melancholy and relief that usually captures me at the end of a tour is totally out of whack. I'm all melancholy and no relief.

The last remnants of bus-following groupies who slipped in from Hollywood Boulevard while we unloaded, collect autographs and kisses from my OG bandbros, Claude, D.G., and Alfie before the lovely ladies scoot their booties toward the clubs. Our temporary brass and keyboard bandmates grab their gear. After a round of dude hugs, they Uber away.

Claude, our rhythm guitarist as well as the voice filling the holes left from our failed attempts at keeping a female vocalist, slaps me on the shoulder. "Holding up the Caliwood, my man?" He offers me his beer bottle. "Top off your tank and help us load in."

D.G., our drummer, wheels out a flatbed trolley. "Leonato says to set up in the Ghost Lounge for the start of the Haunted Hollywood Bar Crawl before we crash."

Alfie groans. "It doesn't start until tomorrow night. We can do it in the A.M.."

Claude downs his beer. "Dude's making us do it now as penance for the bus overtime." He sniffs his underarms. "I need fifteen so I can get fresh before my baby sees me."

Alfie carefully lifts one of D.G.'s drum cases onto the trolley. "Which baby?"

"The only baby that matters, my men—the beauteous Hero."

I explode with the hybrid of a snort and guffaw. "Beauteous, is she? I'm shocked you remember her name." After Claude's social media-documented tomcatting across the U.S., I can't believe the dude is deluded enough to think the daughter of our boss, Leonato Andante, the Caliwood's owner and C.E.O. of our label, will greet him with anything less than a kick to the balls.

"Yes, beauteous, Captain Moody," says Claude, tossing his empty bottle into the trash can by the Caliwood's service entrance.

Residual whiskey from last night mixes with disdain for Claude's callousness toward Hero to gift me with acid stomach. "You broke up with her before we left on tour. Hero's a worthwhile woman, Claude. Don't go sniffing around for a replay of something you discarded."

"Says the reigning king of the relationship fuck up," says Claude.

Heat explodes along the back of my neck. My face must telegraph imminent combustion because Alfie and D.G. step in.

"Claude, dude, cut Ben in on your intention," says Alfie, nudging Claude out of the reach of my right hook.

"Ben, I'm not talking about a quick trip to *Pound Town* with Hero."

I aim a finger between his eyes. "Says the reigning governor of *Pound Town*."

Alfie taps a finger to his chin. "I think you mean mayor of *Pound Town*. Towns don't have governors."

"He could be the count of *Pound Town*," says D.G. "Count Claude of *Pound Town*."

My three bandbros laugh. Usually, I'd dive right into their bawdy banter, but the thought of Claude going after Hero again because she's the closest thing available disgusts me. Hero became Beatrice's closest friend when we all lived in the Caliwood before this tour. I feel responsible to defend her since Bea isn't here to do it.

I must look tame enough because Claude clutches my shoulders to stare me in the eye. "Truth, bro. Before we left on tour,

I liked Hero. I ended things because it would be a shit move to keep her tied down while I was gone."

I shrug him off. "You broke up because you wanted to screw your way across America."

"And you didn't?"

Claude's right to call me out. I slapped multiple coats of one night hook-up paint on my miserable carcass to assuage a splintered soul after Beatrice disappeared without even bothering to flip me off. The series of women I used during the first half of the tour didn't deserve my disrespect, my indifference to satisfy anything besides the package behind my zipper and the freakin' Beatrice shadow in my heart. I was a selfish bastard. Claude makes empty sex look easy, but the aftermath of guilt for me only confirms I'm a self-serving piece of crap.

My dick-flinging behavior came to a grinding halt, pun intended, after an insane night at an upscale bar in Louisville where I indulged quite publicly with a post-show hookup against what I thought was a dark and secluded wall. Discretion had left the building, but cell phones had not. My social media shaming was one hundred percent deserved. I was not only mortified by my lack of decency but gutted at the thought of Beatrice seeing the pictures. I went cold turkey on hook-ups after that.

The sound of Claude's voice pulls focus from my musings back to the dingy alley.

"Ben, swear I'm going to do things right with Hero this time."

"I'll believe it when I see it." I walk away from him to our pile of equipment and suitcases.

Claude grabs my arm and spins me to face him. "Seriously, Ben. The shit I pulled on the road was meaningless. Flings without the feels. I'm ready for heart. Hero has always been the one for me, I just denied it. I'm going to go for it, bro, the whole deal. Hero Andante is the person I want to become a lifer for."

I stare at Claude. His sincerity is out of sync with the player he's been on tour. The shift is jarring.

"Truth, Ben. My man, Claude, is totally all in," said D.G. "Hero's more than a knuckle bulge for him." Our drummer grabs his crotch to illustrate.

Before Alfie can school D.G. to tone down his crassness where Hero's concerned, Claude flies at him and shoves the drummer so hard, he ass plants on cement.

Claude looms over D.G. shaking a fist. "Respect only when it comes to my baby."

I dart between the pair to drag Claude away as Alfie helps D.G. to his feet. "Dude, chill. We've got whiplash from your romantic lane change."

Claude gets right in my face. "I get I screwed up, Ben. You of all people should know how much Hero means to me."

I give him a gentle push away. "Claude, there's not a drop of blood in your body able to be seriously touched with love. Hero is a whim, a convenience. Not a forever."

"Shut it. You know she's a keeper. She's smart and sweet, and tolerant."

D.G. and Alfie snort in a duet at Claude's last adjective. Clearly, we share the opinion that anyone involved with Claude must be the essence of tolerant.

I shake my head. "If you're trying to talk me into the idea of the two of you, Claude, forget it. You had Hero, and you blew her off."

He meets my gaze with no hint of backing down. "I don't need to talk anyone into believing Hero is a rare jewel. She is as beautiful in looks and spirit as the first day of spring after a harsh winter."

Those aren't bad lyrics. Maybe I should tap Claude for words to my music. I level a look at him. "What do you know of harsh winter, dude? We live in L.A."

"It's a metaphor, Ben. Try a few and you might pull decent lyrics out of your ass before Leo kills our next album."

My mouth bobs open and shut at the low blow.

"New flash, Benedict. We're sick to death of your lectures on the evils of falling in love. You can preach all you want, but I've seen you sick in love. I bet a hundred bucks I'll see you that way again if you can ever cut your Beatrice cord."

"Claude," says Alfie, giving him the *lower your volume* signal we use on stage.

I purposefully raise my volume. "You'll see me sick with anger, with fever, or with hunger, but never again with love. If freaking Cupid comes sniffing near me, I'll stab the bastard with his own arrow."

The pity on their faces makes me wish I had an anti-love arrow to drive through every heart, sparing humanity from the pain surging through my body. I spin toward my suitcase, preparing for a spectacular mic drop of an exit. My step falters. These dudes are my band, my creative partners, my family. Our dynamic will repair itself over the next few weeks and when we get in studio after we've decompressed from a year of relentless togetherness. It's wrong of me to project my pain of being home without Beatrice on them. Time to rip off my emo bandage and assume my proper place as the decent and productive leader of *Ben and the Boulevard Bunch*.

A human whirlwind spins through the service entrance doors, and Santino Fedele lands in our midst. "The warriors have returned from battle. Welcome home, gents."

His positive energy dilutes the tension I splattered over the band. After what Santino endured, it's a freakin' miracle the dude retained his gift of erasing shadows. Fading scars crisscross his face from the multiple skin graphs and other surgeries that put him back together. Santino barely survived a massive explosion on the night he led the charge along with the singer, Justin Time, to free pop diva, Zeli, from Grant Gothel's stronghold, Rampion Ranch.

In the aftermath, Gothel landed in a prison that burned down in a killer fire. Justin and Zeli got hitched and now run Rampion Records. It was during Santino's convalescence the musical duo hooked Santino and me up. His cyber makeover for *Ben and the Boulevard Bunch* resulted in sweet ticket sales for our tour. I snagged him pronto as our permanent Internet marketing magician.

Santino scratches at the riot of tight brown curls on his head. Our tour stylist once attacked me with a perm in an attempt to create a fresh look after Beatrice bailed, and we returned to four fellows making music. Epic fail. What works au natural on Santino makes me look like a tool in search of a hip vibe.

"Lookin' good, Tino," says Alfie, embracing our friend.

Santino bounces on the balls of his feet. "I'm a dude filled with grati*tude*. Glad it shows."

Damn. Everyone comes up with better lyrics than me.

Claude nods to the superhero print high-top tennis shoes on Santino's feet. "Those fellows have nothing on your superpowers, man."

The two bust out a ridiculously complicated handshake routine before dissolving into laughter when it falls apart.

Claude raises his palms to beg off. "Out of practice." He grabs a beer from our dwindling supply and twists the top off with a flourish before presenting it to Santino.

I remember Claude encouraging the choreography of their goofy handshake in the days when Santino was rehabbing movement in his hands. It reminds me to appreciate the good guy Claude is at his core. I'm being too snippy about his renewed focus on Hero. Sometimes a dude must run the gauntlet of being ridiculous before he realizes what's important in life. If Claude is ready to appreciate Hero and thoroughly return her feelings for him, who am I to cut that down?

I wish I'd drunk from a romantic well of truth before I chased Beatrice from my life.

Santino takes a long swig and then smacks his lips. "You guys always stock the good stuff. What's with this swill?"

D.G. roots around in our Styrofoam cooler and lifts a handful of ice that he lets cascade through his fingers before shaking the water off. "We did when Caliwood, Inc. was footing our beer bill. Here's hoping Leonato stocked the Ghost Bar with primo brew for the bar crawl."

Santino windmills his hands. The guy's energy is a renewable resource that could power all the neon on Hollywood Boulevard. He's having a good day. Occasionally on video chats during the tour, he'd go dark and angry over what I thought was insignificant crap, rip me a new one, and then disappear for a while. Later, he'd hail me full of embarrassment and regret. It broke my heart when he confided in me that his hair-trigger rage was lingering nastiness from his accident and painful recovery.

"Speaking of..." Santino jerks a thumb over his shoulder. "The boss wants to meet as soon as you're finished unloading."

I whip out my cell to check for a Leonato summons. Nothing. Hopefully, he just wants to brief us on any last minute deets of the crawl tomorrow night before we crash in our own cozy beds.

My lonely bed.

It'll be the first time back in it without Beatrice.

As I help Alfie lift the last piece of equipment onto the trolley, my gut drops to my shoes.

Shit. I'm sure Leo's going to troll me for an update on lyrics and a title for the album.

All I have to offer is a flatline.

2

THE GHOST LOUNGE

WE'RE GREETED WITH A SEA OF TOURIST PHONE CAMERAS AND heartfelt shouts of "Welcome home," as the band makes their official entrance through the lobby of Hotel Caliwood. At the behest of said gathered fans, we rock a few poses in front of the imposing multi-tiered fountain in the lobby.

The cold trickle of spray on my neck zips me back to a Christmas Eve not long ago. The singer, Tressa Divine, appeared to use the ghosts of the Caliwood to construct a bizarre wall of ice to trap Beatrice and me while the woman spouted words sounding eerily like a spell or other nonsense. Tressa was pissed I'd chosen Beatrice to join the band as our new female singer instead of her. Even now, echoes of the ice shards I'd felt that night chill my blood.

"Ben?" Claude elbows me and nods to the grand stairway with its blood red carpet and gilded bannisters.

I swipe the moisture off my neck and follow the band, climbing the steps to the mezzanine where the Ghost Lounge bar and performance space awaits.

No one apart from Beatrice and I witnessed Tressa's phenomenon that Christmas Eve. Instead of attempting to convince Leo and the band we'd had a high-level Caliwood Hotel ghost encounter, we kept the weird to ourselves. We chalked it up to the sour grapes of rejection. Beatrice scoffed when I suggested her rival, Tressa, had a bit of otherworldly presence with her odd glow and effect on those she targeted. Claude and I swore we'd imagined snowfall in the Ghost Lounge during Tressa's audition.

Despite her attempt at skepticism, Beatrice became obsessed for a while, hunting in old newspaper archives and tons of websites for evidence to prove a similar ghostly event occurred at the Caliwood. She uncovered some strange stuff like a testimony from guests swearing they'd walked in on an awards ceremony from the 1920s in the main ballroom and lost time until they found themselves back in their rooms. In the end, Bea landed on Tressa being guilty of ghostploitation and a form of targeted mind control on us.

As the rest of the band approaches the entrance to the Ghost Lounge, I run a finger along a full-length mirror in a Rococo frame outside the door. It is well documented ghosts and Hotel Caliwood exist in an ethereal partnership. The spirits pipe up when and where they choose, not necessarily when guests attempt to initiate contact. The hotel is a hot spot for ghost hunters and visitors seeking an experience with the other side. Being neither seeker nor skeptic, I'm cool if the ghosties hang in their plane and me in mine. Nevertheless, I toss out a silent message for the Caliwood's spirits not to feel obligated to offer me a personal welcome home. I'm in no shape to deal with melting wallpaper or incomprehensible mutterings wafting through the air. Facing Leonato with non-existent lyrics is scary enough.

We strut through the door into the dimly lit Ghost Lounge. It's closed tonight while preparations are made for tomorrow night's crawl. Leonato Andante is behind the counter in a heated discussion with the bartender. Leo points at certain bottles of liquor and stashes others beneath the bar. I hear the boss bark something along the lines of "*Hiding the good stuff.*"

I smile at the antics of the King of Micromanagement. The sole hint Leonato is in his sixties is scant streaks of gray in his hair. The dude is more fit than I am and equals Santino's energy level. Hero's pop runs Hotel Caliwood and the Caliwood, Inc. record company with the hands-on capabilities of an octopus.

Claude's voice booms through the space. "Good sir, Leonato, we have returned."

Leo lifts the hinged portion of the bar top and meets us halfway across the floor. He pats the side of Claude's face too hard to be affectionate. "You're late."

Before Claude can grovel, Leo's expression downshifts from hard-ass to benefactor as he grabs Claude's shoulders.

"Welcome home, you mangy scoundrels." After a round of wrist grabs and embraces, Leo waves a hand at the end of the bar where six shots of what I assume is the good stuff await us. He throws a fatherly arm around my shoulders. "Going solo, Ben? I assumed you'd arrive with a feminine conquest on your arm."

Dig received. Thank goodness the lighting in the lounge is too dim for Leo to see my face deepen into what I'm sure is a rusty blush. "I will cop to my less than gallant choices in temporary companionship at the beginning of the tour."

"Do I detect a dollop of regret from Bad Boy Benedict?"

I cringe at the less than flattering nickname social media saddled me with.

Leo gives me a shove. "Infamy raises the bar on ticket sales and downloads. Dangle it wherever you choose, Bad Boy Benedict."

His praise of my shady behavior feels like another layer of grunge added to what I already wear. "I was working through some shit."

Leo's expression softens. "And?"

I swallow hard. "Have you heard from her?"

He presses his lips into a line that sprouts age crinkles at the corners of his mouth. The arm around my shoulders tightens. "No, son. Neither has Hero."

So be it. We're all part of the same dust cloud Beatrice left behind in her lightning-fast exit. Not even a word to Hero. Damn.

Leo clears his throat and drops his arms. "So, Benny. Let's talk album. I've booked your keyboardist from the road to work with you in the studio. What else are you seeing? Horns? Maybe violins on the ballads?"

"Are you still set on hitting the studio on our original timeline?"

Business Leo stiffens. "It's the only way the album has a chance in hell of dropping on time." My head pounds from the less than delightful combo of hangover and stress as Leo lowers his voice and leans in. "Make no mistake, you're still on a short leash, Benedict, since you and Beatrice trashed my hotel with your breakup. Consider yourself lucky internet hits and the success of the tour still clock you as a major draw for the label."

The virtual collar attached to Leo's leash tightens around my neck.

"We'll cash in on the playboy's back-in-town angle. In fact, Prospero Tempesta wants to book the band for a charity gig next month to create grants for up-and-coming artists." He snaps his fingers. "We'll use the forum for you to tease a song from the new album."

There's no point lying to him. My stakes in this album are his stakes as well. "I've got music that'll rip the heart from your chest, shred it, and then put it back together, but no lyrics." I swipe a hand down my face. "Leo, I'm totally blocked. Nothing I did, not the screwing around, climbing a freakin' mountain in Appalachia, or meditating made lyrics flow. I speak the language of notes, not words. My attempts are heartless shit."

His barrel chest expands and then settles before it can pop the buttons on his shiny dress shirt. "You've never been a damn poet, but you made it work."

"It ain't working, Leo." I'm on the verge of collapsing into a pile of bones under the weight of his disappointment. "We're going to need to hire a lyricist."

This close, lights behind the bar illuminate his face. It's red on the way to purple rage.

"With less than a fucking month left? We can maybe milk a song or two from a third party if anyone bites given our deadline. Hard truth, Benedict—get your head on straight and give me freakin' poetry." Leo bypasses the shot glasses and grabs the bottle of *Musician's Tears* whiskey. "I should send your sorry ass to the pop factory in Sweden for a rebrand if you can't produce."

He tilts the bottle to his lips and takes a long, slow drag topped off with a percussive growl.

The rest of the band freezes with half-raised shot glasses in their hands.

Santino clues into the virtual fireballs flying between Leo and me and plays peacemaker with his signature cheeriness. "Here's to a kick-ass kickoff to the Haunted Hollywood Bar Crawl."

I grab a shot and join my band in the toast. After slamming the glass harder than necessary on the red glass top of the bar, I move my arms conductor style. "Let's rock this set up so we can count Z's before rehearsal tomorrow."

"Rehearsal," groans D.G. "Damn, Ben. We've been rehearsing for a year. Call the set order, and we'll deliver."

The rumble of a bellhop with our equipment trolley interrupts the impending mutiny. I swear Santino kangaroo hops toward the stage. "I'll give you a hand until Hero gets back and I'm relegated to décor duty."

"Hero's on the way?" says Claude, glancing around the lounge. He flaps his T-shirt away from his sweaty skin and runs a hand through his hair.

"Any minute," says Santino, lifting the top drum case onto the edge of the stage. "She's been road tripping to every Halloween outlet between Santa Barbara and San Diego to grab discount creepy ghost shit and a slew of skeleton band projectors she preordered to do up the lounge for the crawl."

Claude smiles. "The woman never does anything halfway."

Alfie waves an arm. "Isn't there enough creepy ghost shit at the Caliwood already?"

Santino chuckles. "If only they haunted on command." He wiggles his fingers. "And don't think I haven't tried to connect." He and Claude double-team D.G.'s largest drum case while our drummer snores, head down on the bar.

Leo's already hot about my impending failure. God knows how he'll take Claude's post-dump reapproach to his only daughter.

Right on cue, I hear the high-pitched, beautifully feminine squeal of Hero Andante from the door of the Ghost Lounge. "Babe!" She bullet-trains it toward the stage.

Claude straightens, his smile catching the glow of the amber overhead LED stage light.

My case of cotton mouth intensifies when my jaw drops. I can't believe what I'm seeing. Is Hero going to forgive the despicable way Claude treated her, not to mention his sexploits plastered all over social media for the last year? I gave her more credit. An urge to block her trajectory and talk sense into that angel-faced head of hers almost wins until she bypasses Claude entirely and rockets into Santino's arms.

Hero molds her body against his in an intimate way while crushing her lips to her lover's smiling mouth. Their kiss is a beautiful thing, the perfect blend of passion and sweetness.

Santino ends it, swinging Hero to his side under a possessive arm. "Wow, if this is what I can expect after three days apart, what will the week away sailing with my dad buy me?"

Hero swats his ass. They beam at each other. I know those expressions. They are totally in love. I've rocked that face with Beatrice. Wonder morphs into panic as my gaze darts to Claude.

My bandbro looks like he's taken a guitar pick to the eye. Rapid blinking swiftly melts into a volatile WTF face.

"Ben, Alfie," says Hero, flitting over to grab us in a hug. She catches sight of D.G. slumped at the bar and giggles. "And the drummer goes down."

Hero's smile fades as she pivots to face Claude, her voice flat. "Hello, Claude."

Before he speaks, she moves to Santino's side and takes his hand. Hero locks her gaze on Claude while Santino fidgets. "We've got news," she says, a shy smile blooming across her face.

Santino stoops to whisper in Hero's ear, and she lays a finger to his lips. Together they face Alfie, Claude, and me. Alfie elbows D.G. to wake him up. Leonato takes what appears to be a protective step closer to his daughter.

I move alongside Claude. Heat flies off his body in waves. Hands, so steady and sure on his guitar strings, tremble.

Claude's voice is as shaky as his digits. "What's up, Hero?"

Santino raises his chin. "Hero and I are getting married."

Hero gestures to the bar. "You're all invited to our engagement bash, right here the night after the bar crawl ends."

"Dude," says Alfie and bear hugs Santino.

Santino laughs as he extricates himself from the bassist. "After my accident and through all the surgeries, I swore from now on to grab happiness and hold tight. If fate tries to wrestle that away from me, it's in for a nasty surprise. From now on, this sucker..." He thumps a fist to his chest with uncharacteristic aggression. "Will come out swinging instead of lying down." Literal Hero worship softens his expression. "Hero is the happiness I will kick ass for."

Hero rests both hands on his shoulder and rises on her toes to kiss his cheek. Santino dons the doofy smile of smitten love as he gazes at her.

Claude is in motion before I can grab him. He gets right in Santino's face as Leo yanks Hero free from the path of the raging guitarist.

"You fucking thief. Did you start sniffing around her the second our tour bus turned the corner?" He shoves Santino, sending him backwards until our webmaster's calves meet the facing of the stage. He plunks onto his ass next to the stack of drum cases.

"Tino," yells Hero, pulling away from Leo to fly toward her fiancé.

Santino's good guy mood darkens. He's charging Claude before Hero can reach him. I clamp onto Claude's arm to swing him out of Santino's path. "Fizz the hell down, Claude."

My bandbro jerks from my grasp with enough force to send pain shooting through my shoulder. He raises fists to confront a red-face and ready-to-boil-over Santino.

Leonato jumps between them, smacking a palm on each man's chest. "Walk away, Claude."

Hero darts to her father's side. "How dare you, Claude?"

Claude grabs her wrist. "Hero, babe, you can't do this. I love you. I screwed up. My head is on straight now. I'm ready to commit."

Now Leo holds Santino back as Hero yanks her hand free.

"Commit?" growls Hero. "Love me now, do you, Claude? Oh, is that what, 'I've got to cut you loose, honey,' translates to these days?"

"I didn't want you to feel tied down while I was on tour. I broke it off for your sake."

Claude sounds so genuine, I'm surprised he doesn't drop to one knee and spout love poetry.

Hero stabs a finger at Claude. "You did it for you. You aren't the real thing, Claude. You never were. Commitment isn't on your playlist." Hero gazes at a panting Santino, concern etched on her face. "I connected with someone who gets it." She whips around to face Claude. "Someone who doesn't swat love aside like his next pickleball shot."

I grab the back of Claude's tee. "Come on. I'll buy you a drink." Looking over my shoulder, I signal Santino and Hero to head out so I can attempt to diffuse Claude. Santino is still hot as hell, but thankfully, Hero takes the hint. Claude stumbles with me to a barstool.

I clench my teeth tight enough for my jaw to give a slight pop when Hero's sobs drift across the lounge. For a moment, I consider following them, but Hero doesn't seem wary of her man's spiking anger. I never shipped Hero and Santino, but damn, they totally work.

Poor Hero. She wanted to share her happiness with us, and Claude shat on it. Happiness, the elusive get I pissed away with Beatrice. It's my job now to mop up Claude's spillage. I wish Bea and her blunt truths were here to handle this with me.

I grab the bottle of *Musician's Tears* and pour a shot for Claude. He downs it. I pour another as I say, "There's never an amp to kick over when you need one, eh, man?"

Claude swipes a hand across his mouth and snorts. "Hero was always the queen of microaggression. She'll come around."

"And you're the freakin' king of macroaggression." I shake my head. No doubt Hero did intend a sting for Claude with her news. I love my bandbro, but I can't deny he deserves a pinch for the way he underappreciated Hero. "There's no crime in Hero letting us know what's what. It was a jerk move to go after Santino. You need to reset, man."

Claude grabs the front of my T-shirt but releases me before he blows. "I'll bet the bastard grabbed every picture of me with women to post on social and then flashed them at Hero. He wore her down, then moved into my space."

I slam back a shot and immediately regret it. Moving behind the bar to the fridge, I grab a water and drain the bottle. An alcohol cleanse is overdue. "You put your space up for sale."

"Ben, I believed she'd appreciate the breather from me and my fucknuttery. I didn't intend to deal her a permanent slice of separation. I am down to commit."

"You're deluded, Claude. You want Hero while we're at home base, but you'd never honor the tether when we tour."

"For her, I'd totally reform. I just need to get her alone and spill my soul."

Claude is a freight train going downhill without brakes when he sets his mind on something.

"May I remind you Santino is our friend and a good guy? He'd never sabotage you." I reach around to scratch an itch on my back. "Face it, Claude, marriage is not the right gig for us. We're transient. Being tied down is the death of freedom to hit the road and rock our tunes. Santino is a grow roots guy. Hell, the dude owns the long block of Hollywood Boulevard from Fedele Costumes to the Caliwood. You've always known Hero digs her Hollywood nest. They make sense together."

"Santino is a fucking thief, and you're a fucking liar with your freedom bullshit. If Beatrice—"

Her name triggers me. I knock Claude off his barstool. "Leave her out of it."

I spike hotter than Claude. The Ghost Lounge turns claustro as Claude's malignant cluelessness, potential album failure, my engagement envy, and the phantom presence of Beatrice close in. I crave air and the Hollywood night.

I grab the nearly empty bottle of whiskey off the bar and head for the one place I can crumble without an audience.

3

UP ON THE ROOFTOP

THE ROOF OF HOTEL CALIWOOD WILL ALLOW ME BOTH SWEET memories of Beatrice and solitude to clear my head. Our first night together and the night we found one another again was under the glow of the ten-foot-high, red neon letters cutting through the darkness to announce the presence of the iconic hotel.

Beatrice and I loved to name the stars in the sky and the stars below embedded in concrete on Hollywood Boulevard. I want to sit on the ratty old couch the band and I dragged up there to build an open-air man cave, close my eyes, and replay good times. Maybe then I'll find my reset.

The elevator shimmies and shakes as it creeps its way to the top floor of the Caliwood. I down the rest of the whiskey, then fold in half to rest my head against the handrail. Mercifully, no one joins me on my journey north. When the doors open, I stare at a tall mirror in a dark mahogany frame topped with a Georgian style pediment against the wall. For a heartbeat, I swear I see the laughing 1950's blond bombshell actress, Audra McLain, blow me a kiss from the glass.

Thank goodness, I'm alone in the hallway and won't be called upon to confirm I've seen one of the famous ghosts rumored to reside here with us at the hotel.

Since there's no witness my lunacy, I'm free to speak to the mirror. "You're on the wrong floor, doll." Ms. McLain is rumored to materialize most frequently in a mirror on the main floor down a short hallway near the elevators. That particular ghost-friendly looking glass allegedly hung in the twelfth-floor suite she occupied here at the Caliwood.

I weave along the hallway past the hotel rooms repurposed into apartments for those of us who call the Caliwood home. I hear low voices in Hero's place and nearly knock to check in on Santino and her. I want to suggest they bop to Santino's apartment over Fedele Costumes since Claude's digs are next to Hero's and the walls here are thin.

Still in avoidance mode, I breeze by her door and whisper, "Sorry, friends. I'm too strung out to be of service." I make a note to send Hero a dozen magenta star lilies, her favorites, as an engagement congrats.

After one last tip of the whiskey, so as not to waste any remaining sweet drops, I tuck the bottle into one of the large, black sconces set on flocked vintage wallpaper. The dark maroon damask pops in sharp relief against its gold backing. Leo poured barrels of cash repapering the walls of the hotel with its original wall coverings. Below the sconce is an out-of-place, modern-looking fixture with a fire extinguisher. Beatrice used to joke that the old-fashioned glass cases with axes were more practical since you could bust your way out of fires and take down invading vandals with the weapon. She even snagged one of the old metal cases complete with axe we found in a hotel storeroom to decorate our apartment wall with it as a nostalgic homage to the Caliwood. It's still collecting dust under the bed, waiting to be hung.

One more thing Bea and I never got around to doing.

I nearly trip when I drop my head back to study the wood parquet ceiling. My bark of a laugh is so loud, I cover my mouth.

Damn, if I were a ghost, I'd choose the Caliwood as my home. Its shadowy, old school Hollywood vibe is definitely on point for ghostly habitation. I imagine our drummer slipping down these halls for eternity. We call the dude D.G. for Dead Guy since we voted him most likely to stay put and haunt the Caliwood after his demise.

When I stumble to the end of the hallway, the handle of the polished wood railing next to the six carpeted steps leading to the library stabs me in the stomach. Am I too drunk to hit the roof? Screwed depth perception could send me over the short rail to splatter Benedict Boyd goo across the 5th Dimension's star on the Walk of Fame. Then again, adding a rocker ghost to the Caliwood's roster could increase its cache even more. Leo's going to kill me anyway when I come up empty-handed for album lyrics. I could spare him the murder charge.

Leaning on the rail for support, I climb to the door of the library. The elevator used to go all the way to the library until Leo closed off the top stop while we were on tour. He never did explain why. I grab the brass knob and turn. It's locked.

Frustration streams up the center of my chest. I'm desperate to get to the roof and attempt to launch the specter of Beatrice clinging to my spirit over the Hollywood Hills. Until I do, there's zip hope I'll pull any lyrics out of my ass. I yank and wiggle the knob with the drunken strength of an entire rugby team, and it comes off in my hand. Poking a finger into the mechanism, I find the release and push the door open.

The knob falls from my grip onto wood flooring as I gawk at the library. Pressing the heels of both hands to my eyes and taking a second look changes nothing. This is not the dusty, cobweb-covered storeroom that used to be nothing more than a pass-through to the roof. The space is utterly transformed.

The once-empty, nearly ceiling-high, built-in shelves teem with stacks of books. I check a few titles to find poetry collections including Keats, Byron, and even Poe. Yeah, Poe tracks for this space where I once encountered a small girl in ringlets who begged me to read her a story before she vanished. Other shelves boast expanses of romance novels from Jane Austen to more modern rom-com flavored love stories.

A Victorian sofa that would look at home in my great grandparents' living room sits before the fireplace now glowing with embers of a spent fire. I never linger in this room. It's a surprise to discover the fireplace is damn big, as high as my shoulder and as wide as the counter in my apartment's kitchenette. Instead of the splintery old piece of furniture formerly occupying the center of the room, a ten-foot-long, cherry oak, trestle-style dining table sits in regal elegance that would be more at home in the Palace of Versailles. Ornate carvings decorate its facing, but I can't make out their design. The light from the resurrected cut-glass chandelier that once held the odd bird's nest from transitory feathery guests sneaking in from the roof is too dim. There's a single, throne-sized, high-back padded chair at one end, but none for guests. Papers and a collection of silver pens are scattered across the tabletop.

Drab wood walls appear highly polished, reflecting light. No dust tickles my nose the way it always did when I passed through here before. The most bizarre addition is the row of four marble statues lined up against the lone wall without bookshelves housing the now out-of-service elevator stop. They vary in size from a childlike figure to the imposing form of an athletic-looking fellow. Each holds a torch with a low but steady burning flame, blue at the center with white around the edges. These unattended fire hazards can't be legal in a room with enough kindling to set the Caliwood ablaze.

The first time I brought Beatrice through the library she swore it had a disturbing energy, but my brave woman powered through the creepy space to share the roof with me. I always assumed its *woo woo* factor as Bea called it, meant the library was a hotel ghost hangout when they weren't toying with guests. Now the huge room rocks a cozy, timeless vibe like an artist's garret. Besides writing detritus on the table, a glass dome rests in its center. Inside, it holds an open book on a pedestal. Not an artist's garret, a writer's nook. Seems Leo, ever the idea man, upgraded this long-forgotten library into a rental space to attract creative types.

Well, the renter better mind their torches more closely. Since there's no laptop or other personal belongings, I assume said author uses the space during the day and skedaddles at night. I'll mention the hazard to Leo. Moving close to the first torch, I'm surprised to feel not even a lick of heat from the flame. I blow on it as a test. As soon as the breath leaves my mouth, every torch in the row snuffs out along with the last gasp of the cinders in the fireplace and the chandelier. I'm plunged into complete freakin' darkness.

Silence screams when you lose the light. My breath comes in short gasps as I edge my way along the bookshelves to the rooftop door.

"Anyone here?"

The hotel ghosts rock a reputation for being mischievous but not harmful. Have things changed since we've been on tour? A clench in my chest sends a spray of whiskey to burn my esophagus.

"Hello?"

A faint bubbling sounds from the end of the room near the hallway door opposite the now cold fireplace. I half expect some brand of new aquatic ghosties, bearing tridents or shark-headed imps to attack as the room fills with water.

Freakin' imagination. "It's the plumbing pipes, you drunk jackass."

My next slap against the wall lands on the knob to the roof stairwell. I throw it open, scramble through the frame, and slam the door to the transformed library. Practically crawling, I make my way up the utility stairs to the rooftop door and fall into fresh air. I lay on my back, willing the stars to help me catch my breath.

My alcohol cleanse starts now. I'm definitely taking the fire escape to climb inside the Caliwood and avoid traversing the WTF vibes I just experienced in the updated library.

I drag myself over to plop onto the couch sitting in the middle of the area rug we pilfered from a hotel suite for our private band hangout. Better yet, I'll sleep off my freak out here under the stars. When I wake tomorrow, I'll be *Back to Work Benedict*, not sloppy, memory hounded, drunk, overactive imagination Benedict.

I stretch out on the couch and stare at the Hotel Caliwood sign above me.

Something is off with the H. There's a lump blocking the crossbar. I squint, trying to make sense of the blight on the sign. It appears the lump has a body and—are those wings? I chuckle. Ah, did Leo finally sweet-talk or money-talk the old First National Bank building out of one of its gargoyles? I'm surprised he didn't install a spotlight to accent his prize.

Being kind to my throbbing head, I slowly sit to reach for one of the blankets stowed in the chest of drawers we dragged up to our rooftop hideaway when a shadow interrupts the red glow of the Hotel Caliwood sign. Standing, I back slowly toward the edge of the rooftop so I can get a better look at the letters. Now a portion of one of the uprights of the H is blocked. Is it my angle or did whatever is chilling on the sign move?

I use my hands to block ambient light to focus on the H and quickly drop them. Shit, there's a big ass bird perched on the sign. My addled mind attempts to calculate the size of a bird big enough to fill the space between the H uprights. An eagle would appear like a sparrow compared to this flying nightmare.

The creature shifts slightly until it's silhouetted against red neon. Its shape comes into clearer focus. It's got jointed ostrich legs and what seems to be a headdress of feathers. And wings that look...

...Holy crap. Those aren't wings, they're arms, and if I'm not totally off my nut, those arms rock bird of prey type claws. The damn thing lifts its wingy arms, poised to take off. I hold my breath and will my pounding heart to chill. What if the thing can sense the electrical impulses of my fear like a shark? I freeze in place to avoid drawing its attention and pray it flies the hell away. Judging by the huge bird's size, it might consider me a juicy dinner.

When it bends its legs and raises its head to the sky, I suck in a breath.

Good bird. Fly away.

When I crouch to be less noticeable, my hand knocks against an empty beer bottle and sends it rolling straight into the low wall surrounding the rooftop. The *clank* of glass against concrete pierces the white noise of the traffic on Hollywood Boulevard below.

My gaze darts to the H. To my horror, the thing's head pans side to side, searching the rooftop as if to locate the sound. Can birds see in the dark or am I thinking of bats? God, I hope it's bats. Just when the thing appears to give up the hunt, its head tilts to point directly —at me.

The roar-screech of the beastly bird flays my eardrums. I bolt to the roof door and leap inside the stairwell. Screw avoiding the bizarre happenings in the refabbed library. I choose unexplained blackouts over the living gargoyle on the roof.

When I slam into the library, it's as bright as Hollywood at noon on a summer day with a now blazing fire, relit torches, and a glittering chandelier. The bubbling sound I thought I heard earlier is replaced with undecipherable low murmurs. There's not a living soul to be seen in the room. I don't stop to question any of the weird and fly through the space to the door I broke getting in.

The knob is back in place.

4

THE SONGBOOK

MY LANDING ON THE COUCH IS TOO ROUGH. I REBALANCE TO KEEP IT from tipping over backwards. Claws embed deep into the cushions. It takes considerable maneuvering to work them free without destroying the fabric.

A second cry of surprise, after the first that frightened Benedict off, rips from my throat into the Hollywood night.

My Benedict is back.

Hero told me the band was returning from tour today, but I wasn't prepared for the agony of seeing the mop of blond hair I used to run my hands through in real time. If I tried now, my overenthusiastic claws could pierce him through to the skull.

My heart skitters. Benedict came up the stairwell. He's been in the library. How? The Dark Vinyl Artists, the quartet of horrors I'm bound to, compelled Leonato to seal off the elevator stop and lock off the one remaining door.

"The songbook!" My screech is nails on the chalkboard even to me.

I clomp across the rooftop, hating my triple-jointed legs and the three wicked talons where five fingers and five toes used to be. I miss fingernails and toenails. What I would give for a mani-pedi with polish to match the outfits Hero smuggles me from Flo and Edie's vintage clothing store.

Feathers along the back of my arms and legs ripple and stiffen in panic. To fit through both top and bottom stairwell doors, my beastly body twists, dips, and contorts. Once inside the library, I'm caught in a whirlwind of whispers repeating the same pair of phrases.

He's the one. He's come.

Ignoring them, I rush to the glass dome in the middle of the table with the songbook. When I see it is undisturbed, I let out a long slow keen and run a hand over my beak as feathers settle back into place.

"How did he get in?" I bumble to the other side of the table and bark at the four statues along the wall. "This could have been a disaster."

Three of the four statues shimmer as each torch they hold snuffs out. One by one, marble casings waver as the trio of my ghostly companions leaks into the room. Their bright blue tinged forms shake and stretch as if stiff from hanging inside the marble. The display is completely unnecessary. The ghost of Audra McLain once told me they do it for my sake to act more human than they are. I wonder if it's also to convince themselves they still hold a drop of humanity within their transparent splendor.

Audra swoops around behind me. I know she's trying to fool with the feathers on my head as if she could train the things into a look she'd deem stylish.

"It wasn't me, sweetie, but I enjoyed the view. Your Benedict is a tall drink of water."

I shake my head to discourage her. "He's not my Benedict."

"For now," she says and floats around to dot a kiss on each of my cheeks. The touch feels like a snowflake landing on bare skin.

"Based on the way you speak after your friend Hero shares news of him, the mantle Bene*dick* fits the man better," says my handsome leading man ghost, Montague Curtz. "I assure you, it wasn't I who allowed him to breech your fortress."

Monty is quite the hottie himself with the physique of a Venice Beach bodybuilder and hair tousled to *Golden Age of Hollywood* perfection. Not even Audra and her coif obsession dare to touch it. Monty is eternally wearing slacks, a button-down shirt open at the top to show a hint of dark chest hair, and a sweater thrown over one shoulder. He's not a Mensa candidate, but his charm reminds me the world can be a positive place. I'd love to get him in jeans and a T-shirt.

"Breech my fortress? Rehearsing for a period piece, Monty?"

He kneel-floats in front of me, pretending to kiss my hand. "'Tis true, Lady Beast. I'm soon to walk the boards in a classic on my beloved Broadway stage. A man must never forget his roots." Monty hisses the double esses. "Graham, will you be accompanying me to rehearsal?"

"I'm sorry, Monty, but I'm off to tonight's festivities. I've got to pick up my date." Graham fusses with his tuxedo jacket and cummerbund.

My fastidious ghost buddy perpetually primps for an award's show that ended eighty plus years ago. It makes me sad knowing if this is his default afterlife loop, he never made it to the event.

"Let's share a cab," says Audra, threading an arm through Graham's elbow to indulge his scripted evening, and with a whoosh and a blast of cool wind the three drift through the library wall. It's heartening they play at life, and it appears to bring them joy. The familiar sense of dizziness that sweeps over me whenever they leave has me grasping for the edge of the long wooden table. Their marble counterparts remain with unlit torches, the sign the ghosts are currently not in residence.

My heart breaks for the trio endlessly replaying their past. Anytime I can jostle my friends out of their repetitive scripts, I do. We've had the crossing to the other side chat numerous times, but they swear the Caliwood is home and have no urge to leave. They play at inhabiting a wider world in their ghostly forms, but it's nothing more than sparkly ghost talk. Here they stay.

I stare at the smallest statue, still literally holding a torch for her past. "Sassy? Is there something you want to tell me?"

A blue sheen overlaying the statue of Sassy Turnbull, a massively famous and adorable child star from the 1930s shakes her head. Even in the transparent image, her chubby cheeks and scores of ringlets are clear.

"You're not in trouble, honey." I tell the little girl. "I just need you to understand Benedict can't come into the library. It's too dangerous. He might ruin the songbook. Do you understand?"

Sassy's ghostly shape nods and then seeps back into the statue, the small blue flame telling me she's present but dormant. When the torch flames blaze yellow-orange, I know my friends are poised and ready for action.

Leaving Sassy to whatever ghosts do in marble, I turn to the table and carefully lift the dome off the songbook. Mentally judging the number of pages left, I take a deep breath. Benedict has returned. The timer on my end game of being Beatrice will speed up its previously languorous pace.

"He can't come in here without warning," I amend to any ghost within earshot. If I'm to have any hope of not living the rest of my life as a harpy, Ben needs to enter this library and connect with me.

My mind drifts to the best and worst nights of my life. I was over the moon when Benedict overrode his bandmate's decision to choose me for their female singer and welcomed me into the group. If I'd only known then who Tressa truly was, my life would be blessed instead of cursed.

I tidy the piles of staff paper on the table and pull out the sheet I keep tucked under the songbook's polished dark wood base. Here are the words Tressa spoke that fateful Christmas Eve. Ben and I blew it by not taking her chant seriously and writing it off as sour grapes. We kept our own personal ghost encounter in Hotel Caliwood on the down-low. What the hell had we been thinking?

The woman I know now to be a powerful enchantress spewed words reeking of bile and revenge. Ben and I had been too into each other to understand Tressa's bitter rhyme held the weight of our potential doom. I read the curse for the thousandth time, searching for any loophole to extend its deadline or show me any alternate way to kill the spell that turned me into this harpy.

In truth, I perpetually search for redemption within its phrases for proof the curse is not my fault.

> *"This dream you grasp with rising joy,*
> *The pair of you will soon destroy.*
> *What once shone bright as future charm,*
> *Will sever bonds and spirits harm.*
> *A curse I summon soon will rise,*
> *When shattered hearts swear to despise.*
> *May pain surround you fated pair,*
> *For slights delivered, souls despair.*
> *While one shall travel forth alone,*
> *The other shackled tooth and bone.*
> *Do not deny that chance does dwell,*
> *Despite sweet torment hope hides well.*
> *Until the day when words reveal,*
> *Broken oaths with truth may heal."*

As is the case every time I read these words, the truth never changes.

> *A curse I summon soon will rise,*
> *When shattered hearts swear to despise.*

My anger-shattered heart prompted me to speak poison to Benedict Boyd, my creative partner, my bandmate, the man I love. Friction was our thing, but never hate. Matching passionate natures don't make for a smooth relationship. At the core of us, there was always love, but that horrible night we burned too hot with the fury of a raging battle of wills, a fight more volatile than any we'd had before. I wanted to punish him, to hurt him. The words I spoke banished me beneath a shitshow of feathers and claws.

"*I loathe everything about you, Benedick. I swear, all that's left in here...*"

I'd pounded a fist against my heart.

"*...with the name Benedict is hatred. I despise you.*"

The devastation on his face will haunt me worse than any ghost can ever manage. I see his teary eyes in my dreams and his lips, slack with disbelief, in my waking moments of despair. I struck too deep with a heartless blow.

Will the man ever want me back in any form? You don't gut a fish and then release it to swim undamaged.

I broke Benedict, and in doing so, ruined myself.

I use these godforsaken claws to slip the paper under the glass dome. Once the curse is safely hidden, I rest my palms against the upper curve of the songbook's case. Suddenly, the glass heats and gives a shudder. Jerking my hands away, I lean down to stare. Starting from the top, a page of sheet music paper from the songbook tears away from the spine and floats to the bottom of the dome.

I slump onto the chair with a thud and drop my hideous face into my arms on the varnished tabletop. Just as Tressa threatened since the first day I wore the beastly skin of her curse, Benedict's return to the Caliwood triggers my last chapter of hope. In his absence, the enchantress placated me by allowing the songbook to gift me with unlimited pages to write my silent songs. I scribed lyrics beneath the empty lines where notes belong but are missing, longing for the day when Benedict would once again complete my poetry with his music.

Now that my love is back, Tressa's curse will signal the songbook pages not to regenerate. They were never an endless gift. As the vile witch promised, upon Benedict's return, my hourglass flips and the sands of my eternal fate in the form of empty songbook pages will begin to fall. If he does not accept a kindred heart to love in the beast that I have become before the last page tears free from its binding, I will forever remain this malformed creature.

How does one prepare for such a trial? I've tried to imagine how Beast could possibly win Ben's heart, but the answer eludes me.

Blinding white light sears my eyes within the feathered sanctuary of my arms. I raise my head to meet the haughty gaze of Tressa Divine.

She primps tight curls of snow-white hair. "Well, Beasty, your man is back on home turf." Yards of glowing, white chiffon bob as the enchantress tiptoes up to the table to tap the top of the dome. "So I did not imagine a tiny rush of heat and the cutest little ripping sound." She traces a finger down the glass to point at the fallen page. "Tick, tick. Lover boy is on the clock." Tressa purses tiny lips more fitted to a doll and scrutinizes me. "Is that what you're wearing?"

I glance at the simple sleeveless print dress barely covering my strange form.

Tressa laughs, way too pleased with herself. "It's not like I can take you shopping." She flicks a wrist. "I hope Benny Boy likes drab green." Her finger aims at a trail of dark spots on the front of my skirt. "And blood stains. Mind your talons, Beasty to prevent..." Tressa giggles. "Spillage."

I press my lips together so tightly, the fangs on my lower jaw poke the bottom of my beak. I've learned to negotiate my bizarre hands fairly well, but there are still minor slips. "How much time do I have?"

She crosses her arms and rakes her gaze from the top of my feathered crown to my huge, clawed toes. "Probably not as much as you need." A *pfft* of air escapes her bright pink lips as she whirls around and vanishes in a burst of twinkling light.

The woman is such an attention junkie. I holler to the empty room. "What would it cost you to give me one straight answer? You stole my life, my love, and my future because Benedict didn't choose you for his band."

Tressa's voice seeps from behind every book, every statue, every sheet of paper on the table. Tendrils of sound bleed into the room until they surround me in an invisible net. "Oh, Beasty. It was so much more. Your smack talk at the audition sabotaged me. The attitude of superiority you wear like that ratty top hat of yours is what defeated you. Not your measly triumph of joining Benedict's skanky little band."

The smell of burnt toast fouls the library, and I know Tressa's off to torment or trick a different target. I circle the table with my clumsy, plodding steps moving faster and faster until my toe claws catch on the border of the hand-tufted, chocolate brown area rug beneath the table. All I want to do is fly up to my nest on the top of the center bookshelf, tuck my head under my winged arm, and blubber.

A quiet knock sounds at the door leading to the hallway steps. I shudder out of my pre-flight stance. No, Benedict can't be here again so soon. I'm not prepared. I scour the library for anything that says *Beatrice*. Tressa mocked my top hat. Did I carelessly leave it out? It's one of my last threads connecting me to Benedict, but it's too early for him to understand why Beast would have Beatrice's hat.

I wonder if its mate is still in the closet of our apartment, or did he stomp it to shreds, burn it, or simply toss it out the window?

"Beast? Are you home?"

Thank my itchy back feathers, it's Hero, the only sweet soul to befriend the hideous anomaly in the library. How I long to tell her Beatrice is trapped inside the creature she calls Beast, but the curse prevents such revelations.

I clomp to the door. Tressa and her cronies had their Leonato puppet design the door so it can only be unlocked from the inside.

A screechy chirp escapes my beak. Unless you're Benedict and manage to break in, regardless.

I clamp three thorny claws around the knob, crisscrossing them to turn it. Hero scoots in before the door is half-open. Her arms are heaped with brightly colored fabric, which she deposits on the table.

"Flo and Edie gave me a bunch of plus sizes from their latest haul they don't need at the store." She starts flipping through dresses. "I know they're flashier than you usually go for, but I'm going to talk you out of drab preferences."

There's a strain in Hero's voice.

"Everything okay?" I ask, concerned.

With a sniff, she drops her face into the mound of dresses.

"Hero?"

She pops up to growl. I stumble on oversized feet. Grace is something I've never possessed as a woman or a bird unless I'm flying. Defying gravity has its perks.

Hero is a tiny thing both in height and build, but she can pack a punch when she needs to. Her hands reach to grab mine, and I steady. "I'm sorry, Beast. It's been a crappy night."

"Crappy how?"

Hero unleashes the emotion she's been holding inside. "The band is back."

The words send a thrill through me. Even though I've seen Benedict, the rush of being in the same building as him lights me up.

"Santino and I shared our news. Why shouldn't we?" Hero's hands close into fists. "Claude goes bat shit and tells me he still loves me and practically jumps Santino. That set Tino off and it almost came to punches. Benedict had to deescalate the whole mess while I convinced Santino to bail." She pounds her fists on the clothes like she's trying to squash them. "It dumped Santino into one of his black moods. I can usually pull him back, but he insists he needs to work through this one alone. He's so afraid people will think he's unstable."

I push my tongue to the top of my mouth, weighing if I should free the question resting there. "Is he—unstable?"

Hero shoots me a defiant look. "He is not. The man literally walked through Gothel's fires of hell. Cut him some slack." Her anger dissipates as she withers. "Leave it to Claude to wreck everything."

"No, Hero." I carefully rest a talon on her shoulder. "Do not give Claude that power."

She grips my claw, her hand barely making it all the way around the damn thing. "The bastard had the nerve to act as if he'd been screwed."

"Key word here, bastard. From what you've told me, Claude is about Claude. Plus, he was probably coming off an all-night bender after their final tour stop. Didn't you say it was last night?" I choose my words carefully so Hero doesn't suspect my knowledge of Claude is first hand.

There's fire in Hero's eyes.

I wave my claws. "I'm not defending the jerk."

Her shoulders droop. "I know, I know." Hero crosses the room to the sofa and plops down. She looks so tiny on the clunky piece of furniture. "It's maddening. I was into Claude for such a long time, dying to hear him say he loved me. When he finally does, it's an attack."

"If he did love you, why wouldn't he have said it a thousand times? What I gather from your history, he wins worst boyfriend of the millennium award." I birdy snort. "Can you even use the term boyfriend for a sleazy commitment-phobe?" My feathers fluff. "You and Santino are a beautiful thing. If you ever had value in Claude's heart, the sore loser would celebrate your happiness and not piss all over it."

Hero nods. "Loser sums it up."

I perch on the sofa back, grateful for the dependable grip of my claws and the weight of the antique sofa to accept my bulk. "Good call." I'm trying hard to keep my cool. I watched Claude dangle Hero at arm's length for years while he screwed around. In his spoiled heart, I do think he thought of Hero as home base. Claude just never chose home base as a permanent gig.

I vow to temper my words. If I spout off about Claude to Hero the way I did as Beatrice, she might suspect there is a puzzle to put together. I need to remain her charity case. The lonely harpy she befriended one night when she found miserable me wedged between the top of the bookcase and the ceiling. From the start, she was kind to the freaky thing I've become. Instead of running, Hero rolled the library ladder over to me and helped me figure out a position where my bulging body could be comfortable. I may be oversized, but I'm not monstrously far off from extra-large humans if they had multi-jointed legs. Later, she brought me pillows and a comforter to fashion a cozy nest.

I missed my old life and Hero so badly, I took the risk to speak with her, painting myself as a pitiable freak who'd happened upon an open roof door to this library. She bought it and came back into my life. I need her to preserve any droplets of sanity I still possess after my transformation. I'm still stunned the assholes who hold my leash allow me any personal connection to my old self. Maybe they figure a happier Beast is a more compliant Beast. They need me functional to do their dirty work, or they'd never allow Beast to maintain a friendship with Hero. I pray Benedict's vital role in the curse prevents them from restricting his access.

Hero sinks deeper into the cushions and raises bare feet. "Thanks for letting me vent."

"Any time." I hop down in front of the fireplace and face her. "Hero, can I ask you something?"

"Only if it's not about Claude."

We both laugh, hers a delightful tinkle and mine a scratchy caw.

"Do you pity me?"

Hero cocks her head to one side and narrows her eyes, as if thinking. "I did. You were pathetic when I first found you."

"And now?"

She shakes her head. "Nope. Not even a little. You're smart and funny." Hero pets my arm feathers. "And soft." She laughs. "Is that shallow?"

I lower my head to bump my forehead to hers. "I take it as a compliment."

She stands on tiptoes, rests a hand on either side of my face, and pulls my head to her level. I hunch a bit to help her get close. "You are a great friend, Beast. I hope I'm the same for you." Hero kisses the side of my beak. "Oh, no." She dabs her pinkie to the corner of my eye. "I've made you cry."

"Happy tears, Hero." If this lovely person can find something to care about in what I've become, maybe there's a sliver of a chance Benedict might do the same. If he can find a way to love the Beast, Beatrice Sharpe will not disappear forever.

5

BAD IDEA

THE BAND AND LEONATO STARE LIKE I'VE GOT HORNS ON MY HEAD AS I barrel into the Ghost Lounge. "The rooftop..." I point upwards. "... giant gargoyle bird." I grab Leo's shoulders. "We need to call the police, animal control, the Air Force, anyone to get rid of it before it hurts someone."

"Jeez, Ben. Drink much?" says D.G., raising his beer to toast my insane call to arms.

The sheer force of my flailing limbs burns off any lingering alcohol in my system. "Hundred percent sober."

The laughter of my bandbros and Leonato echo through the empty lounge. Barely perceptible chuckles reverberate around the space as if the ghosts of the Caliwood question my sobriety as well.

"Yeah," says Alfie, slapping me on the back. "Giant gargoyle sightings appear most often from stone cold sober individuals."

D.G. chicken struts, bobbing his neck forward. "Huuuuuuman dinner. Squaaaaawk. Attack." He rushes me, pretending to take a bite out of my arm.

I flick my wrist. "Fine. Head to the roof. I'll sing at your funeral."

"How'd you get to the roof, Benedict?" Leonato wears an intense look of concern under knitted gray eyebrows.

"The usual way." I wrestle with whether or not to bring up the library transformation.

Leo cuts in, making the decision for me. "Sorry, fellows, but the roof is off limits from now on."

"Dude, you're not buying into Ben's giant chicken story, are you?" says D.G.

Our boss man shakes his head. "As if," he scoffs. "I've rented the library, and the tenant wants privacy."

"I hope your renter is into arachnids and dust," says Alfie.

"Boss, we need our rooftop hang. Being outside is like, inspiring." says Claude.

Leo waves him off. "You're welcome to the balcony over the pool in the V.I.P. suite if it's not occupied. There's your fresh air."

Claude's interest exasperates me. Except for our occasional bro-hangs, the dude saved trips to the roof for one-night stands he didn't want discovering which apartment in the Caliwood he calls home. Beatrice and I took the most creative advantage of the retreat, writing songs beneath the night sky. Now that there's a mythical bird of prey up there looking for a snack, I'm up for a new venue.

Claude snaps at Leo. "You can't cut us off from our dedicated creative space."

Leo dishes it right back. "Fine, Claude. Use the fucking fire escape to get up there, just stay out of the library."

I hold back a laugh at the image of Claude coaxing a conquest in a clubbing dress up the fire escape. Leo finds no humor in the situation. His Ferragamo leather loafers carry him across the floor of the lounge and out the door.

Claude better cool it. After messing with Leonato's future son-in-law, I'd guess the boss is one click shy of banishing Claude from the Caliwood.

The bartender clocked out so Claude ducks behind the bar to draw a pint of a random IPA for himself. After his all-night partying, which continued throughout the day into this evening, the dude must be reaching a critical blood alcohol level. I get that his world was rocked in a bad way with Hero's engagement, but he's heading for the red center of a danger bullseye.

I approach slowly and drop an arm around Claude's shoulders. It's time to play my band leader card. "Last call, okay, dude? I know this has been a shit homecoming, but you need food and sleep to be in shape for tomorrow's bar crawl. We'll be doing sets for three or four hours."

"Fuck you, Ben," says Claude, shoving me away.

I raise both hands in surrender and start mentally trolling for a local replacement rhythm guitarist in case Claude's too burned out to perform tomorrow for the Haunted Hollywood Bar Crawl.

Alfie brings me a water bottle. "Let Claude purge his own poison."

"Wise," I say, accepting Alfie's offering and making my way to the stage where my guitar sits on its stand, ready for action. Instead of picking it up, I lay next to it, staring at dark stage lights. Resting the cold plastic of the water bottle against my forehead, I will my cyclonic thoughts to settle.

I credit the library weirdness to Leo's tenant. Maybe the dude rigged the place for illusions. The library could already be prepped for a dress rehearsal, and I cued a blackout trick when I blew on the torch. When we left for the tour, the Magic Palace magicians club a few blocks away was in the throes of new ownership. Leo was attempting to broker packages with the club for his hotel guests. A potentially haunted library could be decent new digs for a magician eschewing the price hike of Magic Palace membership. I wouldn't be surprised if one day soon a placard in the lobby advertises magic show times.

As for my gargoyle friend...

...nothing. No reasonable explanation except drunken hallucination. I've seen my share of hawks and even the rare California condor perch on the sign. It's possible I need glasses. I do stare into high-powered stage lights for an unhealthy amount of time.

Claude's voice from the bar is rough and pitched low. "I realized I loved Hero when we were on the road. I should have told her as soon as I knew."

"Yet, that didn't keep you from dropping your jeans in every city," says Alfie.

"Dude, he was still a free agent," says D.G.

I'm seriously questioning the morals of my band.

"As was Hero," says Alfie, the voice of logic. "You can't fault her for connecting with Santino."

"Maybe it's a mercy hook up?" says D.G. "The dude rocks a Frankenstein vibe with those face scars."

I swallow my urge to jump in. Let Alfie give Claude a shot of reality. I've already tried and failed.

Alfie huffs in disgust. "You're determined to write your own fantasy, Claude. Good luck." Through slitted eyes, I watch Alfie head for the door. "G'night, Ben."

The energy to answer him eludes me. I'm emotionally and physically spent. I'll cat nap here on stage until I muster enough energy to face my empty apartment.

Claude's harsh whisper catches my interest. "Is he asleep?"

"Ben, your dick's hanging out," says D.G.

I force myself not to react, dying of curiosity as to what they clearly don't want me to hear.

D.G. attempts to whisper. "He's out, man."

My face is in shadow so they can't see my eyes are not completely closed. The stage is raised just enough to give me a good viewing angle. Blurry forms of my bandbros retreat to the far end of the bar. I could laugh. Distance won't keep their convo private. Neither Claude nor D.G. have a low volume setting when they're drunk.

"Santino Fedele is not going to get away with stealing Hero from me," grumbles Claude.

I bite back a groan. Claude's lament is getting stale.

"What are you going to do, man?" says D.G. "Kidnap Cupid and force him shoot a Claude arrow into Hero?"

Claude's voice sounds unnervingly sober. "No need. Cupid conquers some with arrows and others with traps."

D.G. slurps his drink. "Claude, my dude, there's the stink of revenge in your 'tude. You're passing through Pissedville into Obsessionland."

Claude releases a groan full of weariness and pain. I feel for the guy. If I discovered Beatrice was with another dude, I'd want to claw his eyes out. I morph a sigh into a snore to enhance my sleep performance.

"I'm damn sad, D.G. It goes deep, limitless."

"So ditch the gloom."

"For what, D.G.? What's my prize? Good guy of the year? Right. The most exquisite Santino Fedele has that locked up. The only role left for me is villain."

Across the lounge, someone clears their throat. "I've got flowers for Hero Andante. The front desk said she was in here."

I'm sure Hero is waiting for Claude to scram before she returns to decorate for the bar crawl. Out of the corner of my not-sleeping eye, I see Claude leap off the barstool and meet a baby-faced teen, wearing a *Boulevard Flowers* reflective vest. Even with Day-Glo vests, the poor slobs pulling bicycle delivery duty on Hollywood Boulevard take their lives in their hands with every trip.

"She'll be right back," says Claude in a friendly bro tone. "I'll see that she gets them."

"Cool," says the kid and hands a bouquet of multicolored roses to Claude. The messenger pauses, waiting for a tip.

D.G. reaches across the bar and hands a beer bottle to the kid. "For your efforts, my good man."

"Uh, sir, I'm not old enough to drink."

"Save it 'til you are," says D.G.

There's a pause while my bandmates wait for the delivery kid to leave.

"Don't look at the note, Claude," warns D.G.

Claude's voice holds the deadly edge of a switchblade. "Sweet, Hero. It's you and me, Babe. Ignore the dark clouds and slide down our rainbow. Forever. X Tino"

Claude wails on the bar with Hero's roses.

"Not so romantic. Definitely, a villain move," says D.G.

"Keep your mouth shut about it, or I'll let Ben in on your sweet little oxy habit," growls Claude.

"It's not a habit, douche monkey, it's a pastime," says D.G. with a definite slur in his voice.

Shit. D.G.'s sluggish vibe takes on a whole new shading. I force myself to unclench my jaw. Will our drummer's pharmaceutical challenge be the next roadblock to derail our album? I add a massively uncomfortable convo with D.G. onto my *fix the screw ups* list.

The scraggly remains of Hero's bouquet sail over my head and crash into the wall next to the stage.

"I will change for her, D.G. I can be a flowers and sweet talk guy. I just need Santino Fedele out of the picture first to prove it to her."

"Okay, this is not my usual gig, but you're sounding ominous and way too fucking dangerous." D.G. pounds a riff on the bar top. "I'm going to be your voice of reason. Whatever you do, remember Hero is the boss's daughter. If you fuck with her, you could fuck the band."

"I'm no shitiot, D.G." Claude growls. "I'll whip up a plan that doesn't come near the band."

"As long as there's no blood or crime, man."

"Only Santino's bleeding heart, D.G."

Bottles or glasses clink followed by a loaded silence. I swear Claude's jealousy-addled brain emits a low buzz.

"I'm calling it, Claude. You know Ben will be knocking on our doors for rehearsal way too fucking early." A bar stool scrapes across the floor. "And you need to sleep off your dreams of mayhem and revenge."

"Lightweight. It's not even ten."

"Being up for almost thirty-six hours requires an early bedtime."

Damn it. Now I have to keep an eye on Claude for shady shit and D.G. for pill popping. Part of me wants to warn Santino and Hero that Claude is wringing *mwahaha* hands. If the dude is simply pissing in the wind tonight with his brags of winning Hero back, clueing in the couple would exacerbate their irritation. Dealing with Claude's shitbird reaction to their engagement news is enough for now.

I'm too deep in my head to hear Claude approach. He kicks me harder than necessary in the hip. "Wakey, wakey, Ben."

I pull off an excellent performance of lead singer rising from the depths of groggy and swat at his foot like it's an annoying bug. "A kiss on the forehead works just as well, Claude."

"Kiss my ass, Benedict." He shows me his back and struts to the door of the lounge to catch up with D.G.

I sit and scrub my face before calling after him. "Rehearsal at three tomorrow."

I feel ancient, triple my thirty years as I stand with moans and groans. My gaze drops to the stage floor. Sleeping here tonight would allow me to avoid the apartment Beatrice and I shared for a bit longer.

I face my reflection in the mirror behind the bar. "Rip the Band-Aid, Ben. Rip it hard, then clean up the blood." Running a hand through my hair to train it out of my eyes, I take the first step toward my empty nest.

6

FEATHERS

THE TOP FLOOR OF HOTEL CALIWOOD IS TECHNICALLY THE thirteenth floor, but to honor the great gods of superstition, it's always been numbered as the fourteenth floor. I never understood why a famously haunted hotel would bother to shy away from a thirteenth floor.

Grunting in the face of superstition, I step out of the elevator on the real thirteenth floor for the second time tonight. Technically, the library exists on the thirteenth floor as well, or at least thirteen and a half.

Unlike my earlier dash to the rooftop, I turn right instead of left, heading to the apartment formerly known as *ours*, Beatrice's and mine, which is now simply *mine*. Standing in front of Number 1413 sets me swaying unsteadily on my feet. Bea used to say the reverse progression of numbers was a reminder we needed to always keep moving forward instead of looking back.

"What would you say now, Bea?"

I lean my forehead against the door that's dark brown on the hall side and painted robin's egg blue with sunflowers on the inside. Beatrice's touch, along with the apartment's white walls to "expand the space." Besides the paint job, the only thing left of Beatrice Sharpe in my life is...

I pull the turquoise feather from my jean's pocket. When we performed, she'd swap feathers in the ridiculous top hat she wore to match whatever latest Bohemian garb costume she'd scored at a weekend garage sale spree.

This was the last feather she'd worn onstage. I press it to my lips and close my eyes. Memories slice through me with the pain of a dull blade. The sweet combativeness of our lovemaking was always a competition with no loser. I summon the sense of warmth of having Beatrice's body next to mine as we drowsed in afterglow, one of the few circumstances when we weren't challenging one another to excel in music, in love, in life. An image of her soft lips, gentle in silence and sharp in speech, bring a smile to my own. I'd give anything to have Beatrice on the other side of this door, poised to strip me of my jeans and tease me until I throw her on the bed to return the favor. The sensation of my fingers cupping those lovely full breasts, tracing the flare of her hips, and dipping into places that unleash her howl sets my hands tingling. Wishing Beatrice would miraculously appear when I open the door is as likely as a kid's wish for a unicorn.

My quick trip back in time makes it necessary to adjust my fly. I slip the feather in my pocket and rest both palms against the door.

I can't do it. I can't walk into the home I shared with the love of my life. Not yet. I spin and stride toward the elevator. I'm too sober to handle this. Shame washes over me at my weakness. Am I going to get in bed with a bottle instead of reality? I tried that and it only added a layer of self-loathing to my base coat of despair. I must learn to live like the door to Number 1413, dark and broody on one side, bright and positive on the other. The difference is my dark side will need to face inward.

I wipe sweaty palms on my jeans and once again face the hallway leading to my apartment. Two steps and I remember the whisky bottle I stashed in the sconce on my way to the roof. Leo's very fastidious about the appearance of his hotel. He won't take kindly to my use of what I'm sure is a pricey sconce as a trash can.

As I reach for the bottle, I catch sight of the stairs leading to the now-occupied library. At some point tomorrow, I suppose I should introduce myself to my new neighbor. Better to warn the unsuspecting tenant that *Ben and the Boulevard Bunch* are cohabitating half-a-floor below him, so if he hangs here at night any strange rantings or bellowed sea shanties at two in the morning should be ignored.

I tuck the bottle under my chin and fish keys from my pocket. I'm prepped to get over my sad sorry self and walk into my apartment when the low sound of singing glues my sneakers to the carpet. Leo's new tenant is here, and she's a woman.

Images of an aging magician in a silk-lined cape disappear. I creep near the door and hear a guitar join the song. Taking one step at a time, I close in on the library to find its door not quite closed. The voice inside sounds familiar. Peeking through the skinny crack, I see Hero leaning against the sofa, guitar strap around her neck, clumsily picking out chords.

"I'm sorry. I can barely strum a tune," she says.

Who is she attempting to play for?

"Your words are so beautiful, and my horrible playing doesn't do them justice."

With a knuckle, I ease the door open a bit more to get a gander at the new resident of the library. The damn thing creaks as loud as a banshee scream. Hero hisses, followed by strange thumping noises.

Is she in danger? Fear sets off fireworks in my chest. I raise the bottle for a weapon as I shove the door the rest of the way to find— no one. No Hero or whoever she was chatting up.

"Hero?" I take tentative steps into the library. It's well lit by the chandelier and a crackling fire. The statues are still there, but their torches are out. Heaps of wildly patterned clothing lie on the end of the long table closest to me. I spot a guitar resting on the tabletop.

"Hello? It's Benedict, Hero. Everything good?"

Moving slowly, I make my way down the length of the table through the smokey scented air from the fireplace. The breath in my chest hitches when I recognize the instrument as one Beatrice lent Hero for the guitar lessons she was giving her BFF. I run a finger across the strings as if I could conjure another piece of Bea's essence. It appears the latest resident of Hotel Caliwood has taken over the guitar lessons Beatrice started.

"I heard you singing, Hero."

No response. I should leave. If she isn't answering, this is a *get lost* brand of silence. Odd. Hero isn't a secrets kind of gal. They probably hightailed it to the roof to avoid me. I guess Hero's had her fill of *Ben and the Boulevard Bunch* for one night.

I'll go quiz Leonato about the tenant to assure myself Hero isn't in a fix. When I turn toward the door, a flicker of firelight reflecting off the tall glass dome catches my eye. The glass is covering an open book on a small wood pedestal in the center of the library table. I lean to peer into the dome. The book inside is filled with blank staff paper, not a single note or lyric graces the page. Resting on the wooden base of the dome is a sheet from the book that looks as if it's been ripped free.

I set my bottle on the table and press my nose against the glass to see if there is anything interesting on the fallen page. The upturned side holds only rows of empty staff lines. Scanning the room to confirm I'm alone, I reach for the sides of the dome to lift it free so I can examine the rest of the book.

"Don't touch it!"

Before I make contact with the glass, there's a shriek like bad air brakes on a big rig. A dark mass shadowed against the chandelier slams me onto the carpet.

The head of the thing is an inch away. Not a head. I swear I see the dark outline of a muzzle, no a big ass beak. My attacker wears a headdress.

I scream, "Oh, shit," and attempt to pull my body free, but the freak straddles me. "Let me go." I buck my hips trying to dislodge it, but it presses down on my body with suffocating weight. Jerking my head side to side, I see it's pinned my arms to the floor with—

Three wicked clawed...fingers?...toes? I can't make out details in the shadows cast by the table.

The smell of a wet down jacket fills my nostrils. Holy hell, is this the creature from the roof? Did the fucker claw its way in while poor Hero was singing? Where's Hero? Where's the new tenant?

I dig my heels in and thrash like a crazy man. "Help. Fire. Fire." I bellow, praying someone on the resident floor hears me.

A high-pitched, low-volume screech heats the skin of my ear. "Calm the hell down."

Did the living gargoyle speak? Nightmares have nothing over this moment, which I'm pissed scared will be my last.

The door to the library slams shut. No, no, no. Now I'm freaking trapped in here with the thing that ate Hero and her music teacher. I squeeze my eyes shut to avoid seeing its jaw, which probably hyper-extends like a great white to consume my head in one sloppy bite.

A voice breaks through my panic. "Benedict. You need to chill. Beast isn't going to hurt you."

The feeling of my hair being pulled out by the roots contradicts the statement. "Ouch." I open my eyes to find Hero, one hand threaded through my hair, the other covering my mouth.

"Hero?" I mumble into her palm and try to raise a hand to touch her. The thing holds me captive.

"Will you shush so we can explain?" snaps Hero.

I enunciate against her lifeline. "We? You and this horror are a we?"

"Rude," sniffs the horror, making a clacking sound.

"Beast," warns Hero. "You chill as well." She pinches my lips between her fingers. "Benedict Boyd, give me your word you'll stop screaming like a little girl if *we* let you up?"

I nod. What I will do is grab Hero and bolt for the door.

"Okay, Beast. Get off him."

The monstrosity looming over me stills while it pulls its head back first and then lifts its claws. Light from wall sconces reflects off its overly large crimson eyes that look disturbingly human.

"Ride's over, dude," I say, straining to wiggle free from beneath the thing that is apparently friendly with Hero.

Massive knee joints squeeze my hips for a beat before it cranks its body upright and steps off me.

For the first time, I see the freak in clear detail as Hero pets its feathers. I'm so stunned, my escape plan fizzles on the spot. I scramble to my feet and back away despite Hero's comfort with the monster. Though now that I get a good look, truth be told, I've seen unfortunate plastic surgery on groupies infinitely more upsetting than the creature's beak and feathers.

"Beast, this is Benedict. Ben—Beast," says Hero as if she's introducing me to royalty. Hero guides Beast's elbow forward until three talons are inches from my chest. "Shake, Ben."

I stare, not sure whether to grab, pinch, or tap the bird-like appendage. Beast engulfs my hand against its leathery palm and moves up and down. It's unexpectedly soft and warm, not repulsive at all.

"Hello, Benedict."

The Beast's speaking voice lands somewhere between squawk and screech. It's bizarre, but not unpleasant. An undertone close to a purr softens its sharp edges.

"How's it goin', Beast? Is that seriously your name?" I study its face. Yep, a definite bird vibe, but not full-on bird, a human/bird hybrid. It's a full head taller than my six-three, but not as massive as I first perceived. The eyes are strangely shaped, cinched at both sides with a high ridge in the middle. They have the whites, rusty red iris, and pupils of a human. A prominent beak for a nose ends in a sharp hook. A wide but definitely human mouth is tucked beneath its beak. Its chin echoes the point of that wicked hook.

"Something wrong with my name?" Beast lets out a chirpy snort.

I hold up a hand and shake my head, still wary of the creature. "If you're cool with it—"

A shiver runs through me. I may be acclimating a teensy bit to Beast but being comfortable around the creature isn't on the table. I toss Hero a questioning look.

She rubs my arm. "Ben, you're not tripping. Beast is real. She's cool once you get to know her."

She? It is a her, a female. My gaze takes a quick slide down *her* body. She is wearing a dress. It looks like one of the vintage numbers from Flo and Edie's boutique on the boulevard. Beneath the dress, I take note of what could pass for the well-toned, athletic silhouette of a woman with an extra layer of padding.

Beast has muscular shoulders to match powerful looking arms. Her legs that skew more birdlike from elbows to hands and strange backward-jointed knees tower over feet the size of serving platters. Even odder is the nearly human skin of her face, upper arms, and chest.

Holy jeez, the feathers. Her head is covered with feathers instead of hair in multi shades of rich browns and burgundies. Rising straight off her forehead, several rows of wine-colored feathers stand straight like the headdress I initially thought she wore. Smaller feathers rise from the neckline of her dress. More feathery mane sprouts from the back of her neck and arms, growing longer at the elbow joints, so I assume she can fly. How else would Beast have been able to perch on the H of the Hotel Caliwood sign?

I chew on my bottom lip, trying to decide if I should ask. Curiosity wins out. "Beast, were you on the Hotel Caliwood sign?"

"No. Why?" She gasps and covers her mouth with her bird hand. "Did you see another of my kind?"

Another? Shit, are there more of these bird women?

The look of panic on my face sends both Hero and Beast into fits of laughter.

Hero swats Beast. "I think we've freaked Benedict out enough for one night." She bumps her shoulder against her tall, feathered buddy. "Beast is one of a kind." Hero threads her arm through Beast's elbow. "A brilliant poet and wonderful friend. You should read her work."

They exchange a look of pure affection.

My year on the road, alcohol-soaked, bone-weary body hits overload. This creature, this Beast—I need to bounce and process whoever or whatever she is. "I'll let you two get back to your..." I nod at the guitar, wave, and retreat to the door.

Hero zips past me in a flash, blocking my escape route. She lays her palms against my chest to stop me. "Listen, Ben. You absolutely cannot tell anyone about Beast. Swear to me."

My bafflement with the situation hits a new high. "Your dad knows, right? He warned us not to bug his new renter."

She shakes her head. "Beast says she isn't the one who rented the library but won't tell me who made the deal with my dad. He doesn't know she's staying here."

I yank Hero away from her beastie bestie and hiss in her ear. "That thing looks dangerous. Leonato should know what's up here."

"She's not a thing, Benedict. Beast is kind. Look at the poor thing. Where else could she go as safe as the library?

I glance at Beast, expecting her to be locked on our convo. Instead, she stares at the book inside the glass dome with a heartbreaking look of melancholy. This creature is a sad song come to life, a being with a story full of sorrow.

"How did you find it, uh, her?"

"I snooped and got caught." She narrows her gaze at me. "Same as you. And yes, I was freaked at first, but poor Beast was more frightened than I was. We hit it off." Hero squeezes my arm. "Give her a chance, Ben. I'm sure she'd appreciate more company than just me."

"Does Santino know?"

A light flush colors Hero's cheeks. "No. I promised Beast I wouldn't tell anyone. I'm asking the same of you."

"You get this is off, right Hero? A beast writing poetry in a library that someone else rented doesn't track."

"Oh my God, Ben, that's it."

Is Hero coming to her senses. Will she come with me to Leonato to reveal there's an ostrich's cousin living in his hotel?

"Beast can help you."

My attention whips to Hero. "Help me?" I almost add 'to hunt rodents or wipe out vandals.' Actually, using an oversized bird of prey to eradicate the criminal vermin infesting Hollywood Boulevard at night isn't such a bad idea.

"I heard my father ranting about the album deadline and your songs without lyrics. I'm warning you, Benedict, he's pretty pissed."

It's my turn to go red-faced. "I'm working on it."

"Get real. You're shit at lyrics."

I drop my gaze to the fluffy carpet. "Truth."

"Beast's poems are kick ass. Maybe you could use them with your music, or she can help you write new ones."

I catch movement over Hero's shoulder. Beast watches us. There's no way she didn't catch Hero's suggestion.

Hero pivots to face Beast. "Would you consider helping Ben? He's acting like a tool now, but I promise he's a good guy."

Beast and I lock stares as we attempt to read one another. Damn if I don't see the tiniest glimmer in her eyes. The room blurs as reality spins a bit too quickly. Am I seriously considering writing songs with a character from a horror novel?

Hero stamps a foot when neither Beast nor I respond. "Don't be stubborn. Partnering is sensible for you both. Ben, you'll get songs ready for studio." She turns to Beast. "Your wonderful words will finally make it into the world." A sheen of tears covers Hero's eyes, and her voice falters. "Even if you can't take the credit, Beast, everyone will hear your heart in Ben's songs."

As far-out as Hero's proposal is, it's the only proposal to my lyrics predicament on the table. I try to see Beast through Hero's eyes. I trust Hero and she trusts this claw-footed bird woman.

"I need to see a sample of your friend's work."

Hero begins to rifle through a pile of papers on the table until Beast stops her.

"It's my audition. Let me choose."

I'm impressed how Beast's huge hands deftly sort through the sheets until she pinches one between two talons and hands it to Hero.

"The first and last stanzas should be enough to give him a feel for my work," says Beast. Her gaze is downcast as she fidgets from one of her taloned feet to the other.

Hero skims the sheet and smiles at Beast. "I've always loved this one. Are you sure you don't want me to read the whole thing?"

When Beast shakes her head, Hero begins.

"Tales are told of errors made,
When hearts burn hot erasing wit.
Triumph loud with fear and rage,
Captures love in barren caves."

Hero looks up to gauge my reaction. Beast's words are formal and fancy, but they do speak to me. She's got meter going on that could work in a song. I spin my hand in a *go on* gesture, and Hero continues.

"People thrive on joy and hope,
As light mutes loss that shadows crave.
Embrace the warmth you now possess,
To vanquish sorrow's harsh caress."

Yep, definite gravitas and depth from Ms. Beast. The words of the poem mingle with my sorrow over Beatrice, and my throat tightens. Am I truly considering partnering with a beaked and feathered lyricist?

"Nice work." I raise a hand. "Look, I need space to synthesize all this." Beast and Hero perform matching shoulder slumps. "You have my word I won't say anything about you, Beast." I point to the door. "May I leave without getting body slammed?"

Beast clomps to the fireplace and stares into the flames. There's a stab of regret in my chest, fearing I've disappointed a being I didn't know existed until tonight.

"I'll walk you out," says Hero, glancing at Beast. "Goodnight, friend."

Beast flutters her feathers with a low chirp. Hero guides me out the door, shutting it securely behind her. Instead of relief, an unexpected pull to return to the library tugs at me.

Nice work.

What an ass. Why didn't I tell Beast her words moved me? Wow, I can't believe I'm bothered for potentially hurting the feelings of Hero's pet creature. Can I attribute humanity to Beast? It—she talks, writes poetry, and exudes an air of humanity. But, fuck, she's a giant ladybird. Never in my drunken revelries, of which there have been plenty, did I ever conjure a conundrum close to this Beast.

"Ben, I need to be certain you'll keep Beast a secret." Hero stares at me with those round, heart-on-her-sleeve eyes.

When I stare at the closed library door, protectiveness tickles my insides. Is it for Hero keeping Beast a secret, or is it for Beast?

"You can count on me, Hero." Her smile is the essence of sweet and trusting. "But can we agree a talking Beast who writes poetry is deep in freaky territory?"

"Agreed and thank you." She grabs me in a hug. "Not gonna lie, she takes getting used to, but once you do, I promise you won't be weirded out around her at all."

I pat her back. "And by the way, congrats to you and Santino." I hold her at arm's length. "Two folks finding true love who totally deserve it inspires this song maker's heart. I may need to find space on the new album to write a song about it."

"That's sweet, Ben, but you're shit at lyrics. You may botch it."

"Ha, ha."

Hero sticks a finger in her mouth and chews. "Has Claude mellowed? Should I talk to him?"

Ugh, Claude. I wonder if the shredded rose petals in the Ghost Lounge are still there. I don't want to alarm Hero that my bandbro Claude is spouting revenge. What I overheard might be no more than a dashed dreamer working through his bummer. I can't wrap my head around Claude being any kind of legit threat to Hero and Santino. If I whistle-blow on empty bluster, the bad blood will escalate from simmer to boil.

"My dude is going to need time to wrap his pinhead around your engagement. You and Tino steer clear of him until he swallows a reality pill."

She pops the finger from her lips. "So don't strangle him in his sleep?"

"Not until I find a decent replacement for him, then squeeze away."

I'm rewarded with a hearty Hero laugh. She draws an X across her chest. "Claude lives and you give Beast a chance. Deal?"

We both look at the library door.

"I don't know, Hero."

She rises on tiptoes to cup my face in dainty palms. "Please, Ben. Her life is so..." Hero shrugs her shoulders. "...dim. A creative challenge might add much needed light."

There was plenty of light when the torches in the library blazed.

"If nothing else, work with her on the love song you just promised me. I'll let you sing it at my wedding." She dots my cheek with a kiss. "Goodnight, Ben. I've got a lounge to decorate."

The elevator arrives, and she skips inside. After the doors close, I whisper. "Sweet dreams, sweet Hero."

Here I am, midway between my empty apartment and the Beast's library, with no clue which direction to take.

7

MY LADY TONGUE

AT LEAST THESE DAMN FEATHERS ARE GOOD FOR WIPING TEARS. WHEN I saw Benedict on the rooftop, waves of excitement, hope, fear, and love mixed into a complex solution I had no time to reconcile.

Before I attacked him.

I tuck my head under a winged elbow. Why couldn't I control my temper and calmly ask him to get the hell away from the songbook? Did something deep in my soul know he would run from a talking monster and never return? With him pinned to the carpet, he had to listen.

Sitting on top of him should not have been a turn on, but the sensation of Ben between my thighs sent feelings of lust, loss, and longing crashing through me.

I free my head and lean against the back of the padded chair, ignoring the poke of feathers against my scalp. "You still light me up, Benedict."

It was dumb luck Hero dropped off a new load of clothes, so I wasn't alone when he showed. I may very well owe her my destiny for encouraging a connection between Benedict and me that never would have happened given the morass of my emotions in an unsupervised birdchick vs. man confrontation.

Night after long night, I've tried to suss out what to do when Ben returned. How will I guide him to my inner Beatrice when this bastard of a curse locks my jaw against revealing its existence or that of my despicable custodians? The irony is Hero would be the first to stick by my side and help me win Ben's love if she only knew her friend is trapped inside the harpy. Dare I believe fate is on my side since it's gifted me with Hero, the most loyal and loving person on the planet as a friend in every incarnation of Beatrice Sharpe? If it's possible to find blessings under a curse, then Hero is mine.

I stretch, and the sight of my giant avian leg joints rising above the seat on either side disgusts me. Every time I hope I've made peace with this body, a new angle, a new ache reminds me of my personal hell.

A gentle knock at the door ruins my plans to stress the entire night over whether I'll get a shot at kindling a flame with Benedict, or if I'll watch pages of the songbook fall one by one until this curse is my forever. Glancing around the room, I try to spot whatever Hero forgot, but see nothing of hers. The darling thing is probably returning to check on me since I was the queen of weepy when she and Benedict left. She has a long night ahead of her, transforming the Ghost Lounge for the Haunted Hollywood Bar Crawl. I vow to force a smile to send her on her way.

My claws clack against the hardwood floor beyond the rug as I wrap my hand around the knob and turn.

"I'm fine He—"

Benedict stands before me. Did I remember how his eyes are the color of irises, a deep blue with a trace of purple? Did I remember his whitish blonde hair flows off his forehead in thick touchable waves? Did I remember his lips are plump enough to bite and kiss at the same time? Did I remember the landscape of his lean muscles as they flexed beneath my fingers? Did I remember the delight of our bodies intertwined like a perfect rhyme?

Yes, I remember everything about Benedict Boyd, and I want it all back.

"May I come in?"

I nod, step aside, and mutely let him pass. Some fine lyricist I am. He walks as far as the table before I close the door and lean against it.

He takes in the room with a wrinkled forehead as if he's nervous another giant bird is going to materialize and knock him to the floor. Finally, his gaze settles on me.

"I thought I should tell you what I really thought of your poem."

I take a few heavy steps to reach him. "Well, out with it?" My tone is snappy, defensive.

Benedict raises a hand. "Hey, if you don't want me here, I'll leave."

"I let you in, didn't I?"

"Yeah, but you're not turning cartwheels over it."

I fan an arm down my body. "You think this is capable of a cartwheel?" The mouth beneath my beak smiles. I've missed our verbal joust so dearly.

Benedict waves his palms like he's erasing a chalkboard. "I don't know you well enough to take that bait."

Yes, you do, my Benedict.

"Speaking of which, I thought we'd maybe hang out a little and chat to see if Hero might be on to something about us working together."

I hop up onto the sofa back to test Ben's scare threshold.

He jerks with surprise but doesn't run. He doesn't come any closer either. "Nice balance."

"Lots of practice." I stare him down. "You must be desperate if you're back..." I pretend to check my wrist for a watch, "...in under fifteen minutes to hang and chat with Beast."

"Is third person your thing in lyrics or just conversation?" He jerks his chin. "I'm more a first-person kind of guy."

"One of the many things I've heard about you." God, I'm having fun, trading barbs with my man.

Benedict purses his lips and shifts them to the side. One of my favorite moves.

"What does that mean?"

"You're known as Leonato and Caliwood Inc's charming, funny man. From what I've seen online, you launch words masked as jokes, but in truth they often set up a sting." My feathers stiffen, a look I know makes me appear even larger and unfriendly. "I'm sure your conquests on the road would agree. Jokes to lure, then a stinger to reject."

Benedict's Adam's apple ripples, the tell he's getting pissed off. "You've got nerve to claim to know me when you don't." He sputters as bewilderment softens an expression I was sure headed toward anger. "You're on social media?"

"Don't let the feathers fool you. I keep up to date."

He pops his lips. "Hero? Right?" Benedict studies my eyes. "Okay, you think you know me. Maybe I've got your number too. You're a sharp-tongued lady who enjoys delivering a dig."

I should stop, but I'm a prisoner to the back and forth with Benedict I've been denied. Every bruise I felt hearing news of his screwing around on tour smarts with fresh pain. This is a battle to be won, and I want to be the victor. "Do you deny it's the package and not the content that attracted those women on the road, Bene*dick*?"

He's visibly jarred at my use of the derogatory version of his name. Damn, he's remembering the title from my Beatrice lips. Time for damage control.

"Did I mispronounce your name? My mistake, but from what I've heard, you can be quite the dick."

Too far. I've gone too far. Benedict doubles over and grabs the edge of the table. He's facing down, and I can't see his expression. His voice is shot through with pain.

"I can be."

I shift so I'm sitting on the sofa, facing the fire. What have I done?

His voice is quiet. "Did you ever meet her? Beatrice?"

What do I say? If I say yes, I'll have to invent a story. The Hotel Caliwood is the one place my two selves would meet up. Any lie can be blown to bits by Hero.

"No."

He draws a loud breath and then releases it before straightening up. Taking tentative steps, he walks around the sofa and sits at the end farthest from me. "I thought if you had, maybe she'd shared her opinion of me."

"What would she say?"

He laughs. "I think you've covered it." My Benedict drops his head into his hands.

I ache to lay a hand on his back. "I've been told subtlety is not part of my charm."

"No shit." Ben turns his head to the side and looks at me. "I hope your lyrics are more nuanced." When I don't answer, he continues. "You've pissed me off, but in my experience challenges work in a collaboration."

"Friction over harmony?"

He springs off the couch to face me. "I've done friction. Beatrice abandoned the band because of it."

His anguish arrows my heart. Ben thinks I abandoned the group, abandoned him? Did he have so little faith in our love that he believes one fight would end us? No questioning? No second chance?

What else could he think? My poison words invoked Tressa's curse and jacked up my existence. I spoke them and instantly disappeared from Benedict's life. Refusing to embrace a healthy fear of what happened to us on that freaky Christmas Eve landed me, landed us right where we are.

Ben faces the fire. Its glow splits Ben into two, a bright half and a dark half. I want so badly to take him in my arms.

He speaks to the flame. "If there's any hope of us working

together, you need to understand Beatrice's words gave life to my songs. She ripped the heart out of my music when she left."

I can't hold back. "Do you regret her?" Have I lost my mind, deliberately provoking him?

"Not for a single second."

One drop of hope for each of his unregretted seconds since we parted fills my soul.

Benedict works himself into a pant. "Hero says you're a poet, a truth-teller, a channeler of emotion. I would hope you understand my art is damaged from losing Beatrice."

He's raw, stripped of any the bravado or conceit I know he wears for protection. Can our broken hearts heal? Does regret translate to wanting Beatrice in his life again?

Ben runs a hand through his hair, training loose strands in place. "It's going to take a lot for me to give you a shot. I honestly don't know if I can open up to a collaboration. It feels like I'm betraying her."

Damn it, my love for this man is equal parts pain and pleasure. His confession makes me believe there's still enough of a thread between us to rebuild. I'm steaming over his sexual antics on tour, but what right do I have to punish him? He believed Beatrice hated him and never wanted to see his face again.

"If we're truth telling, you should know I consider my poetry the pursuit of art and truth, not a vehicle for ambition or the insta-fame of a hit song."

"Poetry no one hears. Is art, art if it exists in a vacuum?" Benedict stares at me too long. I'm tempted to fly to my nest on the bookshelf and hide until he leaves where I can collect my thoughts.

If I was Beatrice, I'd grab his T-shirt to start a fight and end in a kiss so long and deep, neither of us would remember why we argued. Combat was always part of our passion play. The drops of hope in my chest ignite like a match thrown on gasoline. Is some part of Ben finding that flavor of language with a beast?

"I don't mean to be rude, but damn, you bring it out in me. The dynamic doesn't stoke my creative well." He shakes his head. "Sorry, I can't picture this working. For the record, it has nothing to do with whatever you are. There's no reason not to trust Hero's acceptance of you." His lips crinkle, and he laughs. "The irony is I may wake up tomorrow and realize this—you are one mother of a fever dream from too much whiskey." He strides to the door. "Goodnight, Beast."

"Wait." I fly halfway across the room and land far enough away to avoid being interpreted as a threat. "You never told me what you thought of my poem."

He pauses with his hand on the knob. "It spoke to me." Without a backward glance, Benedict leaves me.

8

DARK VINYL ARTISTS

A SHUDDER FROM THE BOOKCASE NEAR THE CORNER OF THE ROOM warns that my alone time is up. Sure enough, the shelves slide just enough to let Rubata Lear squeeze through. Behind her in the hidden suite, I hear the low tones of Grant Gothel and Sulaa Kylock. Here they are, three of the four D.V.A., Dark Vinyl Artists, fiends and criminals hiding behind the façade of an up-and-coming music company. Add in the enchantress, Tressa Divine, and the unholy quartet is complete.

"You salty Beast. Soooo close, there was a moment I thought Benedict was going to bite at a partnership." Rubata chomps her teeth at me, and then launches into one of her cringy raps, spinning her hips in a circle like a burlesque dancer wannabe.

> "*If you want to hook up,*
> *Wear the eyes of a pup.*
> *Plump your lips,*
> *And shake your hips.*
> *Make him swoon,*
> *To have you soo—ner*
> *Than later.*"

"Ugh, terrible ending. Write me something prettier to post, Beastie," she says with a pout.

Thank goodness, Rubata's younger sis, Chorda, was the songwriter for the Lear sisters singing group. True, the older two sisters, Rubata and Glissanda, had gorgeous voices, but judging by this one's attempts at music and lyrics, that was their only contribution to the trio's success.

I cock my head to the side, infusing my voice with enough sarcasm to play Rubata's game, but not anger her. "Who will you be posting as this week?" I fan a hand from her head to her platform heels. "Do share your latest bio so I can nail its voice."

The voluptuous curves and cherry red hair of Rubata Lear pixilate and reform. Instead of the red-headed witch I know, a platinum blonde with a waiflike fashion model body and pixyish features struts across the room before performing a spin worthy of a runway. "Hello, Beast. I'm Brandy LaCroix," she says in Rubata's voice.

"Like LaCroix sparkling water?"

Rubata/Brandy wobbles her head, her short bob swaying side to side. "Okay, no." She taps her lip with an index finger. "Brandy Beaumont, heiress to the Beaumont estate in Barbados, and rising star with Dark Vinyl Artists."

"Brandy Beaumont Barbados? On the nose alliteration, don't you think?"

Rubata smacks her palms on the table, making the glass dome with the songbook tremble. "I'm not illiterate, Beast."

"Ah-literate, Rubata, as in six slimy snakes sliding slowly southward."

"I know," she huffs, sashaying to the sofa. "Give me a better name."

You can take the Lear sister out of house arrest in Daddy's Hollywood Hills mansion, but you can't take the spoiled heiress out of the sister. The AWOL middle daughter of Midas Lear, president of Golden Pipes Records, is high and mighty even without her influencer make-up mogul status and role on the hit reality TV show, "Kickin' in With Midas." Technically, she still has TV visibility going for her with on-demand streaming.

Benedict's exit encourages the pricklier part of my nature but continuing to snipe with Rubata will only bring trouble my way. The woman is a witch. I never believed the Lear sisters' claims to be legit magical until I witnessed Rubata's shape-shifting. She's perfected the skill since being holed up here at the Caliwood with a low-level sorcerer or whatever category Gothel's fire hands fit into, an enchantress, and a sea witch.

"Thoughts on Brandy Winter?" I ask, riffing off the ice cube that is Rubata's heart to come up with a name for her creation. Trite is as nice as I can manage in my current foul mood.

Rubata claps her hands. "Snappy. I love it." She spins and holds her arms wide. "And accepting the Band Beat award for rising star is Brandy Winter." Blowing a kiss, the Lear sister or whoever she is today, flounces closer. "As a reward, I'm going to give you a tip for catching your man."

I can't wait for her vapid bit of wisdom. When she was out in the world, Rubata was infamous for treating men as disposable.

"Don't bust their balls if you're hoping for a chance to tickle those beauties later."

"Helpful. Did the Mórrigan teach you that?"

Rubata's expression turns stormy. "I don't answer to her anymore. My sister, Glissanda, can keep kissing the Mórrigan's disappointing goddess toes. Sulaa is a mentor much more in tune with my current goals." The former internet influencer fingers the thumb-sized necklace she wears. It has the look of a flattened opal or the inside of an abalone, an appropriate gift from a sea witch. Rubata looks thoughtful. "Toes, goals...does that rhyme?"

"Not even a little." I always considered Rubata as nothing more than a zip-brained, attention addict, but her devotion to the Sulaa reclassifies her as potentially dangerous.

I loathe the fact my quest to win Benedict's love is

entertainment for Rubata, Sulaa, Tressa, and the foulest of them all, Grant Gothel. The fire-wielding fiend who treated pop star Zeli like his personal puppet for her whole life deserved to be taken down on live TV. He should have burned in prison. Prospero Tempesta, head of Tempest Tunes, flung accusations of attempted murder at Sulaa Kylock, the mother and manager of the singing group, The Mermaids, but she was never caught to face justice. Talk about a family feud. Prospero's own daughter, Azure, is the product of his fling with the sea witch. At least that bunch is free of Sulaa. The cosmos must be broken if Gothel, Sulaa, and Rubata manage to dodge the retribution they deserve and remain free to plot new mayhem behind a sliding bookcase in the Caliwood.

And I spend every damn day under Dark Vinyl Artists' toxic magical thumbs because of the power Tressa's curse holds over me.

"So Beastie, *Ben and the Boulevard Bunch*'s number two man, Claude...discuss."

"Discuss what? That he's a jerk?"

"I think he's hot. Is he a boob or ass man?" Rubata lifts her breasts and finding them lacking, rubs a thumb against her necklace. Her Brandy Winter chest pixilates and shifts from a B to a D cup.

Of course, the bastard who strung Hero along for years and then popped her joy balloon when she announced the engagement to Santino would appeal to Rubata. Dark attracts dark. I should stand by without a word as Rubata uses Claude to scratch her itch the way he used women every night of the tour, but as usual, I can't keep my mouth shut.

"When Claude isn't trying to woo a groupie under his sheets, he turns into a pouty sour ass. A conceited, pouty sour ass. Picturing his face gives me heartburn."

Shit, I just described Rubata. The two are a matched set.

"Do you think he's over this?" Brandy pixilates into Hero.

A chirpy growl rises in my throat. "Don't you dare."

Rubata trails a finger across my shoulder, ignoring my anger.

"But from what I hear, Claude craves a nibble of a sweet he can't have."

A voice like oil refusing to blend with vinegar oozes from the suite behind the bookcase. "Rubata, invite our dear Beast in," says Grant Gothel.

Rubata fragments back into Brandy Winter and jerks a thumb over her shoulder. "Time to earn your keep, freak." She fluffs her hair and heads for the door. "I'm going to go discover what other sweets Claude likes to nibble."

"Beast," calls Gothel, an edge to his tone.

I long to sink my talons into his smarmy chest. Does he bleed the same fire that pours off his fingertips when he wills it?

Shouldering the bookcase farther aside to fit my bulk through, I step into what I consider the fetid lair of the Dark Vinyl Artists. The main room of the suite echoes the style of the library with dark wood and dim light. It's set up grand salon-style with a long crimson leather couch facing a more modest fireplace than the one in my library and other conversation circles sprinkled around with cushy armchairs and fancy side tables. Heavy mahogany cornices cast shadows along the upper edges of the walls.

An alcove the size of a formal dining room lined with huge aquariums is cut into the wall opposite the seating areas. Low diffused lighting and bubbles from the tanks give the nook an underwater feel. Sea witch-spelled miniature menaces swim in oval and figure eight patterns within the confines of their glass sea. Varieties of sharks, barracuda, kraken-like squid, lionfish, stingrays, and assorted sea snakes stare with dead eyes. Most frightening of all is the woman whose stature would make a Valkyrie jealous seated with closed lids on a Queen Anne style, indigo leather armchair in the center of the alcove. Sulaa Kylock, sea witch, soaks in her virtual ocean to fuel her powers.

I stomp my annoyingly large feet, moving to the center of the room.

"Step lighter, Beast," Gothel scolds from where he leans on the fireplace mantle, dressed in his signature black suit. "As you can see, Sulaa is recharging before we exit for the night."

Individual shades of blue strands in the sea witch's ropy hair light up in sequence, chasing across her head. It's eerie as her locks throw streaks across the glass of the aquariums.

Gothel strides to a cabinet embedded in the built-in floor to ceiling bookshelves, their facing carved with the same swirling leaf pattern as the carnelian and black carpet. Next to the case is an archway leading to a long hallway with several doors on each side.

I was shocked to learn of the secret residence built by the original owner of the Caliwood for his private use. Who knows what's gone down in this clandestine hideout? I'll bet the ghosts have salacious stories about its history they aren't sharing: secret trysts—jilted lovers—Hollywood power plays.

It didn't make sense Leonato would settle for an apartment suite in the hotel when a luxurious hidden home existed until I learned he had no clue of the world behind the bookcase. Poor Leo is under Tressa's magical influence to serve the D.V.A. without any awareness of their manipulation. Gothel knew about the space. I'd never take a bet against Gothel knowing every nuance of Hollywood: schemes, magic, hidden places, and the vulnerabilities of every soul in the city.

"You may visit the child while Sulaa finishes her meditations," says Gothel, easing the cabinet open.

The blaze of light from inside is so bright, I raise a clawed hand to shield my eyes. Pinprick spots dance through my vision. Pink glass bottles the size of liquor flasks line shelf after shelf. The liquid inside each vessel glows with golden light. This rare treasure ill-gotten from an innocent should be the purview of angels, not a devil and his troupe of she-demons.

Gothel counts his prizes the way he does every night and then selects three. He drinks the contents one at a time before smacking his lips in a satisfied way. The creep lifts glowing hands, bouncing a sizzling arc of tiny lightning from palm to palm. Teeth I'm sure he bleaches on a regular basis, shine against his olive skin and licorice black hair.

Oh, if only I had enough courage to scratch the villainous smile off his face, knowing what his next words will be. Attacking any of the Dark Vinyl Artists is out of the question given the restraints of the curse.

"Refill these three," he orders, holding the drained bottles to me. "We'll be gone before you're finished. Don't open your door to anyone until after we return at dawn. The traffic volume through your library is getting to be a bit much."

Gothel is heartless enough to thwart my efforts to win Ben back. My chest tightens with a larger worry. After my fresh bickering with Benedict, will he even want to seek me out again? To avoid irritating Gothel, I'll need to be mindful to plan any visits from Hero and hopefully Benedict for after the D.V.A. leave each midnight or during the day when they usually stay within the confines of their apartment.

I flip my hand, presenting my palm. Gothel settles the bottles inside the cage of my claws. He brushes hands on his suit pants as if to cleanse himself from contact with me.

"Tressa is late. When she shows, tell her to meet us at the usual place."

A pop of light in the arch of the aquarium nook wakes Sulaa from her trance. The sea witch growls like a bear with a spear in its paw as Tressa Divine leans in to poke her.

"Helloooo, Sulaa."

The sea witch clasps the gold trident necklace that glows against her skin while sparks flare in her plum-colored eyes.

Tressa shakes a finger. "Don't even think about using your puny little trident magic on me. As if your power comes anywhere near mine this far from your precious ocean." She skips to the middle of the room. "Any and all gods, if someone had told me I'd be spending so much time in this dusty rat trap with its chicken shit ghosts, and that—" Tressa flicks a finger at me and wrinkles her nose. "I'd have spelled them bald."

Gothel reverently closes the door to his stash before turning to Tressa, palms pressed together. "Patience, my angel. Soon we'll be lording over the city from our new accommodations."

They can't be gone soon enough for me.

"Oh, Beastie," trills Tressa. "I believe you dropped this." She shakes a ragged piece of paper at me.

I surge across the room, bottles tinkling in my palm to grab it. "You didn't."

"Oops," she laughs as I stare at a fresh page of the songbook, ripped free from the binding. The vile enchantress stole precious time from me. "I don't know why I bother holding you to any curse. Even if you and Benedict hook up again, you'll ruin each other with no help from me."

I want to rage—tear this room and the people in it apart. That's exactly what Tressa wants. It's why she baits me day after day. If I harm anyone in Gothel's cabal, she's sworn to separate me from Benedict forever and hit me with a curse that'll make the one I already wear look like tissue to steel. Her vindictiveness knows no limits.

Driving the hook of my beak into chest feathers to keep my temper from erupting, I clomp down the hall to the last door on the right and step inside.

A scream meets me as the child wakes, breaking off another piece of my heart. I use the tip of one claw to switch off her rainbow unicorn nightlight. I'm afraid if the eight-year-old, golden-headed innocent can see my eyes, she'll recognize the sorrow and regret I feel when I'm forced to visit her every night.

She cries for Gothel. "Papa, Papa."

I summon a voice with the clacks and growls of a true beast. "Call louder, Maisie. Let him come. I'll enjoy a fine feast of his bones."

"No please, I'll be good for you, Beast. Don't hurt my papa."

With a single jump, I'm behind her. I wrap one arm around her small frame to hold her against my feathered chest while I press the bottles one at the time beneath her eyes to catch the flowing tears. The whole time I whisper of unspeakable tortures I plan to inflict on Gothel so she will continue to weep. Oh, how I wish I could fulfill my threats instead of using them to terrorize a helpless child. When full bottles shine with the enchanted tears that power Gothel's magic are wedged between my claws, I rasp my farewell.

"Go to sleep, Maisie. I will let your Papa live another day."

I slam the door as any heartless monster would. Revulsion rises in my chest, and it takes effort to breathe. I have no choice but to continue this despicable routine. Tressa's curse binds me to it. If I dare defy her, the enchantress would not hesitate to rob me of any chance to win Benedict's heart. Turning back to the door, I rest my beak against its beveled wood and whisper to any power listening, "Bless this child with sweet dreams."

Trudging back into the now empty salon, I place Gothel's treasures in his cache. Tressa maintains that if I break the curse, all memories of what I'm forced to make Maisie endure every night will disappear along with any knowledge of my time with the Dark Vinyl Artists. Can such an ugly stain on a soul truly be wiped away? I pray Benedict will never know Beast terrorizes a child. How could he love such a thing? I long for the day I am Beatrice again with no memory of what Beast has done.

9

SONGBIRD

I JOLT UP TOO QUICKLY AND BASH AN ELBOW ON THE WOODEN INSET OF the loveseat's armrest. It takes me a moment to get my bearing. Either someone's banging on my door, or apartment 1413 has been hit by lightning.

Rrrrrumble—crack

The floor beneath me vibrates. "Are you freaking kidding me?"

The guests below my apartment in the suite with its own pair of bowling lanes are at it early even after they pulled a wee hours bowl-a-thon last night. I'd grown deaf to the muffled growl of the ball against the wooden lane and the smack of pins before I left on tour. I'll have to acclimate again like people who live next to train tracks.

Pain shoots along my back when I attempt a shoulder roll. My spine may be permanently twisted. I couldn't sleep in the bed I shared with Beatrice, not yet. There's still too much of her there, throw pillows with dingle ball trim, a knitted afghan from an anonymous granny tossed over our wicker Chesapeake-style footboard, right down to the tacky mustard and mauve paisley print on the sheets she snagged at a garage sale. Flo and Edie always poked at Bea to start her own line of what they labeled

Bohemian Chic products, featuring those garage sale bargains she loves that most people can't get out of their houses fast enough.

Beatrice is everywhere. She walked away with her favorite guitar, the clothes on her back, and nothing else. It's as if she didn't want to keep any reminders of our life together. Those all belong to me. I can't brew a cup of coffee in our kitchenette without seeing the *Pinch the Cook's Ass* dish towel and flashing back to Bea's generally terrible cooking, except for macaroni and cheese, meatloaf, and those mini sausages simmered in barbeque sauce. The woman was a wiz with comfort food. Even in the shower, still stocked with her products, I close my eyes and imagine her beautiful naked body encased in steam. My lips remember following the trail of water sluicing between her breasts down to the alluring place between her legs that drew me in again and again and—

"Hell." Another muscle pops from spending the night on this righteously lumpy and too-short loveseat. I roll and twist to my feet, adjusting my T-shirt and boxers to the way they were intended to fit a human frame. Judging from the gentle light pouring in from the balcony, I'm up much earlier than I planned. It's the universe reminding me I'm the leader of a band with responsibilities. My bandbros are counting on me to present them with an album's worth of both tour-worthy and potentially hit-making songs. We're riding the crest of a decent wave from the tour, but a band's gotta keep momentum going. Feed the fans with juicy new material to keep interest high. I've watched too many groups grasp for lost ground after killer gaps in their productivity. I can't let that happen to us.

Alfie pestered me to share what concept drives the new album. When I told him love and loss, he gave me a very Alfie *get over yourself* look and unleashed a rude buzzer noise.

"That'll get the audience dancing in their seats," he'd come back with.

He's right. Fans don't buy tickets to be reminded of the negatives in their lives. A soul-searching song or two is fine, but an entire album of boo-hoo will send listeners under their covers for a week. After his reaction, I leaned into a mix of upbeat and emo even though upbeat is not my current mental jam. Artistry plus marketability is everyone's expectation. It's my responsibility to deliver.

I step onto the balcony for a dose of fresh air. It's September's last hurrah, but the Hollywood morning already promises a scorcher of a day. The two days of fall L.A. ponies up won't hit until sometime in November. The city still rocks full-blown summer.

In the distance, a crew below the Hollywood Sign services the fairly new innovation of high-powered lights illuminating the landmark after dark. It always struck me as a missed opportunity those unlit iconic letters disappeared into the nighttime hillside while below, Hollywood proper indulged in revelry and mayhem. For years, Leonato has been jonesing to purchase patron rights to a letter since Rampion Records, Golden Pipes, Miaqua Music, and Tempest Tunes had already scored the H, O, L, and L as they came up for grabs. Leo was finally able to score the D when its guarantor dropped dead last year.

I pray Leo is in a generous mood today. He and I are meeting at noon to unwrap what he's calling my lyrical impotence. Whatever the outcome, which must be to hire a lyricist, will cost me a healthy chunk of my profits on the next album. I grip the black iron balcony rail until my knuckles turn white. "Damn it, Benedict. Pound out workable lyrics like you used to."

The Hollywood Sign stares me down. I point a finger, daring it to intimidate me, and a bubble of inspiration hits.

"Dancing on the Hollywood Sign."

The last song Bea and I were working on together will be my entry point into lyrics. In fact, we should call the album *Dancing on the Hollywood Sign*.

If I can produce any semblance of decent words and music for the title cut, maybe I can coerce the boss to push our studio date back. Opening the drawer of the bedside table that used to be Beatrice's, I free a legal sized yellow pad, her preferred stationery for lyric writing. I thumb through its pages—all empty. The stupid part of my brain hoped to find a song fragment, an idea, or God help me, a note from her that I'd missed before. Nothing.

I dive into the drawer again to grab one of the aqua colored gel pens Beatrice favored. Slowly, I move onto the bed, expecting the pain of memory to slap me. Gifted a small miracle, I make it to the middle of the mattress and sit cross-legged. This is progress. If I'm able to hang here on top of the multi-colored, log cabin patterned quilt—a Christmas gift from Flo and Edie after one of their east coast sojourns for vintage goodies—without falling apart and pound out lyrics, there's hope for me. I tap the pen against my bottom lip, close my eyes, and go back in time to when Bea and I first conceived the song.

"Dancing on the Hollywood Sign," I singsong to the apartment. The perfect upbeat, fun-loving, ditty we were toying with. Grabbing my cell, I flip through my sound files and open the music. It's catchy, not too pop, not too moody.

"Dancing on the Hollywood Sign with my baby,
Puts me in the mood to grab that lady…"

Do baby/lady rhyme? What did my granddad call it when he started to lose his hearing? A tin ear. I've got a flippin' tin ear for rhyme, more evidence I am shit at lyrics and always will be. I Frisbee the pad onto the bed next to me as the brief creative surge dribbles away.

It's time to face the music with only music. I blow through a shower, pushing aside my earlier memory of sharing the tiles with Bea, and throw on khakis and the rugby shirt with *Ben and the Boulevard Bunch* appliqued on the back to go grab breakfast on Hollywood Boulevard before I meet with Leo. Maybe I'll trip over to *Fedele Costumes* and see if Santino wants to join me. We need to start brainstorming online marketing magic to build anticipation for the album yet to be completed. Hanging with the Prince of

Optimism will gird my loins to handle the inevitable sucker punch from Leonato.

I give myself a stern talking-to to play nice and accept whatever solution the boss presents since I've got nothing to bring to the table. For the flash of a moment, I entertain the thought of Hero's gal pal, Beast. The notion leaves as fast as it came. It's too out there to consider partnering with that abrasive, probably control-freaky poetess. She irritates me and not like sand irritates an oyster to produce a pearl. The giant feathered thing plain pisses me off, not the formula for a productive pairing.

I lean on the tile counter of the kitchenette. Then again, I don't need to fall in love with her to appreciate her words.

> *"Tales are told of errors made,*
> *When hearts burn hot erasing wit.*
> *Triumph loud with fear and rage,*
> *Captures love in barren caves."*

There's no denying her poem sticks with me. The word choice is too formal, but it does dig straight into emotional truth. I snort. My emotional truth. Would Beast consider reshaping her personal style to fit *Ben and the Boulevard Bunch*?

I let my head drop, tugging at my already sore shoulder muscles. Am I dismissing Beast too quickly because of loyalty to Beatrice? Or am I just too weirded out by the prospect of writing songs with a giant bird?

The next crash of bowling pins below and a grumbling stomach send me through the apartment door. As soon as the latch snicks behind me, a faint, distant squeal fills my ears. No one else would mistake the irritating whine as anything but the elevator in need of TLC.

I however, suspect something quite different.

The hallway is empty. Leonato being an early riser won't be in his huge apartment at the far end of the hallway from library. My bandbros are not familiar with the term *early*. After listening for any signs of life in the direction of Hero's room and finding none, I hurry along the carpet to the foot of the stairs leading to the library.

Sure enough, the unpleasant warble is slightly more audible here even though it's mostly masked by the library's heavy oak door. I ease up the steps, thankful the carpet muffles my sneakiness and press my ear to the wood. Beast's voice makes the roots of my teeth ache. I clench my jaw and soak in her words.

> "Faith is a thread too easily broken
> When thoughtless words ring true.
> Temper thought before speech if hearts wring raw
> Or fate will punish you."

It's an awful din. Scratchy and shrieky. Chords played sloppily on a guitar punctuate the lyrics. If the words were not so compelling, I'd cover my ears and flee to the elevator. Instead, I'm riveted to her racket.

> "Where is a chance to right the wrong?
> Has the essence of mercy fled?
> There is no truth that perfect souls,
> Claim their freedom from fault instead."

A thousand questions race through my mind. Why does it seem this creature writes only of sadness? What awful things has Beast been through in her life? I feel a pang of gratefulness in my chest Hero made a sanctuary for the bird woman in the library. Leonato's sweet daughter is right. Where else could such an anomaly find shelter and safety?

Beast's singing, if you can call it that, stops abruptly, and she stage whispers, "Hero?"

Too late I realize in my wonderings I've clunked my head

against the door. If I bail, Beast might be afraid someone is poking around her digs.

"It's Benedict. May I come in?"

The words are out before I consider what I'm doing. A laugh escapes my lips.

Temper thought before speech if hearts wring raw.

Beast might as well be writing about me. I'm so strung out by my situation, my filters are full of holes.

The harsh *clomp, clomp, clomp* of Beast's steps approach the door. Her hesitancy to open it is palpable.

I swallow my trepidation. "Can I talk to you?"

The loud thump against the door sends me scrambling backward in surprise. A long, slow whistling exhale follows, and I move in closer. One click at a time the knob turns until Beast looks down at me through the partially open door. She's a foot, give or take, taller than me. One peck of her amble beak against the top of my head could do serious damage.

A quiet squawk I assume passes for her version of a whisper breaks the silence. "About what?"

The answer to her question propels me across a line I never imagined crossing. I'm on the verge of negotiating a deal to create songs with an abrasive, lumbering, bird gal. This is what happens when a guy is out of options.

"I'd like to reopen Hero's idea of you writing lyrics for me."

Without a word, Beast moves aside, allowing me to step into the room. She reaches over my head to shut the door and stares. Her bulk blocks me from going any further into the library. "Decided I'm not a drunken dream after all?"

I raise a hand. "Okay, I deserve that. I teetered on asshat territory yesterday." Taking a risk, I pat the feathers on Beast's arm. They are alluringly soft. I have an urge to stroke them like I would a friendly cat. I swear she leans into my touch. "I apologize."

Beast's curvy eyes squint until a fraction of the irises show. "What changed?" She flaps an arm wing.

Breeze from the motion wafts the scent of a freshly laundered comforter my way. I shrug. "Clearer head?"

She gives a sound I interpret as an avian *humph*. "Or growing desperation?"

"Not going to lie, some of that too." I gesture to the sofa. "Can we sit?" Crap, does Beast sit or just perch? Did I offend her again?

Those super-sized eyes flick a look of concern toward the bookcase next to the door.

"Whoa." The torches of all four statues are ablaze with hot blue centers surrounded by golden flames. The entire library is as bright as a fully lit football stadium.

Beast reads my discomfort. "Ignore those. They won't burn down the place, I promise. I prefer a lot of light. It makes me feel less cooped up."

I gesture at the door to the rooftop stairwell. "You can always grab some air?"

She crooks a talon over her beak. "Only at night, and even then, it's a risk."

My chest tightens in sympathy. Of course, Beast can't risk exposing herself during the daylight. How claustrophobic to be stuck in this large but nonetheless confining space every day.

I scoot past the lit torches, hugging close to the long library table. Does Beast worry about singed feathers given these energetic flames? As I pass by, there's no rise in temperature, just brightness. Odd. Something else strikes me halfway to the sofa. "Where's your fancy book?"

Beast snaps her beak. "Away from sticky fingers like yours." She nods to a shallow alcove next to the sealed elevator doors. Heavy drapes frame the arch beyond which sits a side table supporting the songbook and its dome. Spots of light reflect off its touch-me-not glass.

I notice there are additional pages piled near the base of the dome. I wonder why Beast leaves those particular sheets there instead of adding them to the stack of lyric sheets on the long table.

As I cross in front of the sofa, Beast glides quite gracefully across the room between table and ceiling. I'm gripped by curiosity to see her fly beneath a starry sky. She lights on one sturdy arm of the classic couch, which adds to her height. Her body looms, drowning me in her shadow. "You were saying?"

I force myself to swallow discomfort, doubt, and a miniscule twinge of repugnance at Beast's inhuman features. "What do you say, Beast, do we dare give working together a shot?"

10

CHARADES

THIS STUPID BIRD HEAD WITH GIANT EYES MAKES IT TRICKY TO HOLD back tears. I don't have the emotional control I did as OG Beatrice. A sniff and a turn of my neck buys me a moment to recover.

He's here. My Benedict. He came to me, proposing a partnership. Do I dare hope this is a first step in breaking my godforsaken curse?

My poetry pierced the tough veneer he attempts to wear. He admitted as much when he said my words spoke to him. I'll thank Hero later for forcing the issue.

We stare at one another. I drink in the strong curve of his jaw and straight nose ending in the hint of an adorable button. My nails itch to stroke the side of his face and listen to the rasp of his stubble. I quickly close my hand. Claws would not produce the same sound. I'd draw blood with my beastly paw.

"I heard you singing," says Ben.

My eyes dart to the door. "Shit." I'm being too loud. If Benedict heard me in the hallway, who else did?

To my surprise, he laughs.

"What's funny?"

He sucks in a breath to stop. "Sorry. Your poems are so formal, cursing seems like a non sequitur busting out of you."

My feathers ruffle of their own accord. "Get used to it." I bob my head forward. "And elaborate on why you're here." Damn it. I'm being too harsh. My tone sounds laced with impending rejection.

Chill, you fool.

I can't give into Beast's crusty default and ruin this chance to get closer to Ben.

He nods. "Here's the deal. My band and I are slated to hit the studio in a month, earlier if we can swing it. I have songs with no lyrics." Ben's gaze slides to his watch. "In a few hours, I meet with Leonato to discuss my inadequacies with lyric writing. I'm scared as piss my failure could jeopardize my band's future." Benedict stares in the fire. "If I can't serve up a decent playlist of completed songs in time, Leonato may decide to disassemble *Ben and the Boulevard Bunch* for spare parts."

Benedict is deeply troubled. He believes what he's saying. My instinct to comfort him nearly drives me to bend and nuzzle his neck with my top feathers. Since Ben's six-foot three, I'm barely a head taller than he is. Thank heavens for tall man genetics. Logistics aside, I don't think either of us is ready for so bold a gesture. A harpy diving in for an unearned snuggle is a surefire way to send him running.

"You seriously think Leonato would do that?" I flap my elbow feathers. "Hero told me your band just came off a successful tour."

He frowns. "A tour he bum-rushed us to start earlier than planned when my ugly public breakup battle with Beatrice here at the Caliwood went viral." Ben drops his head onto fists. "I'm on a short leash with him as it is. I've got to make good with the album to protect my band." Slowly, he raises his head to meet my gaze, eyes pleading. "I haven't heard much of your poetry, but what you've shared tears at the heart. I need that level of depth in this album." He waves a hand. "With a counterpoint of upbeat, of course."

"Crowds gotta dance too," I say.

Benedict rewards me with his full, unfiltered laugh that I've missed to the core of my being. He studies me more closely. "Aha, there is a sense of humor beneath the feathers."

Oh, Benedict. If you only knew besides Beatrice's humor, her body beneath my false covering longs for you.

"What do you say? Will you invest time in a journeyman artist who's not even close to a people-going-through-my-garbage level of fame?"

I trill at him. "Cut the humble, Benedict. You stopped being a journeyman the moment the group's first album tore up the charts."

Benedict rakes a strand of hair off his forehead. "Okay. I own that, but it doesn't stop me from feeling like an amateur every time I start writing a new album." He pulls a digital recorder from his pocket and lays it on the sofa cushion. "All the music for the album is on this." Flustered, Ben grabs it. "Crap, sorry. Can you work the control with your..." He gestures to my talons.

"I'm very handy." I use claws to lift the device and press the play button on and off.

"I shouldn't assume. It's just..." He trails off.

"What?" I watch him at war with his thoughts, trying to decide what to say.

He bounces a fist off his thigh. "Well, it doesn't seem fair your body—I mean you're quite balletic flying across the room. What I'm trying to say badly is it's a curse your voice..."

I flinch at the word curse. He doesn't appear to notice. Does he really think this bulk I wear appears graceful, or is he just being polite?

"Not to be insulting, but you deserve the voice of a canary instead of a crow. It would add some appeal."

I flare my claws at him. "Appeal, you say. Perhaps I must wait until I fly through the gates of Heaven and find eligible bachelors who will tolerate my voice and form. Then I might have a shot at being appealing."

"You don't believe you'll get a shot while you're earthbound?"

"Do you? What sane man would pursue a harpy?" What am I doing? It sounds like I'm trying to convince Benedict there's no point in my ever entertaining the prospect of love when that is exactly what I need from him.

The intensity of his gaze sends flashes of heat beneath my feathers.

"I suppose you're right. You voice can be off-putting and even scary." He shakes his head. "Reality is the cruel master of love."

In a flurry, I dart to the carpet and start pacing. His words hurt. I can't help it if I sound like tires on a wet highway. The noise I make offends my ears as much as I'm sure it does everyone else in my company.

Ben stands, clasping his hands and holding them out to me. "I didn't mean to hurt your feelings. Sometimes, I dip too deep into frankness. I'm sorry. We are what we are." He approaches cautiously, as if to prove he feels no fear or revulsion. In his eyes I find softness, compassion. "To me, Beast, your words hold beauty that is doomed to remain hidden in the Caliwood's library unless you find a vehicle to send your poetry into the world. Will you do me the honor of letting the band introduce your art to a wider audience? The lyricist credit will be all yours, I swear."

He thinks my words are beauty. Until he thinks the same of who I've become, this is all we'll ever be to one another, a musician and his secret lyricist, unless he can break the curse and uncover Beatrice inside Beast.

I've endured the pain of what I am and what I lost, but I've been ignorant of the new levels of hurt awaiting me as Beast attempts to win Benedict's heart. There is no direct line from him to me. I long to embrace him and tell him who I am, enlist his aid in ridding me of a harpy's guise. The curse forbids it. I must win his trust, his love with strategy and patience. Is there enough patience left in my soul to allow him the space to come to me?

I meet his gaze, hopefully encouraging him to draw closer. "Maybe the library is the only place my words are meant to be heard."

Ben erases the distance between us. "I don't believe that." He offers his hand. "I'm fully aware I'm the one benefiting the most from our partnership. Tell me what I can do for you, and I'll do it. Guide me to erase any reasons that would keep you from giving this a whirl."

I stare at his long fingers, capable of coaxing love songs from guitar strings and pleasure from my body. This man holds my heart. He's had it since our first night in the Ghost Bar nearly three years ago when we danced and ended the night making love beneath the stars on the rooftop of the Caliwood. Benedict Boyd reclaimed my heart a second time when he defied his band to name me their new lead female singer. I tainted our future, professing to hate the man I dearly loved. Our matching pride and relentlessness led to the fight, but it was my words that triggered the curse.

My heart that belongs to Benedict alone, believes he will be my curse breaker.

Again, his hand reaches for me.

I take it.

"Deal?" he asks, the hope in his eyes harmonizing with the same emotion in his voice as he carefully threads fingers between my talons.

I gently squeeze, curving my claws around his wrist. Damn it. I'm too choked up to answer. Maybe it's for the best. The horrid timbre of my voice may spoil the moment.

Benedict moves our joined hands in a shake and then slides his free. "Write lyrics for one ballad and one up tempo, and we'll see if we're a fit." He snaps his fingers. "I'll go print out a playlist of the titles in my head and the visions I have for each song. That'll give you a jumping off point to choose what you want to work with first."

My heart flutters like my feathers do in a California breeze. So it begins again—Benedict and Beatrice making songs together.

He hurries to the door, but stops, not turning back. "I'd love for you to start with cut five, 'Dancing on the Hollywood Sign.'"

A surge of joy turns my heart flutters into a dance. He wants Beast to put words to the last song we worked on together. More proof Beatrice is still in his heart.

"How long do you need to see if any of your existing work will fit my music, or to write something new for a couple of songs?"

"How many days do you think you can string Leonato along?"

Ben looks desolate. "Maybe a week before he'll want to see progress. We hit the studio in a month. I'll be vague and tell Leo I may have found someone to work with. He'll be distracted with the Haunted Hollywood Bar Crawl for the next three weeks, since it's his brainchild. Any forward progress should placate him for now and buy me, buy us, some time."

Us. Ben isn't as shit at lyrics as he thinks. "I'll try to work fast. I believe I've got tons of material to potentially fit your music."

"Here's hoping," says Ben, holding up crossed fingers. "I'll grab the playlist and slip it under the door so I don't disturb your flow." His forehead creases. "Is there a way to get in touch with you?"

I ask a question I already know the answer to. "Are you a night owl?"

Ben snorts. "I'm the lead singer of a rock band."

"Point taken," I laugh-squawk at him. "Knock on my door after twelve-thirty every night. I'll answer if I've got something for you." I shake my wing feathers. "Hero visits all the time. We can communicate through her as well."

He flashes me the smile I've seen every night in my dreams and lets himself out. As if to mock my hope, the songbook flares in the alcove as another page tears free and shivers to the bottom of the dome. Before vanishing time sours my mood, a stream of light like a blue comet's tails streaks around the room, extinguishing the statues' torches.

My four ghostly companions pour out of marble and close in on me.

"A definite thaw, sweetie," says Audra as she beckons Graham to waltz with her on the library table. "Don't you agree, Monty?"

Montague strokes his chin. "Aye, the gallant seems drawn into your sphere."

Ah, crazy Monty and his classical affectation. In his heyday, such verbiage probably screamed sophistication with the rich and famous.

Sassy tucks her chin to her chest and gazes at me through her nearly transparent lashes. "Will he read me a story?"

I raise my beak and wiggle my tongue, which always entertains the kiddo. "Soon, little one. I don't think he's quite ready to meet you."

Her lips push into a pout. "He saw me before when the library was dark and icky. He didn't read me a story."

"He did get a good peek at us the night of Tressa's curse," Audra says, toying with a loose curl on her head that always springs back into place no matter what she does to it.

I shiver at the memory of my spirit pals trapped inside Tressa's blue wall of ice. The masks of panic and despair on their faces as they clawed against the enchantress's frozen captivity will never leave my memory. If Benedict and I had given that moment in time the proper balance of belief and wariness, I might not be standing here with clawed feet and a beak.

"I love reading you stories, Sass," I say.

"Will you read one now?"

"Can you wait a little while until I finish some important work, sweetie?"

Drops of black liquid begin to spill from Sassy's eyes. They leave tar-like tracks down her cheeks as she wails before zipping through the wall.

"Kids," says Audra. "I don't envy the next person she runs into." She twirls Graham on their tabletop dance floor.

Without ceremony, the three remaining spirits grow fainter as they disappear through the library wall. Off to the job of day-haunting the Caliwood, I suppose.

I retrieve Benedict's digital recorder, hit play, and close my eyes. I feel his music. It resonates through my bones and into my soul. It's gritty. Identical pain to what I've felt this past year infuses every note. There's comfort knowing I haven't been alone in my personal darkness. Benedict was always there with me.

I pause after the first song to savor its after effect. This is who I am. With his music and my lyrics, I am home. As I languish in memories of what was and what will hopefully be again, a single sheet of paper slides under my door. Ben doesn't knock or even call out. Did he hear me playing his music? Does it pain him to hand his creations over to Beast instead of beloved Beatrice?

If I am still his beloved. I must believe I can be, or my efforts will be in vain.

With a corner of the carpet pulled up, I'm able to free a floorboard and access the old vent system running through the hotel. It's wide enough for me to sneak down until I land above a corner of the Ghost Lounge. It may be wasting valuable writing time, but I can't resist listening to *Ben and the Boulevard Bunch* playing live each night of the bar crawl.

It's been a week since I agreed to collaborate with Ben, and I've matched nearly all of his ballads to existing poems. It's as if we've been writing the album together despite our separation. We conceived the concept together. It makes sense we'd be on the same page creatively. I haven't made the mental shift from soulful to fun-loving. Two of what I think of as his *dance party songs* still beg for lyrics. Listening to my former bandmates in real time stokes my own creative juices to write or adapt a few of my lighter poems into claw tapping lyrics.

Ben taps at my door every night. I've let him in to reassure him I'm making progress, but I've only shared the lyrics for two songs to convince him I'm the real deal. Watching his intensity as he picks out the chords on Beatrice's guitar while he sings is a sweet reward. I mistook his surprise at first as dislike. His gentle touch on my arm, grateful tone, and the barest dot of a tear in the corner of his eye showed me the truth. He loved the songs. I indulged in moments of glimpsing a featherless future but stopped myself. Benedict and I still face a journey together with no guarantee of any future.

Each night, he stays a little longer, never pestering me about the lyrics. Benedict respects process and I've told him this is mine. We talk music. He entertains me with stories of tour performances and audiences, never his offstage antics. Last night, he stayed longer than usual, making himself comfortable lying on the couch while he regaled me with details of the night's bar crawl set. If only I could tell him how much even his mundane chats are a gift.

My gut tells me what the turning point must be. Ben must be blown away with my lyrics for "Dancing on the Hollywood Sign." Nailing that song is the next crucial step in strengthening Ben's bond with Beast. I pray the completed song will work to tear down the walls surrounding his wounded heart. With so much riding on it, I've been afraid to dive in.

Tonight feels electric. I'm enjoying a performance high by osmosis. The energy nudges me past my fear, and I know it's time to work on our song.

When their final set ends, I scoot back to the library. Hero visited earlier to slash and resew some of the new dresses she brought from Flo and Edie to accommodate my shape. I avoid wearing any of the new pieces when I flap through the dusty vents. I slip into one now. I may be feathered, but my vanity isn't entirely lost. Looking nice for Benedict's next visit is high on my list. Hearing his soft rap on the door would be welcome.

I rifle through the sheets of lyrics I wrote when the songbook was generous and replenished any sheet of staff paper it gave up. Benedict and Hero call them my poems. Only I know they were always lyrics waiting to be born into songs with the power of Ben's music.

The one song I need is the one I can't find in my piles, and panic crushes my chest. I wrote what I hope are killer lyrics for "Dancing on the Hollywood Sign," months ago. I hope they hold up.

"Where are you?" I growl at the stack of pages.

My gaze drifts to the ceiling with its rooftop beyond. I vaguely remember penning the song under the stars. I probably stuffed it into the chest of drawers, knowing it would be months before the band would return from touring and hit their rooftop man-child clubhouse.

I crack the door at the top of the stairwell to check for any life beyond pigeons under the red neon letters. My birdy brethren always fly off once I appear. The space is empty, so I step out under the full midnight moon and breath in a lungful of air with the blend of breeze and whiff of exhaust from Hollywood Boulevard. An acrid snap of something foul slinks in from the other side of the framework supporting the huge letters of the Hotel Caliwood sign.

I fly to perch on the center of the H where I blend in best and peer down at a ring of knee-high stones. Sulaa conjured these for Rubata on the darkest part of the rooftop away from Hollywood Boulevard. There's no equipment to maintain on this half of the open-air space. It's a perfect shadowland to cobble together a witch's circle. Sure enough, Rubata twirls in the middle of the stones, giggling. I'm surprised to find her up here. Even though I know there's a second roof access from the Dark Vinyl Artist's lair, Rubata rarely misses the opportunity to pass through the library and taunt me. I wonder how often she sneaks into the open air here for rituals and witchy mischief.

A creak of metal from the east side of the Caliwood's roof draws my attention. Claude's face beneath his slicked-back chestnut hair appears at the top of the fire escape ladder. Rubata hears it too. Beneath me, Rubata Lear disappears, leaving a perfect replica of Hero Andante in her place.

What the hell?

"Hello," whispers Claude. He takes a few steps and in a louder voice, calls again. "Hello."

The urge to soar down and grab Rubata's "Hero" in my talons and drop her over the edge of the roof puffs my feathers. My gut tells me to keep silent.

Rubata slips out of her circle and hurries across the roof toward the band's hangout atop a rug pilfered from one of the hotel suites. A rug Benedict and I rolled around on plenty of times.

"Hi-eee. Are you Claude?"

Claude turns to the shape approaching him from the shadows. "Yeah. I see you made it here okay." There's wariness in his voice. "Where's your friend, Brandy Winter?"

How does Claude know Brandy Winter, one of Rubata's fake skins, and what in the name of the Caliwood ghosts is he up to?

"She brought me through the bar next door and as far as your scary bridge. I thought I was going to fall." Rubata/Hero purses her lips. "Then Brandy bailed to go clubbing."

I follow the direction Rubata points to discover a trio of wood and metal planks bridging the gap between Caliwood's rooftop and the empty upper deck of the *Kicks and Kinks* bar next door. Hero told me Santino, who owns the property housing the sleazy bar, had finally been able to terminate their lease after a year of trying to oust them after questionable dealings with boulevard vandals and numerous run-ins with police.

Rubata slides from the darkness into red neon light and flips a strand of hair over her shoulder.

Claude gasps, seeing her clearly for the first time. "Holy shit. You could be Hero's twin."

"So I've been told," giggles Rubata, gliding within inches of Claude. "Brandy told me you're eager to get naughty with this." She drops her head back, brushes hands along the sides of breasts, to her waist, her hips, and around to her ass, which she slaps.

For once in his life, Claude doesn't have an obnoxious retort. The dude must be in shock at the Hero.2 closing in on him.

Rubata grabs the waistband of Claude's jeans to pull his hips flush against hers. She gyrates against his crotch and then steps away to admire the bulge growing behind his zipper. "I see I'll do even if I'm not the real thing." She runs a fingertip along his groin.

Claude answers in a throaty rasp. "We need to pretend we're getting naughty to mess with some buds."

Bile rises in my throat. Nothing good can come of Rubata pretending to be Hero no matter who Claude plans to punk. I'm righteously offended for my friend. I should soar down and scare the living piss out of them.

Except, Rubata wouldn't be spooked. She'd find a way to plunge my life into an even greater hell than it is. Joints in my legs feel like they're going to buckle. Is this the curse warning me not to screw with any Dark Vinyl Artist? Even if I managed to mess with whatever is going down, the vindictive Lear witch would love to use any excuse to ruin the progress I've made with Benedict. I can't risk that. All I can do is watch.

I open my beak and inhale deeply. I may be stressing about nothing. This could just be Rubata's way to rid Claude of his pants.

"Uh, huh," purrs Rubata. "But why pretend when the real thing can be oh, so much more convincing?" Rubata fists the front of Claude's T-shirt to pull him close. I see her tongue push between his lips. The kiss barely has time to get steamy before she's hitched a leg over his hip.

Claude's moans nauseate me. Hero told me of his confessions of love, yet here he is doing the nasty with someone he knows damn well isn't her. I look away, stuck here until they leave. Soon enough, I hear Rubata telling Claude exactly what she wants and the sound of skin slapping skin. Claude's rhythmic expletives confirm he thoroughly enjoys delivering on her requests.

Over the sounds of their lustmaking, I miss the footsteps on the walkway between the rooftops.

"Hero?" Santino's choked whisper is laced with shock. He and D.G. stand beneath the C of the Hotel Caliwood sign not more than ten feet from the copulating couple.

Santino stumbles, and my heart skips with fear he's going to back off the edge. I wish I could swoop in and assure him what he thinks he's witnessing is all lies. Santino bolts across the planks and vanishes.

D.G. trails Santino and returns a few minutes later. "Our man grabbed an old bottle off the bar in Kicks and Kinks, cracked it against the wall then skated out onto the boulevard."

Claude slings an elbow over the back of the couch. "Think he bought it?" He leers at Rubata's bare breasts.

"That's a hard, no shit," says D.G., who takes in the amount of naked on the couch. "Lotta hard going on up here."

"Does ole Tino suspect we saw him?"

"Nope."

Claude points at the adjoining rooftop. "Get lost. Make sure our dude doesn't run into traffic." He dives into a kiss with Rubata, breaking it off to yell over his shoulder. "Keep your trap shut, D.G." Claude mimes popping a pill into his mouth. "I'll do the same. And pull the damn planks. I don't need any more visitors."

With a quick flip, Claude has Rubata on her back. I ache to launch this pair of bastards off the edge of the roof without Gothel, Sulaa, or Tressa finding out. The damned curse prevents me from doing or saying anything that would compromise the Dark Vinyl Artists or their nasty plans. Everything about tonight is wrong— Santino's pain, my silence, Claude and D.G.'s dark purpose.

Oh, dDear stars above a town made of both wonder and villainy, why is my redemption shackled to the treachery below me?

There's nothing I can do or say to right this wrong without forfeiting my chance at being Beatrice. If I even try to chastise Rubata to her face, she'll go straight to the enchantress and insist my curse be permanent. I'm forced to bear the guilt and shame of being party to Claude and Rubata's deceit by the silence of self-preservation.

On the day I thought my path finally turned toward the light and Benedict, darkness once again consumes me. I fly to the farthest space on the rooftop away from them and duck my head under a wing.

11

GHOSTLY ADVICE

MAYBE I SHOULD HAVE BEEN AN ACTRESS INSTEAD OF A SINGER. MY Beatrice self, that is. No one in their right mind would call Beast a singer. For the first few nights after Ben came knocking at my door after Claude's rooftop villainy with Rubata, I managed a convincing brave face despite a stomach that felt like I'd swallowed razor blades. It's all I can do to hold back a tirade about what a low life Claude is when I'm face-to-face with Benedict. I'm dying to spill the ugly truth of his bandbro's nasty charade and enlist Ben to help glue Santino's heart back together.

If only this curse didn't have my truths pinned to the wall.

Ben's companionship is the only thing keeping me sane. He's taken to bringing me stupid little gifts at our sessions together. The first was half a cookie with a dangling fortune he'd clearly attempted to stuff back inside that said, *Your future is about to take flight.* We mock-argued over whether that meant he was going on an airplane or that I'd fly him over the city. I loved the way his eyes sparkled at the thought of a harpy piggyback ride above Hollywood Boulevard. When I had to dash his daydream given the dicey aerodynamics involved, I don't know who was more disappointed.

Then there was the pamphlet from the cultish church down the block forced on any poor passerby who didn't dodge their aggressive recruiters fast enough. Ben and I laughed at the plastic-looking, too-happy people in the pictures and then busted out spontaneous dramatic oratories of the doom awaiting those who refused the cult. Benedict stood on the library table, using his rowdy call-an-audience-to-attention voice that brought Hero to the door to tell him to dial it down. Thank goodness if anyone did hear, it was Ben's voice they'd recognize and not mine.

Amidst those weeks of sharing coffee drinks, dissolving into fits of laughter over Ben's disastrous latest headshots, and fitting my lyrics to his music, something I desperately hoped for began to happen. It's a progression we skipped before—friendship before sex. There's warmth and comfort to defining a mutual rhythm. We had that once. If Ben can somehow embrace the Beatrice within Beast and rediscover love, no curse will keep us apart. Despite my longing to be in Benedict's arms and his bed, I celebrate this joy of finding a way back into his life.

It feels cosmically unfair that my joy wears a shadow of dread over potential fallout brewing over Santino's discovery of Rubata and Claude on the rooftop. I worry for Hero and Santino. My inability to intervene and expose the deception weighs second only to the curse on my heart. Considering his fragile emotional reality these days, I can't imagine Santino isn't an unexploded bomb. God, I hope I'm wrong. It's as if Hollywood Boulevard wavers in borrowed stillness. Any day a storm will break. For now, I allow myself to revel in the growing bond with Benedict.

Ah, my Benedict. He's been patient, agreeing to wait for "Dancing on the Hollywood Sign" to be the last song we complete even though it was the first he asked for. As our friendship deepens, I sense his growing trust to make the song what it must be. We both need it to be perfect. I love the lyrics I've created. They're straightforward to match the upbeat pace of the tune, but will Ben be able to handle the blunt, simplistic recap of our story? To our audience, "Dancing on the Hollywood

Sign" may read as a puff piece, but Benedict will know it's anything but.

The familiar drop in temperature and light breeze announce the arrival of half of my ghost posse. Audra's bluish glow illuminates the alcove as she leans over the songbook's dome. Graham floats next to her.

Her lips draw up in a petite bow of concern. "The book is looking a little thin."

I wave a talon in her direction. "Don't remind me."

Graham peers through the glass. "Thinner perhaps, but not in its last throes."

My gaze lingers on the spot in the wall they faded through. "Where's Monty?"

Graham slowly shakes his head, but his mouth curls into a lazy smile. "Doing what Monty does best, schmoozing."

"Big spirit bash at the pool tonight," says Audra, primping her blond bob. "The big doings even inspired Sassy to trade whining for a tap dance. The girl is quite a talent. Who can resist those adorable bobbing ringlets?" She sighs.

I wait for Graham to weigh in on the ghost party, but as usual, he anxiously checks his watch. Poor guy, he can't even enjoy a diversion, stressing over perpetually arriving late to his blasted award show. How I wish I knew the secret to permanently snap him out of his anxiety loop.

I sneak a glance at the door. Benedict is due soon. "Why are you two up here instead of whooping it poolside? Run out of ice?"

Audra floats to sit on the edge of the table near where I've planted myself in the oversized, padded dining chair. "Graham and I were chatting. We've decided tonight's the night."

I smooth a drooping feather off my cheek. "Who's the lucky guy?"

Her hand strokes the air as if she's petting a cat. "Not for me, my lovely. For you."

My face heats. "Tell whatever hot harpy ghost you've got your sights on that I'm already taken."

Audra's face hovers inches from mine. "This is the night you should play Benedict 'Dancing on the Hollywood Sign.'"

I stand and begin to pace. "I'm not sure he's ready to hear it. I need more time for him to feel connected to me before I spring it on him."

Graham's concerned expression reflects off the glass of the dome. He sighs and drifts out of the alcove. "Time is the one thing we cannot help you with."

Audra keeps up with my nervous stride. "You're stalling for no reason."

I stop. "No reason. What is he going to think when a stranger hands over lyrics that narrate his damn life?"

Graham flanks my other side. "You are hardly a stranger to him."

I move to the fireplace and both ghosts trail me.

"We've been watching you two these last weeks," says Audra. "Don't tell me you haven't noticed he sits a little closer to you every day. A whole lot of shoulder bumping and other excuses to touch you. And those eyes with purple shading the blue..." She lays a hand over her heart. "They drink you in, Beast."

Graham moves his hands through the air as if he's conducting a symphony. "The fellow hangs on your beautiful words, relishing the way they weave into his music."

"Okay, so we click with the work. You can't call it more than that after only a few weeks."

Audra imposes herself between the mantle and me, causing me to take a step back. "Maybe this body has only had a few weeks, honey," says Audra, making a patting motion on my shoulder. "But your hearts have loved far longer." She slides onto the sofa, crossing her legs at the ankles and smacking her knees. "I've always believed when you laugh as easily with a man as you do with Benedict, it's the sign of an undeniable connection. I'm sure he feels it too."

Graham strolls around the sofa. "Dear Beast, we are certain comradery with your paramour is in its bloom."

"He's hardly my paramour." I reach over to squeeze the edge of the mantle with my talons. "Yes, I'll admit we've grown closer. I, I... I'm afraid if I push too hard, I will push him away."

"From what I've seen," says Graham, straightening his suit coat and taking another furtive glance at his watch. "It would take a mighty push to counteract the pull between you two. Fear is the foe to defeat."

Cold seeps into my ear as Audra moves her filmy lips across its shell. "Play him the song."

Before another protest has a chance to form beneath my beak, they're gone. Damn those ghosts for throwing me into a panic I've got to get under control before Benedict knocks on the door tonight. I'd breathe into a paper bag to keep from hyperventilating if I had one big enough to fit over my beak.

Are they right? In some intangible language is Ben's heart speaking to Beast's? I want to believe it. What more can I do to coax his friendship past its boundary into affection, the first fragile steps toward passion that has a shot at turning to love? Where is the tie between Beast and Beatrice that Benedict can feel without words?

I squawk. Ugh, I detest that sound.

Words—they are my domain. The urgency to use them to further my cause is mine, yet I am speechless.

Play him the song.

The ghosts are right. It is time. I must trust their observations and my rising hope that Ben is indeed seeing something in Beast worth valuing.

I want him to hear our story in the lyrics. I want him to remember us.

12

MUSIC AND LYRICS

BEAST DIDN'T OPEN THE DOOR FOR ME LAST NIGHT. NOT A GOOD SIGN. I've been charged up by the progress we've made, and to me, our collaboration totally rocks. I can't believe I'm reading the situation wrong. Beast seems as into our work as me. Plus, the boss totally bought into my story of a lyricist who wanted to remain anonymous. As long as I keep ponying up completed songs, he wouldn't care if the words were lifted off a to-go menu.

I tried knocking on her door several times, but Beast didn't answer. Maybe it's part of her process to go zero dark thirty on a deadline, but the delay is making me insane. The bar crawl, our buffer from Leo, ended tonight. The band has started rehearsing the songs we've finished which are kickin' perfect, but the most important lyrics have yet to arrive. To me, without "Dancing on the Hollywood Sign," there is no album. It's the essence of the message this album is destined to deliver: loss does not steal hope, it merely shadows it until we allow the light back in.

My time with Beast has allowed my soul to begin to reclaim its lost luster. Beast chases my shadows away. Our time together has felt timeless even though it's still so new. I need to tell her what's she's done for me.

I hug my guitar to my chest to push down my rising anxiety. Less than week from now, we're in studio. What if I hate the words she's written?

Deep breaths, Benedict.

How could I hate Beast's words? The closer we've gotten these past weeks, the more I swear I've glimpsed her soul, her spirit. It's a lovely thing, vulnerable yet giving. My appreciation for her has softness around its edges.

Hero shuffles the last of the bar crawl crowd from the Ghost Lounge and starts ripping down strings of skeleton head lights with a broom handle. The woman is consumed. Her engagement party is tomorrow night, and clearly haunted Hollywood décor isn't the right vibe.

I duck to avoid getting cold-cocked by a giant rubber bat. "Hey, Hero, why isn't lover boy here helping you?"

"He's still at his folk's place up the coast." She knocks another bat off a hanging light fixture. "Tino's dad needed help with a major DIY project. After Pops fell off a ladder last year and wrecked his back, Mrs. Fedele won't let him near a ladder."

"It must be a big-ass project to keep him away this long?"

Hero sighs. "When they finished the house project, they headed out on their annual father- son sail from Santa Barbara to Lalale Island and then on to Catalina."

"Sailing can't be easy on Fedele the elder's back."

"Leeni told me that Uncle Nico went with them to handle the heavy lifting his dad used to do." Hero leans on the broom. "Tino was supposed to be back this morning, but he texted to say they were taking an extra day.

"And has he been enjoying his sojourn with the waves?

Hero wrinkles her nose. "He's been a man of few words, mostly emojis, not many messages. Just enough to let me know he's safe and busy." She smiles wistfully. "I text enough for the both of us. I'm sure I'll get all the briny details when he gets back."

I grab another broom and rid the room of a couple bats and assorted spider webs a bit baffled by Santino's prolonged absence given his obvious adoration of Hero. "Sounds like someone is dodging bat cleaning duty."

Her frantic wave of flying rodent destruction stalls as she chews on her pinkie nail. "Who can blame him for hiding out. I am obsessed when it comes to decorating."

"And it's always a masterpiece," I say, fanning my arm in a circle around the room. "So, what's your theme for the engagement party?" Melancholy kidney punches me. There was a time I totally believed Beatrice and I would head to the altar. She was my person, and I took it for granted.

"Falling for fall," says Hero, a wistful look on her face. "If the seasons won't show up for us in Hollywood, we'll take them by force."

With obligatory chitchat in the rearview, I ease into the real topic on my mind. "Has your library friend mentioned anything about a meet up tonight?" I strive to hide my disappointment. "She wasn't in a door-opening mood yesterday."

Hero looks baffled. "I texted you."

I slide my cell from my pocket. "Nope."

Hero retrieves hers from her crossbody bag. "Crap, I never pressed send. Here."

My phone dings with the message Beast does want to see me tonight. A thrill tickles my insides. I'm dying to hear the lyrics she's come up with for the song that matters the most to me. Strangely enough, it's also the prospect of clocking time with her also has my toes tapping. These past few weeks in my new friend's company have made me begin to feel like the Benedict that's been dormant since Bea walked out. Besides, Beast is quick-witted and crazy talented. I'm charged with the energy surge that comes with successful collaboration, and if I'm honest, an important friendship.

Hero scrolls through her messages and sighs. It doesn't take a genius to know she wants more attention from her man. If Santino knew he was bumming her out, I'm sure he'd find a way to send a dozen messages despite crap boat reception. Dude would probably swim to shore, holding his phone above the swells to put a smile back on Hero's face.

"Tell Be–," Hero darts a look around to see if anyone heard her near slip. "Your friend, I need my laptop back. She said she's been using Garage Band to work on your stuff."

"Why would she need...never mind." I guess Beast wants to tinker and my digital recorder doesn't cut it for the perfectionism I've come to expect from her. "I'll grab your laptop."

"Sweet. Bring it down when you guys finish."

"We might be awhile."

Hero shoots me her *are you thick* glare. "Same. Transformation takes time, Ben."

I feel guilty leaving Hero to decorate solo. "I'll come give you a hand after. Do you want me to ask the guys to help out?"

Hero glances to the stage where D.G., Claude, and Alfie are packing our gear. Her lips form a tense line. "Pass." When Claude catches her gaze, Hero swiftly looks away. "Hard pass."

"Understood," I say and lean in close. "Too bad Beast can't lend a wing. She could handle the high stuff."

Hero shoves me away. "As if." Her gaze lifts to the ceiling. "I'll bet she'd love to get out of that stuffy old library, poor thing."

"You're a good friend to her, Hero."

She levels a stare at me. "You be good to her too, Ben."

"I mean to," I say, and I do. I feel I have been. If our partnership continues to pan out, maybe I can help Beast expand her territory, give her a bigger life so she isn't caged. Damn, if I accept her, why can't others? A rush of purpose fills me. Beast doesn't deserve a life of confinement.

"Later, Hero."

"Yeah, yeah," she says and returns to whacking shit from the ceiling.

I book it to the elevator, checking my watch. It's after 12:30am. I'm good to go. At the door to Beast's library, I raise a hand to knock when sound from the other side of the door stops me dead.

"They're calling it the Battle Royale of Hollywood Boulevard. Last night following their win for best song and best album of the year at the Band Beat Awards, Benedict Boyd and Beatrice Sharpe, the lead singers of the skyrocketing band B & B +3 trashed the famed Hollywood landmark, Hotel Caliwood, with their soon-to-be legendary brawl. Sources say the pair started in-your-face shouting at the afterparty in the Ghost Lounge where they broke a good portion of Leo Andante's crystal champagne flutes and turned over a line of bar stools before taking the conflict to the main lobby. Many lamps gave their lives in battle along with a seven-foot-high palm near the famed portico fountain. Combat resumed poolside where lounge chairs, tables, and a full cabana setup including tent and wicker couch ended up submerged. Video from a dozen cell phones don't conclusively show if Benedict pushed Beatrice and her ten thousand dollar, floral appliqued, tulle designer gown into the water, or if he tried to keep her from slipping. Neither singer is available for comment, but Leonato Andante, president of the Caliwood, Inc. music company as well as owner of Hotel Caliwood, insisted he would seek reparation from the damages caused by two of the biggest stars on his roster."

Shame covers me like plastic wrap on leftovers. I can't breathe. My heart feels wedged between two ribs. I relived our fight a thousand times since it happened, and Beatrice disappeared from my life. Always alone. No one dared bring it up to me, except for Leo, who promptly booked a series of last-minute venues to drop kick the band on the road early for our yearlong tour, hoping our absence would allow the story cool off.

I insisted he only charge me and not Beatrice for the chaos. Luckily, insurance took the brunt of the financial ding after I ponied up Leo's deductible, a chunk of change that seriously thinned out my savings.

Now the fucking fight that fragmented my soul is going to be the elephant in the room between Beast and me. Will she even open the door or is the stink of Benedict Boyd something she'll choose to avoid at all costs?

I don't want her to walk away. Yes, I need her lyrics, but the essence behind those lyrics, the essence of Beast, I don't want to lose. Art seeks art and the artists who make it. It brought Beatrice and I together. It's the same pull making Beast's acceptance of me a powerful want.

If either of us bails on writing together, my one remaining option will be to throw myself on a spike since I've screwed over my band not providing them with a complete album to record. Maybe they're better off without me. Without Beatrice, my drive to create has dwindled. Complete atrophy is imminent. Unless...unless... Beast doesn't turn away from me.

I raise my hand to the door, suck in the breath of a dead man walking, and knock. From behind the door, I hear the slam of a laptop being closed, and then silence. I wait.

Come to me, Beast.

Silence stretches until I can't bear it another second. I knock again. Hero said Beast wanted to see me. My insides begin to go numb. That was before she watched the video. She knows about the fight so why is she watching the damn thing unfold again?

The sound of claws scrape against floor, and my throat clenches. Then silence.

Please, come to me, Beast.

I ache to call out her name, but she is a secret, my secret, Hero's secret. I won't betray that. If Beast won't see me, maybe Hero will agree to run interference. She can vouch for my regrets, hell, my devastation over the fight and the responsibility I fully accept for Beatrice's leaving.

Scrape

Is she moving closer? I jump back a second later when a floor shaking *thud* sounds on the other side of the door. I picture Beast flying across the room and landing close enough until only two inches of oak separate us.

The knob begins to turn so slowly, I yearn to twist it the rest of the way in a fury. I wait. Patience is the right call. The same patience I abandoned during the terrible fight with Beatrice.

Click.

The lock disengages and the door opens a crack, no more. Gently, I push, and it yields. I slip inside, close the door, and lean back against it. Beast has already crossed the room and stands in the alcove, staring at her songbook in its dome. I walk to the table where Hero's laptop sits but go no closer, giving Beast space.

Is she going to stand there and give me the silent treatment? After weeks of learning what makes each other tick, can she not even look at me? Is Beast the mirror to remind me what a useless bag of skin I was that terrible night? What does it matter if the messenger making me face the memory still eating away at my spirit is fair or hideous? The memory is hideous. Why not the messenger?

But Beast has stopped being hideous to me the way she was that first night. It hits me that I'm beginning to find unique beauty in her strangeness.

"I didn't push her," I say. When Beast doesn't answer, I go on. "But I didn't do what she asked." Slowly, I step to the edge of the alcove. "Beatrice insisted if I jumped into the pool with her and ruined my expensive tuxedo to match the total loss of her loaner designer dress, we had a chance. Proof of solidarity."

Beasts wings rise and fall as her breathing quickens.

My fingers grip the molding around the alcove's arch. "I didn't jump."

I knock the top of my head against the wood. "I should have jumped." It feels right to bare my soul to Beast. She's part of my life now, part of my music. I can trust Beast with my truths.

After a stuttering breath, I continue. "Beatrice constantly hit me with those kinds of tests. She had a tough life. Trust issues. I understood her unhealed bruises and always did my damnedest to give her the right answer." I raise my gaze to Beast. "But during the fight, I failed her. Callously wrote off her request as ridiculous and refused to play the game. It cost me my soul."

Beast's voice is quiet. "What was the fight about?"

Something in the tone of her voice makes the question feel like one of Beatrice's tests. Only Beatrice and I know what sparked the not so merry war between us. I could bury the specifics, but an ache behind my breastbone propels me to tell Beast everything.

"It was over firing Claude. Beatrice found out he'd cheated on Hero."

A low growl rumbles from Beast. "Claude is human filth."

"I admit Claude has a faulty moral compass, but he's a damn fine musician and he's been loyal to me and my vision since day one. The band would never have come to be if it weren't for Claude sticking it out through our garage rehearsal phase until we finally got our break. I felt like I owed him."

"Do you still feel that way?"

"Let me be clear. Beatrice turned the fight into a choice between Claude or her." I press the side of my fist against my chest. "I refused to acknowledge that. My tunnel vision escalated the conflict to volcanic proportions."

Beast thrusts her chin forward causing the tip of tiny fangs to peek out of her bottom lip. Not her best look, but I don't turn away.

"You didn't answer my question."

I fill my lungs to steal a thought-gathering moment. "I still rock some loyalty to Claude, but Beatrice was my life. Given the chance, I'd fall at her feet and give her anything she asked for, including giving Claude the boot, but she dropped completely off the grid. God knows, I tried to find her."

I'm surprised at the tickle against the skin of my forearm as Beast rests her wing on my shoulder. "Your Beatrice's ultimatum hits me as out of balance. Claude in the band or her in your life. She owed you the choice of a compromise, not an all or nothing proposition."

"The band was our life. Beatrice and I are both to blame for allowing our relationship to become so singularly focused. Beatrice was it for me. I wish I'd gushed every day how deeply I loved her and dreamed of us making little musical babies. Mumbling I love you without elaboration in the half-second before you fall asleep doesn't cut it." I shake my head and grunt. "I told you I was shit at lyrics. That goes for real life words as well. Idiot me assumed we had plenty of time to draw the map of us. Ambition came first with me. I have the teeth marks on my ass to prove it."

"Beatrice wasn't ambitious?"

I laugh without humor. "She was, but not a captive of it like me. The artistry of music making drove her. It was an extension of a beautiful heart and soul. Passion for Beatrice was in creating our songs not the number of downloads."

Beast's wing trembles against me, and by reflex, I stroke the feathers of my companion. The gesture surprises me at first. When she doesn't protest, I continue. Comforting her feels like a natural progression in our growing closeness. "The reality is, Beast, you don't shit on fate and come out unscathed."

She pulls her wing free of my hand and with one impressive hop lands on the table as if she's no larger than a sparrow on a branch. "Don't I know it."

A question nags at me. "Why were you watching the video? Don't tell me you're a tabloid junkie. If you want dirt on me, just ask. I own it all."

Beast pecks at a stack of papers next to the computer. The human skin of her face flushes a lovely shade of cranberry. It compliments her feather headdress. "Maybe I was looking for the Benedict hiding underneath the bad press."

If she searched me, I'm sure she got an eyeful. Especially after the series of wound-licking terrible choices I made on the first leg of the tour. "Any chance you'll still consider working with me after seeing—" I jerk my chin at the laptop. "What a useless bastard I can be."

"I think," says Beast, preening her feathers as if deliberately avoiding my pointed stare. "You should stop assuming all the blame for your fight with Beatrice."

I expected judgement or condemnation from her after watching the damn viral video. Beast's kindness is unexpected but not unwelcome. I've worn a hair shirt over our fight for a year. As long as I refused to relinquish blame, in a weird way, I still hold on to Beatrice or at least the concept of Beatrice. Beast's kindness begins to loosen my choke hold on a situation I do not have the power to change.

"And I think," I say, attempting to deflect. "We should talk music if that's still a thing with us?"

Her voice is uncharacteristically soft. "It's still a thing."

I'm so relieved this person who has become part of my life isn't going to reject the prick from the video, I could hug her.

What an odd urge? Or is it? We've grown closer both intellectually and physically to a point. Hell, I just stroked her feathers. Would she welcome my embrace? What would Beast feel like in my arms? Is she squishy beneath the feathers or tough? I clasp hands behind my back and lean toward the pile of what I hope are lyrics. I don't need to add more tension to an already strange evening between us. The unexpected sensation to touch her lingers. "So whatdaya got for me?"

Beast's eyes fall to the top sheet.

"May I?" I nod at it, and she nods. The first thing I notice is the horrible penmanship. I squint to decipher lyrics. They remind me of scrawlings I recorded in the song journal by my bedside during middle of the night inspirations.

She lets out a *pfft* and grabs the sheet. "I can barely read my scratches." She waves a clawed hand at me. "Ever try to write with one of these? Party in a box."

I hold my breath afraid to laugh if this is a sore subject with her. Thank goodness, Beast is first to chirp a giggle, clearing the way for my own.

"Considering your...challenge, I'd say you've done pretty damn well."

"Ready?" she asks, flapping the sheet and peers at me over the top of the page. "It's time I gave you the song you asked for first, 'Dancing on the Hollywood Sign.'"

Suddenly I can't swallow. Will accepting Beast's lyrics to this song be the final admission my days collaborating with Beatrice are truly dead. I force my head into a nod, driving fingernails into my palms as this turning point begins.

Beast clears her throat with a squawk I'm getting used to and sings.

"Take my hand and come with me
To a place neither you nor I have been.
Hillside magic we will find
When we dance together on the Hollywood Sign.

On H so high, we'll taste the sky.
Around the O our steps will glow.
A pair of Ls will kiss and tell.
Dear Y spins promises to fly.
W presents a view.
Where O and O brighten your soul.
Last, darling D frees dreams to be.

I understand life's fear and doubt.
Alone such things will seek you out.
I'll chase them from your heart in time
When we dance together on the Hollywood Sign

On H so high, we'll taste the sky.

Around the O our steps will glow.
A pair of Ls will kiss and tell.
Dear Y spins promises to fly.
W presents a view.
Where O and O brighten your soul.
Last, darling D frees dreams to be.

Will you dare the climb at all,
If I swear, we'll never fall?
As one, we'll grasp sweet love divine
When we dance together on the Hollywood Sign."

It isn't the way Beast's voice abuses the lyrics that brings tears to my eyes. The story she tells is so heart-rippingly on point with what Beatrice and I planned this song to be, I'm stunned. It's snappy, jaunty, and springy with the deeper message of promising to be there for one another if you dare to take a risk on love.

Beatrice dared, and I wasn't there. I didn't jump into the pool.

For the first time thanks to Beast's perfect lyrics, I begin to truly believe the album will be all I've envisioned—messages of hope and love.

I lift my gaze to Beast's and feel the pull we've been cultivating strengthen between us. I'm desperate not to screw up this fragile new connection. It's not just relief. Is this attraction the joy of speaking the same creative language, or something more we've forged over weeks of togetherness? Beast understood my music and nailed its message. Am I transparent, or is this creature that wise? Has fate sent me her feathery presence to share the perpetual emotional prison holding me away from the light since the day Beatrice left me?

Maybe I found another soul who truly understands the darkness of being alone.

Beast's eyes are wide, questioning—waiting for my reaction. She wants approval, appreciation, and my damn throat is so locked

I can't manage a sound. I do the only thing I'm capable of in the moment to express the gratitude to this beautiful poetess. I throw my arms around her.

It takes her a few beats for her to adjust to my hug attack. At first, it feels as if I'm embracing someone in a huge, padded puffer jacket, but as she relaxes her feathers smooth, gripping her body. Beast's true shape melts against me. Her head dips low to settle on my shoulder, and I rest my cheek against hers. The stony, unforgiving wall around my heart softens.

Beast is definitely a woman. The form beneath the baggy dress and layer of feathers possesses feminine curves I'm quite familiar with. When her hips press more firmly against mine, I give a final squeeze and release her.

An odd sensation courses through me as I look up into her face. If possible, in the moment she looks more human than harpy.

I wipe hands down my face to settle back to reality and snatch the sheet where it had fallen to the carpet when I grabbed her. "Wow, Beast. You nailed the song."

Her smile stretches beneath the beak, giving me a better look at her mouth. Now that I take the time to study her more closely, I appreciate the fullness of her bottom lip. Has she ever been kissed?

She catches me staring. Her voice is softer than I guessed she could manage. "I'm glad it works for you."

I take a step back and nearly trip on her guitar. Grabbing the neck before it falls to the carpet, I lift the instrument across my chest. Beatrice's guitar. I force composure into my bones. "Let's run through the second half of the album. I'll play, you sing."

She eyes me with a combination of wariness and disappointment before gathering a pile of papers in a huff. It's as if Beast expected something from me I didn't deliver. A familiar refrain from the song of Benedict. I go through the motions of tuning the guitar. I don't dare ask after Beast's feelings when I've got my own tangle of strange emotions about her to unravel and an album to lock down.

"I want to tackle the rough edges of cut three," she says shuffling through the stack. Beast levels a gaze at me. "Are we keeping the working title: "*Colossal Regret*?"

I begin to wonder if my heart will survive an album's worth of Beast's spot-on lyrics.

13

LONELY PEOPLE

HE LOVED THE SONG, OUR SONG. TEARS OF RELIEF BLUR MY VISION. I lean against the closed door as if it will lessen my distance from Ben. It was exquisite torture to taste his embrace, a delightful shock for him to launch his body at mine. How I've missed feeling his heartbeat against my own.

Even though my Benedict tried to hide it, I recognized the pain on his face as my words matched his intention for "Dancing on the Hollywood Sign." No denying, I was on edge the entire time, worried he'd question how an exiled harpy read the messages embedded in his music with such clarity.

"Love, Benedict," I whisper to the door. "That's how I knew."

He was so thankful and relieved his music became whole with my lyrics there was no probing into my insights. Not yet at least. Will those questions come? What will my answers be? The curse robs me of the ability to speak plain truth.

I fly across the room and settle on the sofa. The joy infusing my spirit as I worked with him again to birth the final song for the album lingers, making me light-headed. Now, Benedict holds in his hands all my lyrics of love. If only he will speak such words to me from the heart, he'll free me from this beastly form of feathers and claws.

Can his battered heart ever fill with love for Beast?

My single tool to get through to him is my gift for words that craft our story. One laden with veiled hints and enough indirect puzzle pieces to sidestep Tressa's curse. The greatest joy in our collaboration is after a year of doubt, our session tonight sets my heart afire with certainty Benedict Boyd will accept Beatrice back.

"Audra? Monty? Graham? Sassy?" I wish the ghosts would return to justify my hope and help me with the next steps to lead Benedict home to me, but their torches are dark. I duck my head under an arm wing.

A flash of light filters through my feathers. My head snaps up in terror at its undeniable source—the songbook. The glass trembles ever so slightly with a faint *hum,* warning another page has fallen. Except this time, two pages flutter to the bottom of the dome.

I dart to the alcove and stare at the songbook, willing it to hold on to its treasures. Fighting the urge to count the remaining pages, I pin my wings to my sides. Is this part of Tressa's cruelty, escalating my deadline the closer I get to Benedict?

"Benedict, oh my sweet Benedict, how quickly can you requite my lonely heart?"

The weight of fear presses down on me. If Ben and I are forever parted, a vast darkness will consume us both. I used to believe we were a pair of destined fools. I still do. Unfortunately, our foolishness outweighed our destiny. It's clear from his reaction to my lyrics we exist inside a burden of shared pain. I can't move on without him, and in his despair and his confessions about the night of our parting battle, I understand he mirrors my overwhelming stasis of loss.

We must find our way back to one another to be free of our shadows.

At the low grumble of the bookcase sliding aside, I slip out of the alcove, surprised the D.V.A. are still at the Caliwood this late. I assumed they'd used another one of their hidden routes out of the hotel that didn't involve the library. I won't give Tressa the satisfaction of enjoying my misery.

Sure enough, the enchantress flounces into the room. "I thought your boy toy would never leave."

I fly and land directly in front of her. She squeaks, taking a series of tiny steps backward.

"Why are the songbook pages falling faster?"

Tressa recovers her haughty coolness. "Instead of sniping, you should be thanking me for the extra time you had with Benedict tonight."

"Thanking you!" The volume of my *caw* silences the conversation in the Dark Vinyl Artist's apartment.

Gothel is at the bookcase in a snap. "Is there a problem here?" His hands glow with feather-scorching heat.

"Nah," chirps Tressa, bobbing past him.

"You're late to your task, Beast, which makes us late for ours." He steps aside, slicing an arm toward the hallway and Maisie's bedroom.

Fury pounds in my chest, threatening to burst my heart. I breathe in deeply through the small openings in my beak and force myself to stay quiet. I fear the closer I get to Benedict, the worse the Dark Vinyl Artists will treat me. I must be their obedient lap bird and not jeopardize any of my scant freedom to be with my love.

Sulaa and Rubata are bickering as usual as I slide past them head down.

The sea witch preens, twisting a strand of indigo hair into a curl she lays over her shoulder. "I told you to cut ties with your over-the-hill goddesses, Rubata. I hear you crying out to those faded entities up in your circle." She imitates Rubata's signature pout. "Bríg forgive me. Mórrigán blah, blah." Sulaa laser focuses on her mentee. "Open your eyes, little witch, I'm all the mentor you need to polish your laughable skills."

Rubata sniffs, turning from Sulaa to block my progress. "Did Benny sing your pretty songs, Beastie? Does he love you now?"

The women enjoy a laugh at my expense.

"You could draw that man a road map to break your curse, and he'd still be too thick to figure it out," says Sulaa in her imperious way.

Gothel strolls closer. "It's too bad you aligned with the likes of Leonato and Benedict's boy band instead of seeking out a place in my stable of talent at Rampion Records. There's no denying your gift with lyrics. In fact, we may expand your responsibilities to include writing songs for our darling Tressa's debut album."

I straighten to my full height, which towers over the whole rancid cabal. "I'd rather pluck every feather from my body."

The flare in four sets of villainous eyes tells me I've gone too far.

Gothel's fingers turn the red-orange of a banked fire ready to burst into flame. "I understand claws can be extremely flammable, and recovery from burns are exceedingly unpleasant. Ask Mr. Fedele, your friend, Hero's lover."

I catch Rubata's flinch at the name.

Yeah, witch. The man whose life you and Claude decimated with your rooftop tryst.

Mist rises from the green and black stone in the ring on Rubata's right hand.

Sulaa points a finger at an agitated miniature mako shark that begins to ram its ugly head against the glass. "My sharp-toothed pet has several relatives offshore who would greatly enjoy a feast of Beast."

Tressa *harrumphs* as if this is dull business and flicks her wrist at me. "Here's a penny for your memories, Beast."

Instantly, I double over with searing pain in every muscle, every bone. The apartment blurs and vanishes as over-chlorinated water rises to cover my body, my head. I can't breathe. I flap my arms to try and break the surface while water floods my mouth, throat, and lungs. The light and color of the world iris down as the black of nothingness bleeds across my consciousness. Then, pop! I float up, breaking free and rising into the sky. Below me I see the Hotel Caliwood pool filled with furniture.

I cry out for Benedict to catch me, but he's gone. The pool deck is empty. The lights of the Caliwood go dark. My body contorts as the points of a hundred knives pierce skin. From each slice, a feather grows. Bones snap and reform as I feel my legs stretch past their limits and then crimp at the juncture of new joints. With an explosion of agony, my face, hands, and feet elongate. I twist to witness my hellish transformation, and I see them for the first time, claws in the place of fingers and toes. Looking below at my reflection in the pool between bobbing pieces of furniture, I see what I have become, a creature neither bird nor human. A beastly apparition. Beast.

Tressa floats beside me in the Hollywood sky. "Once you bested me, Beatrice. Now it's my turn to best you. You and Benedict chose to ignore my warning, and this is the consequence. I've unleashed the harpy in your soul to claim your body."

Lightning in the black night blinds me and sight returns. I'm in the library. Tressa taps a fingernail against a glass dome holding a book, resting on a wooden pedestal. "Before the last page of the songbook falls, Beast must win the love of Benedict or remain a creature forever."

From far away, I hear Gothel's voice. "Enough, Tressa."

The villains surround me in their lair. I've collapsed on the rug near the fireplace.

Tressa sniffs. "Everyone needs a reminder of their proper place now and then."

"Get up, Beast," says Gothel.

I lift my head to find my enemies staring at me in disgust. I'm pissed at myself for losing control and encouraging Tressa to drive the hot poker of memory through my brain. I must pretend to roll over for these fiends until I win Benedict over. These bastards won't hesitate to deliver on their threats to keep Beast in line, safe in the knowledge once the curse is lifted, I'll retain no memory of them or their stink.

Gluing my eyes to the carpet, I choke out words. "I apologize. Get me the music tracks for Tressa's songs, and I'll write lyrics for you."

Gothel slaps five empty pink vials into my hand. My skin sweats from his not yet cooled fingers. Playing my subservient role, I trek down the hallway sickened by what I'll have to do to Maisie to fill all five vials.

"We're off then," says Gothel as if he's inviting his cronies to a dazzling night in Hollywood. The lead vandal and his toxic trio pass through the library. Through the quiet, I hear the snick of the library door closing and picture them slithering to the panel in the wall leading to the hidden staircase they use to disappear into the night.

I pause at Maisie's door and stare at the small glass bottles cradled within my claws.

I hate this. I hate this.

I—hate—this.

So why do I force myself to do it night after night?

"For you, Benedict. For us."

Doing the despicable bidding of Gothel is the single path open to me. There is no other way for me to buy the time Beast needs to win Benedict's heart.

How am I any better than the Dark Vinyl Artists when I continue to perform the soul-sucking action of terrorizing an innocent little girl to fuel the powers of a demonic asshole?

Is this a sign Beast is subsuming Beatrice?

Shame crawls up my spine leaving a trail of pain as I face the truth. The egocentric part of my brain keeps forgiving Beast the bitter task since all memory of it will disappear once I'm Beatrice again.

I grip the door frame with my talons to steady myself. None of what I do should be forgiven. How despicable of me to trade

Beatrice's triumph for a child's ongoing torment. I am lying to myself not to accept I'm a trashcan fire of a human being for devoting every ounce of who I am to win Benedict back when the real soul in peril is the golden-haired child behind this door.

I can't reclaim Beatrice at the cost of forgetting what Gothel is doing to Maisie. His exploitation must stop. Revelation hits with dizzying force.

Beast is the only one who can stop Gothel, not Beatrice.

One of the bottles rolls off my palm. Thankfully, it lands on the carpet and doesn't shatter. Gothel keeps a tight count on his supply. He'll fry two of my feathers to the shaft for every bottle I break. He's done it before.

I stare at the bottles aghast at the selfishness my fear has manifested. A Beast who allows the theft of tears to continue does not deserve redemption. The right thing to do is to fight for Maisie even though the cost to my future may be cataclysmic.

The rustle of sheets and a childish snuffle inside the room return me to the moment, to my duty. I can't avoid the tear harvest tonight. Playing along is vital so I don't tip off the Dark Vinyl Artists to this destiny-shattering epiphany to work against them. I've been tragically single-minded as Beast. Tears pool in my eyes as I face the hard truth, the resurrection of Beatrice cannot come true at the cost of Maisie's freedom.

My soul can't live with that as Beast or Beatrice.

I wipe my eyes on shoulder feathers. I can't think like a defeatist. Believing there's a chance to achieve freedom for both Beatrice and Maisie is the only way forward. Otherwise, Beast should fly off the roof into the Hollywood night.

I am not alone. Ideas begin to sizzle in my mind. Benedict will help. Hero too. I must be smart, trickier than the vermin who hold my leash, and find a way to outwit the curse and let my friends know a child is in danger here within the walls of the Caliwood. They will do what it takes save her. I know they will.

Sadness splashes over me, and I clutch the wall for balance. Oh,

Benedict. If I take this risk, your Beatrice may never return. First my curse-triggering words broke his heart, and shifting Maisie to my priority, may prevent it from every being put back together.

His pronouncement returns to me in a rush.

"The reality is, Beast, you don't shit on fate and come out unscathed."

A sinking feeling tells me fate will favor a single outcome. Maisie must not be the one scathed.

I'm lost in my own head when I carelessly stumble through the door and walk into a fully lit bedroom. Despite the late hour, the kiddo is not asleep. Our gazes meet for the first time in full light, and it's too late to turn back.

Her bow mouth turns up at the corners as she takes me in. "Hello, pretty bird."

Under bright light, Maisie's similarity to the pop diva, Zeli is jarring. The singer was the last child and then young woman whom Gothel held sway over until Justin Time came on the scene and helped her escape. Zeli was the last source of magic tears to fuel Gothel's firepower. Now Maisie is trapped in the role. Gothel is clever. This time, he protects his investment by convincing this child he is her father. She loves him dearly. Did he ever form so deep a bond with Zeli?

Maisie scrunches her little nose as her assessment strays lower. "Except, you have chicken legs." She covers her mouth, abashed at the thought of insulting the giant birdwoman in her bedroom.

What has the kid seen in her short life to not think me a horror?

I reach for the light switch and snap it off, my heart thundering. She was supposed to be in dreamland. All Maisie should see of me is the horror of shadow and beak from the scant light leaking in under her door. "I'm not pretty. I am the Beast who will eat your Papa."

To my dismay, Maisie laughs.

The joyful sound works as a catalyst for hope. I hit the switch and the room is bathed in a warm yellow light. Maisie gets out of bed and faces me.

"Your feathers are beautiful. They look soft. May I touch them?"

I bow, and she pets my headdress. Her childish hand is warm, loving. If I needed a clear sign this little person must be my priority, this is it. I ruffle my feathers to make her laugh. The sound is contagious. I laugh with her.

Maisie jumps onto her bed and stands, attempting to look me in the eye. "Have you been the one making me cry?"

I want to gather her in my arms and croon a thousand apologies. "Yes, and I'm very sorry for it."

She drops onto her bottom, making the bed bounce. "I'm not scared of you now. Are you magic like a unicorn?"

I shake my head. "You are more magical than I could ever be."

When I sit on the edge of her bed, the mattress dips, and Maisie comes tumbling into me, inciting another round of giggles. Kids are so wonderfully trusting. They accept the fluid edges of reality adults define as immovable.

"What are you then?"

"I'm Beast."

She cocks her head waiting for more.

"Some people call what I am a harpy. I'm part woman, part bird."

"Do you eat worms?"

"Good God, no. Disgusting," I say with a muffled squawk. "The eating part of me is human."

"Are you Papa's pet?"

No, baby girl. I'm his prisoner, like you.

"Let's say I work for your Papa."

She nods as if being an employee is the status quo of anyone in Gothel's sphere.

I rattle the pink vials caged inside my claws. "We've got a problem, Maisie. Your Papa needs tears. He'll be angry at me if you don't cry and fill his pretty bottles."

Her lower lip quivers. "Crying makes me so tired."

"I know sweetie, but it makes your Papa happy. Don't you want him to be happy?"

Please, kid. Start the water works.

Maisie trades her lip wiggle for a lot of blinking and a yawn. What the hell am I going to do if I can't wring liquid gold out of her anymore? Her pout reminds me of Sassy. Two tiny, lonely souls. The little ghost girl and this one could be great friends.

Ghosts! That's it. If I can't freak the kid out, maybe the ghosts can. Haunting is their raison d'être.

"It's super late, kiddo. Time for you to go to sleep." I pull her covers back and she snuggles in, hugging a fuzzy pink pillow to her chest. Gently, I tuck her in. She's so helpless. More than ever, I want to clamp my talons around her tiny frame and fly her away from Dark Vinyl Artist's twisted world of grudges, curses, and revenge. "Good night, Maisie."

Her words are slurry coated with sleep. "Papa's tears?"

"Let me worry about that." I wish I could dot a kiss on her golden hair. The best I can do is lay my free palm against her curls. Watching her drift off softens the prickly edges of my Beast personality and sets my mind wandering. What would the children Benedict and I make look like? Would they inherit his blond hair or my natural burnt crème brûlée locks? His iris-tinged eyes? A musician's long fingers? Would they favor writing words or music?

Quietly, I leave the room, shutting off the lights and book it to the library. Luckily, Graham's torch blazes.

"Graham, I need you."

His torch snuffs out as his twinkly transparent self floats above the long library table. "Yes, my friend?"

"I have an emergency sitch for Team Library."

He releases the long-suffering sigh of one who's always at the beck and call of others. "Do you need everyone?"

"Yep. Immediately."

He's gone with a tip of his hat and a feather-ruffling *whoosh*.

I stare at the vials in my hand, hating the need to involve my ghost companions to frighten Maisie into filling them up.

14

SHAMED

HERO WORKED HER MAGIC. THE WALLS OF THE GHOST LOUNGE ARE lined with trees. Each row of white trunks sports a myriad of silk foliage from gold to crimson, chocolate to tangerine, and blood orange to saffron, creating the feel of partying on a quaint New England patio in fall. The ceiling is draped in black velvet, peppered with individual strings of icicle lights that appear to drip electric stars above the engaged couple. Hero's showstopper is a huge, illuminated full moon bobbing over the stage. Along the bar, several large steaming vats of cider infuse the room with the crisp sweetness of ripe apples. Pub tables wear drapes of rust and burnt sienna fabric capped off with red lanterns aglow with candle flame as centerpieces.

Hero claims she hired a local band to give *Ben and the Boulevard Bunch* the night off after our bar crawl gig. I suspect her choice of entertainment has more to do with not wanting Claude to play at her engagement party. *The Moonrakers* fill the room with the sound of fiddles and folksy tunes. I stuff my face with bread dipped in baked brie and bacon, the only snack Santino requested be put on the menu, giving his darling Hero free rein to choose the rest of the finger food.

At the end of the bar, I spot Hero, arms flailing, either chastising or encouraging the bartenders to sync their mixology with her theme. She shouldn't be working. The woman should be dancing with her fiancé and reveling in their big night. I scan the room for Santino and locate him at a table with his sister, Leeni, and her boyfriend, Snapper Bakke, in a dark corner of the room. Leeni Fedele, with her mop of orange Creamsicle-colored hair, repeatedly pounds a fist against her brother's biceps. Santino's gaze is pinned to the tabletop.

Snapper stands, his over six-foot, linebacker frame towers above the siblings. He whispers in Leeni's ear, motioning to the dance floor. She flicks her wrist at Santino in an *I'm through with you* gesture and twirls into Snapper's arms.

I'm getting a weird vibe. This is Santino's night. He buzzes like a live wire on a normal day, right now he should be arcing with the force of a downed power line. Hiding in the shadows is not his thing. I start across the room to see if the dude needs someone who will not pound on his biceps to talk to. Before I reach him, Santino chugs the dregs from a glass of beer and adds it to an ample collection of empties on the table before he slips out of the Ghost Lounge.

Leeni must have pissed him off if he needs to bail for a few. An arm slips through mine, and Hero pulls me in. There's no hint of whatever bad taste is in Santino's mouth on her. She's lively and absolutely beautiful with the countenance of a woman in love.

"Dance with me, Ben."

"You sure Santino won't kick my ass for stealing his bride-to-be?"

Hero laughs and takes both my hands. "I want to show you a secret." She dances me through the couples on the floor, spinning to a rockin' tune, and then into a grove of prop birch trees. "Look high—in the corner." Hero guides my chin upward.

Behind the stage above a remote corner of the room, is a small patch of ceiling Hero left uncovered. A single wood panel has been removed to reveal a dark shaft beyond.

"What am I looking at, Hero?"

She pulls my head down, her lips against my ear. "It's Beast. She can slip into the old air vent system and watch from there."

I search the shadow but can't see my winged collaborator.

"I wish she could be here with us to celebrate but..." Hero shrugs.

"I'm sure she'd love that."

"Go dance with her, Ben."

I release Hero. "What?"

She clutches my arm. "In the library. Leave the vents open, and you can hear the music. Please. Make her a part of our night."

My gaze drifts to the ceiling. It felt unexpectedly nice to hug Beast the other night. I'm curious to explore what sort of sensation dancing with her might bring.

A twinge of disloyalty to Beatrice from my desire to dance with Beast makes me hesitate. I've got to quit beating myself up. Beatrice is gone. We are over, and it's not like I'm moving forward in a relationship with someone new. Beast is a friend, a collaborator. She's helping me dislodge the yoke of guilt I've been carrying since Beatrice walked out. Beast's take on the pool fight nudged me into believing maybe I'm not the sole cause of our breakup.

Hero watches me, a hopeful expression on her face. How can I deny her this favor on her special night?

"For you, Hero. Anything." I kiss her forehead and head for the door of the lounge. This isn't just for Hero or an act of charity for Beast. I find myself eager to dance with her and want Beast to know I've moved past her strangeness, her otherness, and am interested in the person—

I stop suddenly and nearly trip as I realize I do think of Beast as a person, not a creature, not a thing. The thought sets off a nice warm buzz in my chest that quickly dies when I glance over the railing to find Santino slumped against the grand fountain in the lobby.

Something is totally off. He's not even on the same floor of the hotel as his intended on the night of their engagement party. Concern for Hero sends me tapping down the carpeted main staircase to join the droopy bridegroom.

"Hey, Tino."

He takes so long to raise his head I wonder if he's in pain. Maybe he is. Days manning a sailboat probably have his muscles barking. Even weirder, he stares at me without a word.

"Dude, you cool?" For a guy who's been in the sun for days, he's awfully pale.

Santino grunts in reply.

"Okay, who the hell are you and what have you done with Santino Fedele?" I bump his shoulder with mine.

"Oh, it's all me," he says.

"You sick? Engagement jitters? Too much brew?"

"Sure."

I crane my neck to peer up into his down-turned face. "Seriously, man. You're kinda freakin' me out."

He raises his head. "Before a show, do you ever feel that you can't step up?" He blinks a few times, clearing his throat. "You know you gotta perform, but everything in you screams 'bolt.'"

"Dude," I say, clapping him on the back. "Classic stage fright." Santino's reticence and off behavior make sense to me now. My man may have once been a step into the spotlight kind of guy, but that was before his trauma. Tonight, Hero's shining a blinding beam directly at him. "It bites us all at one time or another. Even after years in front of an audience."

The turmoil in his eyes doesn't dim. Is this too much stress for him to handle?

I lean closer. "How can I help?"

Another grunt. "You can't, Ben. I just need a minute before I go in."

His voice sounds clear, not sloppy mumbles brought on by a massive buzz. Suspicion blooms in my mind. I want to ask if Claude screwed with him again about the engagement, but I chill. If Tino needs to vent, a bandbro of Claude's may not be his first choice of sounding board.

I lift the phone from the back pocket of my white jeans and shake it at him. "Hit me if you need to."

Santino gives me a half-nod and resumes his staring contest with the water in the fountain.

On my way to the elevator, I keep checking on him. He doesn't move. I've never seen Santino Fedele stay still so long. Despite my urge to poke and prod until he talks to me, I keep going. Hero asked me to dance with Beast. Include our mutual friend in the night's gaiety. I'm more than happy to oblige. In fact, I haven't looked forward to dancing this much since my last spin around the floor with Beatrice.

On the top floor, I skip along the carpeted hallway to the library. At least for tonight, I'm relegating the past to the past. I want to dance.

Beast doesn't answer my knock right away. When she does, I find the library bathed in a golden glow from the chandelier that sets off highlights in Beast's feathers. She looks softer, painted with watercolor instead of etched in sharp lines. Her dress is a forest green and gold pattern overlaid with a transparent claret wine-colored silk. Even though its cut allows for her unique build, the fabric is strategically draped to hide her more avian assets. A thin circlet of gold rests on the feathers forming her natural headdress. A crown for a regal being.

Beast catches me checking her out and nervously smooths her skirt. I meet her gaze.

"You look lovely." I bow, and damn if she doesn't blush.

"It's on the frou-frou side for my taste, but a bird's gotta take what a bird can get." She checks me out. "You're put together rather nicely yourself." Her claw glides through the air in front of me, taking inventory. "Black shiny button down, white jeans, black leather high tops."

"I didn't know what my date would be wearing, so I went with black and white, the safe choice." I lift a pant leg to reveal dark green socks and jerk my chin at her dress. "It seems I guessed right with my one splash of color."

"Your date, huh?" Beast crosses her arms. "Very presumptuous, Bene*dick*. I don't recall being asked out."

I startle at Beast's use of the derogatory twist Beatrice would use for my name but shake it off. It's a natural slur, and Bea certainly wasn't the first to use it.

When I meet Beast's gaze, she's rattled as well. I wave her off. "You are correct, madame. Only a dick would assume a lady isn't previously engaged."

Her squawky laugh warms my insides. I like making Beast laugh.

"Ms. Beast, may I request the honor of your company as my date for a dance in this most excellent library to celebrate the upcoming nuptials of our mutual friend, Hero and her beau, Mr. Fedele?" I offer her my arm.

Beast's feathers ruffle, pushing against the inside of her dress as she puffs up. "I accept."

I lead her to the front of the sofa and shove the coffee table aside with my foot. When I try to scoot the sofa out of the way, the damn thing is so heavy it barely budges. With a single kick of her muscular leg, Beast shoves the ornery piece of furniture against the library table to clear space for our personal mini ballroom in front of the fireplace.

I give a proper clap. "Well done." Looking around, I try to locate the floor panel leading to the air shafts, but Beast already snugged it back in place. "Hero told me we can hear the music if you slip the vent cover aside."

Beast sets a claw on her hip. "If I didn't know better, I'd say someone is trying to set us up."

It's my turn to be a little flustered. Is that what Hero's doing? I write it off. No, Hero wants Beast to share in the happiness of the engagement party, and I'm the one who knows there's a lonely harpy in the library. My lips twitch. It feels wrong to think of Beast as a harpy with all the negative connotations that go with it. She's a lonely birdwoman, a singular creature like no other I've ever known or will ever know again. Beast is a friend.

Beast is a gift.

Beast hooks her claw under a rather large square of parquet flooring in the corner between the fireplace and the alcove and leans it against the wall. True to Hero's word, music from the Ghost Lounge drifts into the library.

Beast's head bobs in her birdlike way. "This is one of *Ben and the Boulevard Bunch's* songs, isn't it?"

I listen for a few beats. My eyes moisten. "Technically, it's one of *B & B + 3's* songs. Beatrice and I wrote it together."

We stare at one another as the first verse swirls through the hint of smoke in the air from the fireplace.

> *I never knew the stars.*
> *You showed me how they shine.*
> *The dark of night will never be.*
> *Much less than yours and mine.*

As the second verse begins, Beast closes her eyes and begins to sway to the music.

> *The heavens rain with tears.*
> *But sorrow's not the end.*
> *For each bright kiss we buy a wish.*
> *True lovers don't pretend.*

Before the verse ends, I move close to Beast and thread my

fingers through her claws as best I can and pull her to me. We dance.

> *Those pictures in the sky,*
> *Tell tales of life to be.*
> *For keeping tight your hand in mine,*
> *Thus draws our destiny.*

She's careful with me as her oversized feet find a workable distance outside of mine. One of my hands drops to her waist and I pull her against my chest. She bends enough to rest her head on my shoulder. I enjoy the new sensation of not being the taller person required to dip lower to meet a partner cheek-to-cheek. We sense the music together through a series of slow twirls.

> *Plain fools will doubt the stars.*
> *That won't be you and I.*
> *These gifts of light show fortune's path.*
> *In stardust we will fly.*

The song ends. Instead of letting go, I hold Beast tighter. "Thank you, Beast."

"Dancing is free, Benedict. No need to thank me."

Her heart beats faster than mine ever could. Is it the bird in her? I reach around her and play with the dark reddish silk of her wrap, lightly touching her back. Can she feel me through the feathers?

"It's more than a dance I owe you. The words you put to my music woke passion I thought would never take another breath. Your partnership is bringing me back to life, Beast." I move away until our gazes meet. "You make me believe I'm not a dried husk who used to be able to write songs."

Reflection of firelight dances to its own melody in her huge crimson eyes. "You'll never be that to me, Ben."

Ben.

Beast's never called me Ben before. The intimacy of the word and her intense stare knock me sideways with confusion. Can I truly handle what seems to be happening between us?

As I try to decide if I should pull away, Hero's voice calling for the attention of her guests saves me.

"It's time for the toasts. Get down there." Beast shoves me, and I stumble. Her clawed hands fly to her beak. "Oops. I forget how fragile men can be."

The arm of the sofa halts my inelegant backpedal. I feel like I should say something, but damn if I know what it is.

"Go!" Beast orders in her coarse trill.

I hurry to the door but turn before slipping out. "Thank you for the dance, Beast."

"Thank you for not stepping on my feet."

Good elevator Karma allows me to zip into the Ghost Lounge before Hero finishes her toast. She's alone at the mic. There's a knot in my gut until I spot Santino at the front of the crowd near the bar. I blow out my worry in a long, slow breath.

Hero is bathed in an amber downlight. Her taffeta dress covered in fall leaf appliques swishes side to side as she speaks. "You hear the words love and loyalty, but it isn't until you and your person find one another that you understand how deeply their meaning enriches your soul. Santino is my soul, my light, my forever." She raises her champagne flute to him as the guests applaud.

Santino doesn't raise his glass.

Hero looks perplexed but covers it quickly, sipping from her glass.

With painstakingly sloth-like steps, Santino mounts the stage. Hero steps aside to yield the mic to her fiancé.

"Love and loyalty are powerful words, Hero, but we both know you're just giving them lip service." Santino's voice is rough, devoid of its characteristic lightness.

Gasps and a low rumble roll through the guests. Hero looks as if she's been slapped but recovers in a breath. She lays a hand on Santino's arm. "Babe?"

He shakes it off. "I thought I could go through with this." He stares at Hero. "I believed I could somehow bear your betrayal because I love you so deeply." Santino presses a hand to his heart. "But I can't." His expression hardens as he turns to the crowd. "Hey, everyone. It's me, Santino, the great guy, the nice guy, the let everyone walk all over me guy."

Off to my right, I see Leonato making his way to Hero. On my left, Leeni, Snapper, Justin Time, and Zeli are moving forward. Alarms blare through my head. Something is terribly wrong.

"Well, here's a news flash," says Santino, with even more grit in his voice. "This time I'm not going to play the fool." He raises his champagne flute and pours the contents onto the stage.

Leonato jumps up next to him. "What the hell is wrong with you?"

Santino stares at Hero. "I didn't return from the dead to be taken advantage of. You say you love me, Hero."

She's crying now and reaches for Santino. "I do. I love you more than I've ever loved anyone or anything. You are my life, Santino."

Santino's bitter laugh is enhanced by the mic. "Do you now? Hey, let's bring Claude up here to see if he agrees. You know, Claude, the man you joined on the rooftop of the Caliwood to play games of savage sensuality."

Hero looks gutted. "What? No. I wouldn't. I didn't. I love you."

Santino's face is as red as the ruby leaves on Hero's dress. "I saw you screwing Claude, Hero." Like a real fall leaf instead of one of Hero's robust artificial decorations, Santino wilts.

"This is utter bullshit," rages Leonato.

"I wish it was," says Santino. He raises his eyes upward and practically wails. "God, how I wish it was." His voice is doused with every shade of sorrow. He lowers his gaze to Hero, and I swear he's about to crumble like the last of the barbeque chips at the bottom of the bag. "I wasn't the only one who got an eyeful,

Hero. Ask D.G." Santino's voice breaks and he barely gets out the words.

My body vibrates with a nauseating surge of *what the hell*. Claude and Hero? D.G. involved? How is half my band responsible for this cock up between Santino and Hero.

D.G. shuffles to the edge of the stage. "Sorry, Leo, dude. I was with Tino when we saw Hero and Claude doing the nasty."

Hero's scream jolts to the marrow of my bones.

It's not the sole cry ricocheting off the walls of the Ghost Lounge. The muffled screech of a mighty bird from the corner of the room blends with Hero's cry and the cacophony of the crowd.

Beast.

She must be watching.

Hero leaps off the front of the stage weeping and flees. The guests part, leaving her an escape route. As she reaches the door of the lounge, the bastard of the hour, Claude, steps inside.

"Hero, babe, you okay?" He reaches for her.

Hero lunges at him, smacking his chest with enough force to shove him into one of the trees. It teeters and then falls, knocking the one next to it over, and then the next. The entire line of Hero's gorgeous fall forest crashes to the ground.

Did I just witness an *I'm going to kill you for lying to Santino about us* or an *I'm going to kill you for letting Santino find out about us* assault from Hero to Claude?

The room goes batshit. Santino's entourage drags him off to a corner. Onstage, Leonato grasps D.G. by the shirtfront and shakes him like a cat with a lizard. Claude hasn't taken another step inside the lounge. I sprint over to him.

"You need to get the fuck out of here," I say, and hustle him through the door, following close behind. In the hallway, I repeat Hero's move and shove him with both hands. "What did you do, Claude? Did you touch Hero?"

He pushes me back hard. "Fuck off, Ben. What goes on between Hero and me is none of your business."

Before I have a chance for a comeback, he flies down the main staircase and through the front door of Hotel Caliwood. I whip my head between Claude's retreating form and the commotion coming from the lounge. I don't know what to do. This is too bizarre.

Or is it?

Hero was into Claude for so damn long. No, beyond into, she was obsessed with him. Could she? Would she risk her future with Santino for one last night to get Claude out of her system? I never took Hero for the farewell fuck type, but D.G. and Santino saw them.

Now, the dude's avoidance of Hero and his slump at the fountain track. Tino's public defamation of Hero leaves a sour taste on my tongue. My man never struck me as an eye-for-an-eye dude. Or at least that was the Santino everyone said he was before he was almost fried to death in the explosion at Gothel's vandal ranch. A memory of him going after Claude the night we got back from the tour flashes through my mind. That was some serious aggression.

I can't go back into the lounge. The urge to punch Santino makes my fists throb. I want to bloody him for turning Hero's engagement party into a public spectacle of humiliation and hate. If it's true, and that's a huge damn *if*, he had no right to handle it this way, no matter how badly life shits on him.

I pound into the elevator and slam the button for the top floor to commiserate with the one person who will be as hot as I am about tonight's cluster fuck.

15

AFTERMATH

HERO'S SOBS DRUM VIOLENTLY AGAINST MY CHEST. I WORRY HER heart will literally burst. She launched herself into my arms the moment I opened the library door. Even though I witnessed the horror show unfold in real time, I'm still in shock at Santino's brazen public humiliation. Sadly, it's no mystery to me what prompted it.

Guilt pours down my throat like an acid cocktail. I want badly to whistle blow on Claude and Rubata's filthy rooftop charade. Even if I could circumvent the gag order of the curse protecting the Dark Vinyl Artists, who would believe me?

Hero?

Hey Hero, remember Rubata Lear, the reality TV show star who was convicted of involvement in the plot to poison her father, Midas Lear, president of Golden Pipes Records? You know the one who disappeared from house arrest? Well, guess what? She's living in your father's hotel right on the other side of a bookcase with Grant Gothel, Sulaa Kylock, and Tressa Divine. Oh, and get this—Rubata is a legit witch who shapeshifts into other people.

Ben?

Benedict, I've got a yarn for you. Maybe we can write a gut ripping song about it. *Your self-serving bastard of a bandbro, Claude, screwed a Hero lookalike in your rooftop mancave and invited Santino to the party to watch.*

I'm kidding myself. The curse and my shackles to the Dark Vinyl Artists will never allow me to out Rubata's foul witchery.

My feathers are soaked from Hero's weeping. I use the tip of one claw to carefully stroke her dark brown waves, beautifully styled for her night that should be made of stardust and dreams come true.

"I don't understand," hiccups Hero, repeating the words she's stuck on since coming to me for solace.

I hate Santino for doing this to her. I hate my impotence at not being able to do a fucking thing for Hero's heartbreak except to coo at her like an overblown dove.

Moving with the stiffness of an octogenarian, Hero releases me. "Oh," she says and dabs at my sodden feathers. "I'm sorry." She tugs at my arm. "Come sit by the fireplace and dry off."

I fluff out the feathers at the top of my chest. "Waterproof. You need to sit." I guide her to the sofa where she crumples. Hands cover tear-stained cheeks.

"How could our love be so fragile that one unproven accusation can destroy it?" Her sobs rev up again.

Instead of answering, my thoughts fly back to the night of my battle with Benedict. Even as the white-hot core of my anger attempted to incinerate him, I never intended for it to be our end. Oh, if only I'd sensed the invisible miasma of Tressa's curse surrounding us, waiting for my words to activate its trigger.

Now Hero and Santino are the fallout of a different witch's folly.

"Beast." Benedict's muffled voice hums from the other side of the door. When I don't respond, he gently raps on the wood. He's being cautious, subtle. I appreciate his care at not giving away my sanctuary.

"Benedict in or out? Your call, Hero."

She wipes the river of drips from her nose with one of the leaf appliques on the hem of her lovely dress, now soiled in more ways than one.

I rise from the sofa. "I'll tell him to get lost."

Hero grabs my silk overlay to rein me in. "No. I want to find out what happened after I left."

Nodding, I take heavy steps to the door. After pulling it slightly ajar, I clamp my claws on Ben's shoulder and yank him into the room to demonstrate how pissed I am at Hero's situation.

"Ow, Beast. What the—" He scrambles around the side of the library table, using it as a shield. "Don't take Santino's psychotic break out on me. I'm losing my freakin' mind about it too."

I advance on him. "*You're* losing *your* mind?"

Hero steps around the sofa, startling Ben.

"Hero?" His attention flicks between her and the volatile harpy bearing down on him. Distress tightens his features. "Holy hell, honey, are you okay?" He rushes to her and takes inventory like she's been hit by a bus. I suppose she has. "Of course, you're not."

"Psychotic sums it up," I say in a rumbly churl.

Given the rapid pace of Hero's breathing, she's poised to reform her broken pieces into anger until she registers the gentle concern on his face. Ben opens his arms, and she dissolves against his chest in the way one does when a friendly face offers an invitation to fall apart.

"Hero, sweet, Hero, I'm so sorry," he whispers into her hair.

A good friend would be all-in with sympathy for what Hero's just endured, but jealousy rips through me, a hot ember to dry brush. I want to be the one in Benedict's arms and hear his soft murmurs against my hair.

"Why, Ben? I don't understand how he could do that to me. Not my Santino."

But it is her Santino or a battered and broken Santino—a man destroyed by a rival's treachery. Here I stand in silence, watching despair rain like shattered glass over two people I love. My silence stokes Hero's misery. I am the cause of every fracture in Benedict's soul.

"I hate to say what I'm going to say 'cause I like the guy, but maybe this is the way Santino is now—more about himself than anyone else. When a man gets a kiss on the lips from death the way Tino did, it changes him down to the core. Screws him up big time."

My insides boil. It doesn't matter what Santino thinks he saw on the rooftop. There is a decent way and a bastardly way to handle it, and he chose the latter, making Hero out to be a cheating floozie at their engagement party.

My angry trill startles both Hero and Ben. "Don't you dare try to mansplain away what Santino did to Hero." I stomp so hard the floor shudders. "It doesn't matter what he thinks he saw or how damaged he is. Santino Fedele did not have the right to shame Hero in front of everyone who cares for them both. His dance with death should make him grateful for love, not give him permission to spit on it."

I realize I've gone overboard when Benedict swivels to face me, shoving Hero behind him to protect her from the raging feathered freak. Propelled by a flurry of rage at Santino and ashamed to be directing it at Ben, I fly to my nest at the top of the bookcase and recede into the shadows. Growly clucks vibrate in my throat instead of the words I should be speaking to assure my friends I'm not a threat.

Beast's short fuse is mortifying. I need Ben to see more of Beatrice and less Beast as the minutes to win his heart are torn from me at an ever increasing speed.

Bless Hero. After the shitstorm she's paddled through on an inflatable kayak, her face shows only concern for me. She swipes remnants of tears from beneath her puffy eyes and manages a weak smile. "It's okay, Beast. I appreciate you being pissed for me." She releases a fluttery breath. "I just want to go to bed." Hero leans against Benedict. "Walk me to my apartment, Ben. Don't let anyone talk to me."

He throws a protective arm around her shoulder. "Whatever you need, I'm your dude." Benedict pulls Hero against his side and guides her to the door. He aims a brief squint at my perch before leaving the library.

I curl onto the collection of pilfered hotel comforters and pillows of my nest. The torrent of my tears makes Hero's weep a meager drizzle in comparison. I cry for my friend's humiliation and shock. I cry for Santino's despair at the false betrayal that drove him to his merciless act. I cry for the distance my anger created between Benedict and me when I should be encouraging the opposite.

The guttural noises streaming from my beak coupled with the scratch of feathers against the fabric of my dress as my chest heaves with sobs nearly covers the muffled patter below. I dread the prelude to the bookcase being coaxed aside to summon me to my distasteful duties for the Dark Vinyl Artists.

The patter continues, and I quiet. It's not the bookcase. I'm hearing fingertips play against wood. Someone is knocking surreptitiously at the library door. I draw farther away from the light. Are the ghosts playing with me? Hero's not coming back tonight. She looked ready to lose the ability to stand. I wouldn't be surprised if Benedict had to carry her to her apartment.

More likely the tapping is a ghost hunting hotel guest whose EMF meter is going bonkers near the library. I snort. They should see their little needle go off the rails when my four ghost pals are present in the library instead of flitting around the hotel.

The taps get slightly louder, and—Is that the clink of glass against the door?

His voice is low and careful.

"Beast?"

It's Ben. My Ben. My heart. My redemption. He's braving the terror in the library.

I drift to the carpet and do what I can to recapture the subtle draping of my dress. The rapping stops. In a panic, I dash to the door and throw it open. Benedict is at the bottom of the few carpeted steps. In his hands are a bottle and a pair of cut crystal Glencairn whisky glasses. I recognize the glassware in an instant as part of the set we bought when the band played an exclusive celebrity wedding in Scotland at a whisky distillery. B & B + 3 weren't a wedding band, but the high-profile couple were close chums of Leonato. It was a win/win. We were his wedding gift to the celebs, and the band got a free trip to Scotland. We chose the set of glasses with the name of the distillery etched on the sides to remember our foray to the Scottish Highlands and islands.

We'd vowed to return. Like many of our future plans, we never got the chance.

Benedict turns when he hears the door. For a breathless moment, we stare, each waiting for the other to speak.

His expression is one I know well. Ben is unsure if I will invite him in. It's my move. He won't push. That's one of the things I love about Benedict Boyd. He's patient without expectation and avoids forcing an issue. I was the ramrod in our relationship. Once engaged, my man will joust with the best, but first he allows the space for permission.

Benedict raises the bottle. "I don't know if you drink, but if I don't pour a large quantity of alcohol down my gullet, I'm going to totally lose it."

He looks stricken. Santino's disintegration into assholery has taken its toll on Benedict. I didn't see how much before. Suddenly, I realize the one hopeful truth in this Armageddon of an evening. Benedict hadn't come up to the library to see Hero. He didn't know she was here. Benedict came to see me. He came to commiserate in my company, knowing we share affection for Hero.

I was anything but hospitable, yet he's here, not giving up on the irate harpy. I don't want to love Benedict more, but I do. Every fresh bud of love for the man has the potential to decay into a new fissure of pain if he is lost to me forever.

"You bet my feathered ass I drink." I step aside so he can pass, then listen for a moment before closing the door. If Hero's sobs punctuate the silence of the thirteenth floor, I'll send Benedict to her apartment.

The hallway is silent. There aren't even sounds of Leonato or the band heading in for the night. The Ghost Lounge must still be abuzz with Santino's act of lunacy and speculation as to the verisimilitude of his accusation. Everyone better get it out of their systems tonight because if I hear anyone questioning or dissing Hero, I'll find a way to dig a claw into their gossipy flesh.

I catch Benedict eyeing my ass.

"Are you speculating whether my ass is feathered or not?"

His smile is tired but there. "I love a good mystery." He sighs. "And a good distraction." Benedict commandeers the sofa and nods to the empty space next to him. "Drink with me, Beast." He smacks the glasses on the small oval table I set back in place between the sofa and the fireplace. "And let's uncover the secrets of the universe." He fills the glasses nearly to the rim.

The surprise on my face wrestles a glib chuckle from him.

He sets the half empty whisky bottle on the table. "I think you'll agree tonight is beyond a two-finger pour." Without waiting for me to join him, Benedict raises his glass. "To Hero who's better off single." He drains three-quarters of his glass.

I watch in fascination. Ben drinks, but not like this. His face flushes. He coughs, wipes his mouth with the back of his hand, and then drains the rest of the glass.

I settle in next to him, my oversized knobby knees poking up higher than the table. He reaches for the bottle.

"Should I get you a straw?" I ask.

Benedict finds this hilarious. A laugh explodes from his lips, showering my legs with spittle. "Damn, I'm sorry." He rubs a hand between my overlarge joints to clean off the evidence of his drunken spray.

The gentleness of his hands sliding over my skin ignites

desperate sensations beneath my skirt. Desire so intense races through me that I have no time to temper the reaction. My substantial tongue rattles, sending vibrations out of my beak, making something akin to the purr of a giant cat instead of a bird. It takes me a moment to realize I've dropped my head back, which is probably for the best since I'm sure my eyes rattle like dice on a craps table.

Benedict clamps his hands on my arms. "Beast, are you okay?"

He probably thinks I'm having an avian seizure instead of a killer wave of lust. I'm dying to shove him down and straddle him the way I did the first night he met me as Beast. I want to feel him between my legs, thrusting his hips not to escape but to lose himself in the pleasure.

"Are you hurt?" When he pops to his feet and scans my body the way he did Hero's earlier, looking for signs of injury, his rapid-fire whisky infusion sends him reeling.

I catch him before he falls. Celebratory drinking has officially shifted to excessive *douse the pain* drinking.

Benedict collapses onto the sofa, leaning against me to stay in a semi-upright position as he stares into the fire. "I always said marriage was bad news." He points a finger at an imaginary audience. "Don't get me wrong, women are awesome. My mom was a woman, and I thank her for bringing me into the world. But a wife? Nope." His finger wags back and forth like a windshield wiper. "There's a recipe for always wondering if they're faithful to you. Trust issues are a bitch, a toxin. If Hero isn't capable of being faithful, then no woman is. So, no thank you. I'll stay a bachelor forever and never deal with the kind of shit that went down tonight."

I can't let Ben slip further into this shell of protection he's attempting to surround himself with. How will he ever pierce my beastly skin with love if he retreats from the concept altogether? "I call bullshit."

He startles as if he'd started to doze off after his proclamation.

Pulling away from me a tiny bit, he twists to look me in the eye. "Excuse me?"

"Swear to me you believe Hero was unfaithful."

Ben's shoulders slump. "Can't."

"Because you don't believe it." I stare at the door to the rooftop stairs. "Don't believe it, Benedict."

His features, slack from drinking, perk up. He stares at me, moving so close his nose nearly touches my beak. "What do you know, Beast?"

I decide to test the boundaries of the curse. See if I can find a way to the truth that won't tie my tongue. "I know Santino has good reason to believe it's true, but it isn't."

I hold my breath. It worked. My statement lacks details or accusation, but it's a truth. I'll have to find a subtle way to string truths together to tell Benedict more. Is it possible to somehow guide him to the Beatrice trapped inside Beast with this method? And what about Maisie? I've got to find a way to partner with Ben to give the child a chance at life away from Grant Gothel and the Dark Vinyl Artists. Once this man I trust above all others is on board, maybe he can recruit the very people who bested Gothel before—Justin Time, Zeli, and Santino.

Dammit. Before I can count on Santino, the mess between Hero and him must be fixed. He deserves a kick in the ass for the way he aired his grievances, but salvaging their relationship may be another task within my power. I need to force Claude into confessing his rooftop rendezvous was not with Hero. The alternative, announcing to the world Rubata Lear is a shape-shifting witch, is a hard no.

Benedict waits for me to continue. I lose courage. I need think time to write out thinly veiled words that will move everything forward. Blurting the wrong thing could easily shut down my plans. If Tressa or any of her cohorts suspect how close I tread to leaking information, they'll lock me away somewhere else, and I lose any chance of Benedict breaking the curse or saving Maisie.

The panic of potential self-destruction from a hasty attempt sends me along a different path. "If you're so anti-love, Benedict, why did you write an album full of love songs?"

Love songs for me.

I want to remind him of his confession about wanting to make little musical babies with Beatrice. That's not what lives in the heart of a man professing he's hell bent on avoiding marriage. My gut tells me it's not the time to bring Beatrice to the surface. Benedict is having this moment with Beast. Beast is the road he must trek to find his way back to Beatrice. I must take care not to be my own undoing.

He blinks as if he lost his train of thought and reaches for the whisky bottle. Bypassing the glass, he guzzles. His Adam's apple pulses to the tune of his personal drinking song for a few beats before he hands me the bottle.

"You write the lyrics to deliver the message, not me. I'm nothing more than wordless beats to a measure, rhythm, melody."

If he wallows any deeper, he'll drown in the muck. "I call bullshit part two. Music speaks without words."

I maneuver the whisky bottle under my beak to my lips and swallow. Ben watches me intently. His head tilts to one side, studying my mouth. When Benedict leans in, I stop breathing. Is he going to try to kiss me? Inch by inch, he gets closer and then his gaze falls on the wicked hook at the end of my beak, and he backs off.

"Fuck all," he says, and to my surprise, stretches out on the couch with his head on my lap. Not two minutes later, he's snoring.

For the first time since our reunion, I have free rein to relearn the landscape of his face. If I didn't run the risk of poking his eyes out, I'd run the tip of my claw over his ridiculously long, sable-brown-colored eyelashes. Their exotic color was the first thing that charmed me the night I met him at Leonato's annual Christmas soiree in the Ghost Lounge years ago. They swept open and closed as gently as flower fluff blows in the wind. Delicate and beautiful.

When we first met, their mismatch with his sun-kissed hair made me wonder if he dyed his whitish locks. Once I was treated to a glimpse of the soft blond hair sweeping across his pecs, I gave him full credit for being all natural.

His lips boast a slight natural upturn as if they're always hiding a merry or mischievous thought. My lips turn down in contrast. Together we balance mirth and sorrow. Will we ever enjoy such balance again?

Carefully, I run the tips of my claws through his hair the way I did to Hero's earlier. Ben sleeps. I dream.

An icy blast followed by a rush of heat washes over us as the ghosts return to their statues and the torches blaze.

"You can come out," I whisper. "He's asleep."

The torches blink out as the quartet forms a circle around us.

"Is it done?" asks Monty, in a low ghostly tone to avoid waking Benedict. "Does he love you?"

Audra gives him a backhanded slap on the arm that of course goes right through him. "If it was finished, we wouldn't be looking at Beast." She lights on the arm of the sofa, leans down, and blows across Benedict's face. His skin turns pale blue for a moment before pinking up again. "He's out cold."

Graham holds his hands to the fireplace as if he could warm up. Sassy stands next to him and names off creatures she imagines in the flames. I wonder what secrets ghosts see that we living folks can't.

I meet Audra's wavering gaze. "There may be a glimmer I'm getting close." Nodding to the whisky bottle, I continue. "I believe he thought about kissing me."

My glamor gal ghost claps her hands. "Oh, Beast. Marvelous."

Monty clucks his tongue and runs a finger around the rim of my still full glass. "Wicked whisky does not a true intention tell."

"Kill joy," scolds Audra.

Monty raises a finger. "Ah, but a sleeping heart is fertile ground from which truth may bloom like the fragrant flowers of early spring."

Audra shakes her head, twirling a hand. "Less purple prose, more straight talk."

Monty plants his right foot in front of his left, turning his forward toe out to the side. His back is stiff as the library door. "My meaning is as clear as a crocus breaching the crust of a winter frost."

I bob my head at Audra. "Your simile meter is in the red, Monty."

He peers down his long, aristocratic nose at us with a sour look that says *peasants*.

It's Graham who sneaks in for the save. "If you want to know what's in his heart, let us have a go at him while he's asleep."

Audra floats upwards to hover over Benedict. "Brilliant. I'll call the pool ghosts and those hold outs in the ballroom to help us." She flies to the blocked off elevator and then turns to me. "Are you sure he's in deep?"

I raise Benedict's arm and let it fall onto his chest. He doesn't stir. "Yep. Dead drunk. Why? What do you mean by 'a go at him'?"

Audra lingers above Benedict's sleeping form. "How about a snap of gentle ghostly intervention to peek at your hottie's intentions?" She claps her hands. "Maybe I should take up lyric writing."

Just as I'm about to eek a few more details from team ghost, voices rise from the other side of the bookcase.

Sassy begins to cry. "I don't want to scare the little girl again."

Graham takes a knee and whispers in her ear. She rests her ringlets on his shoulder. They barely dip past the boundary of his form. I wonder if the ghosts feel each other's contact.

"She can come with me while I gather the troops," says Audra, holding a hand to Sassy. The child drifts to her, and they both disappear through the wall.

Monty gives a long-suffering sigh. "I shall frighten your charge tonight, dear Beast, while the others ready our exploration of your lover's psyche."

Whatever they're up to sounds too much like an alien probe scenario. "New plan. Leave Benedict alone to sleep it off."

Monty swoops in front of me, lingering at eye level. "Let us do this for you, friend. We shan't harm him. You have my word." Monty's gaze falls on the thinning songbook. "He'll never suspect our visit is more than a dream."

I press the back of my hand to Benedict's warm cheek. "It'd better be a sweet dream."

"Time for—" Rubata's voice rings out as the bookcase is thrown aside. Eyes wide, she stares at Benedict. "Shit," she hisses and begins to slide the faux wall closed.

Fear gut punches me. Will she hurt him? Will Gothel, Tressa, Sulaa? How could I be so careless to keep him here during their departure window? I should have shooed him to his room, but the ghosts and their talk of dream probing distracted me. I wave a wing at her. "It's okay. He's passed out."

Rubata stalks to the couch and peers at Benedict. "Why is he even in here now? You know the rules."

Anger pumps blood painfully through my heart. I want to scream accusations at Rubata that she is the cause of tonight's catastrophe. Her appetite for Claude brought madness on all of us. The weight of Ben sleeping on my lap reminds me to shut the hell up and not confront her.

"I swear to you, Rubata—"

She swipes the air and jerks her chin at Benedict. "Don't say my name, you idiot bird."

Grasping for the last vestiges of my patience, I continue. "He's checked out until noon at the earliest."

The smirk on Rubata's face brings Beast's rage far too close to the surface. Fury that grows stronger as each songbook page falls.

"I see you haven't forgotten lover boy's nocturnal habits."

Jostling Ben as little as possible, I slide out from under him and kill every light in the room apart from the fireplace. "I'll go to Maisie."

Rubata studies Benedict too long for my comfort level. Her eyes fall to the vicinity of his zipper. "Once you're totally out of commish, maybe I'll give blondie a little treat. I'm sure he's capable of raising a girl's temperature."

The thought of Rubata and Benedict together sickens me enough to spray whisky back up my throat. The witch laughs as I choke before she crooks a finger to lead me into her lair. Unbeknownst to her, Monty accompanies us through the bookcase.

16

DANCE OF THE MIRRORS

M*y* throbbing head rests on a pillow soft enough to rid the world of all its troubles. Fingers trail against my scalp, promising peace, rest, and better times to come. Once, twice, and again they stroke, easing the pain of memories just out of reach. I'm wrapped in a cocoon of perfect warmth. I'd be content to never leave this stolen peace.

Like imagined voices on a breeze, barely audible words drift through my mind.

"Rest Benedict. Sleep Benedict. Dream Benedict."

My body floats in a world of dim firelight like a babe rocked in a cradle. I let the sensation carry me along until my feet touch solid ground. I open my eyes to find myself in the library alcove behind Beast's songbook. The rest of the room is visible through the glass dome protecting her precious treasure, but it's not the library I know. Flickering torchlight distorts the room, elongating the bookcases until they begin to crawl across the ceiling. Each book liquifies and drips down onto the enormous cherry oak table, melting into pools of color—burgundy, chocolate, dusty blue. The fluid tomes run together to form a pool where words from each volume float across the surface, leaves on a pond.

The fireplace has grown to consume one entire wall, setting the library ablaze with orange and yellow light. In place of heat, the flames radiate sensations of joy and hope. I'm digging this.

Slowly, I ease around the songbook's table into the library. I want to dip a finger into the trickle of watery books. As I approach the library table, now grown to gargantuan size, my gaze falls to the carvings on its facing edge. I've never studied their detail, but now I see they tell stories of dashing heroes swinging cutlasses toward a horde of charging horses. Couples with windswept hair drive in vintage convertibles along country roads. Not a natural wind, but the result of giant fans pointed at the car. Farther along the table, an airplane chases down a man, running along a highway. On the steps of a palazzo is a woman in a sundress with pin curls upon her head holding a bouquet of flowers. A little girl dances with a man in a tailcoat.

The oaken reliefs continue with images of cameras and clapper boards, and lines of folding canvas chairs with names embroidered on the back. As I round the end of the table, I find scenes of a red carpet flanked with paparazzi, snapping pictures of men in tuxedos with women in flowing gowns, award show finery, a limousine waiting at the curb. This is the story of old Hollywood with its movies, studios, and stars.

I pause before the carving of one such starlet, blowing kisses. She looks familiar, but I can't place her. Suddenly, the figure begins to move. Her hand taps her lips and then flings the kiss away from the table in my direction. A droplet of light flies through the air and lands with a *smack* on my cheek. I raise a hand to touch it and stumble backward when the woman breaks free of the wooden tableau, transforming into a shimmering form nearly as tall as me.

All along the table's four edges, figures begin to wrench themselves free. They float around the room showing me stories of an era full of grandeur, elegance, and good times. Beach balls fly between bikini-clad beauties and men with sculpted bodies and devil-may-care attitudes. Light bulbs flash at the red-carpet scene.

Wind machines blow my hair. The ring of metal swords sounds behind me. The library table disappears to make room for the living history.

I move between and through images, totally enchanted by the show. I'm a voyeur to a world long gone before I became part of the Hollywood scene. Sadly, the vignettes fade. The room fills with blue tinted light emanating from transparent forms sliding around and through one another. Firelight adds a reddish outline to each figure. I'm in the center of a cerulean ring of light pouring off these beings, free of their wooden prison.

A little girl in ringlets and tap shoes dances to me. Recognition sizzles through me. She takes my hand. I know this kid. I've seen her before, here, in the library. I search my surroundings, or what was this library. She asks me to read a story and then disappears.

Memory tingles and then bursts free, nearly knocking me to my knees. I whip my head from side to side, taking in the figures. My visitors aren't just visages of Tinseltown past, these are the ghosts of the Caliwood. The last time I saw them was with Beatrice on the night Tressa Divine turned the spirits into a wall of ice. The night I chose Beatrice over Tressa to join the band. The night Beatrice and I found one another again after losing a year because of my stupidity. The night under the stars and the gaze of the Hollywood sign where I truly fell in love with Beatrice Sharpe.

I search the room, looking for a sign Beatrice is with me in my dreamscape. The room transforms into walls covered in vintage flocked wallpaper adorned with a series of tall mirrors. The music of violins fills in what's now a grand ballroom. I'm thrown into the arms of one partner and then the next. I'm never allowed to lead as the ghosts hand me off to the next and the next. I twirl down a seemingly never-ending line of dancers until I waltz alone. Ghosts break around me, a boulder in their supernatural stream.

The whisper begins like a rumble in my heart and then grows louder into lyrics to match the melody of strings.

Benedict. Oh, Benedict. Draw out your gilded key.
'Tis you who must decide the path to find the soul engaged.
Beneath the sheen. Beneath the shell. Beneath the borrowed cage.

Benedict. Oh, Benedict. Draw out your gilded key.
For only you can shine the light on evil's cursed lock.
Love shan't be lost forevermore if passion's path you walk.

Benedict. Oh, Benedict. Draw out your gilded key.
The pages fall with rapid pace and soon time will be lost.
If shadowed eyes do not see truth, two hearts will bear the cost.

I'm again tossed into the center of an ethereal circle of whirling blue light. The ghosts are moving so quickly, it's hard to tell one from another. Am I supposed to waltz with them? Sing an answer to their enigmatic song?

In perfect synchronicity, each ghost raises an oval handheld mirror that looks like it leapt from the pages of a fairy tale. Every frame is gilded with jewel-encrusted, curlicue designs. Reflected in each looking glass is my face.

Benedict. Oh, Benedict. Draw out your gilded key.

I spin, searching for someone to tell me what the hell key they're talking about. A cold snap rises inside me. I'm sure this supernatural host is trying to deliver a message. The problem is, I don't speak ghost.

The ghosts close in, their color shifting from blue, to purple, to gold, and back to blue. In every mirror, I see the same reflection of my bewildered face. A force spins me in place, the hundred faces of Benedict blurring into a pulsing silver streak. One by one, ghosts abandon the circle to advance on me in a line, always moving with the grace of a waltz. When each is upon me, they thrust the mirror before my eyes, and I see her.

Beatrice.

No, Beast.

Beatrice.

Beast.

Beatrice.

Beast and Beatrice side by side.

The faces of the two women blend together in a never-ending procession of mirrors, and the ghosts take up a chant.

Love. Love. Love.

The ghosts glow crimson as their melody shifts back into the song about me and keys and falling pages. I hear it now as a sweet longing that matches the crimson melody yearning in my heart for Beatrice while growing ever closer to Beast.

Choose love, Benedict. Choose love, Benedict.

Mirrors, ghosts, images of Beatrice and Beast twirl and spin before me. Everywhere I turn is a face playing my heartstrings. The song rises in volume, urging me to obey. I want to do as they ask. I want to love. I want Beatrice. I want Beast.

The moment the thought takes root, the ghostly dance freezes like a car slamming on the brakes. To both my right and left, the mirrors multiply, one after another in endless rows. One direction reflects infinite images of Beatrice's lovely face, gifting me with the smile she saved for our most intimate moments. The one proving she trusted me to keep her most guarded vulnerabilities safe in my heart. A look that promised love and partnership. Oh, how I miss the light in her eyes.

My body swivels as if I'm poised on a turntable determining my direction. Before me is a never-ending highway of Beast. Her larger-than-life expressive eyes with their pointed edges dazzle beneath the feather headdress. A trust, fresh yet at the same time familiar, swims in their burnished depths. I sense promises not yet spoken. Possibilities.

The images change. Down one avenue Beatrice and I swirl in the ecstasy of a deep and carefree kiss. A turn of my head reveals Beast and I swaying to silent music, my arms holding her close, one hand stroking the feathers on the back of her head. A warm and sunny place opens in my chest. This Benedict is happy with Beast, so happy. Is my vision the harbinger of a new beginning or a balm to tell my bruised and battered heart that hope of love isn't dead?

The mirrors begin to shrink until once again they're held by a legion of ghostly hands. On and on they come, lines of ghosts and mirrors, showing me Beatrice, showing me Beast. They push me to the edge of a chasm filled with rising mist.

Choose love, Benedict. Choose love, Benedict.

How do I choose? Whom do I choose? My lips move but make no sound as my mind flickers, a strobing light between these choices set before me.

Beatrice. Beast. Beatrice. Beast.

I lose my footing and trip into mist and blackness. The shine of the mirrors, the incandescence of the ghosts, and the library itself grow smaller until they are mere pinpoints of color and light. I fall into the oblivion of indecision. As I open my mouth to scream the name I gamble will stop this merciless descent, blinding pain silences me.

My eyes snap open. "Son of a bitch." I grab the left side of my head where I collided with an edge of the small table in front of the sofa. I'm drenched with sweat in a heap on the carpet in front of the library's fireplace. The statues' torches blaze, adding their flickering light to the hearth fire.

I scramble to my feet, turning to face a library devoid of any ghostly onslaught. There are no mirrors, handheld or otherwise. No music. No dancing. No edge to trip over into a black void. The carvings on the library table are static, their stories once again frozen in time. I am alone.

"Holy hell."

I see the empty whisky bottle and wipe hands down my face. My drinking companion is nowhere to be found. Shit, did I say something in my freaky ghost dream that hurt her feelings? The library feels stuffy and claustrophobic. Bile rises in my throat, and the air feels laced with too much smoke.

I dash through the stairwell door up to the rooftop. The wind is up. Grit from the world above Hollywood Boulevard, where lost souls seek solace under the stars, blows into my face. I search the red neon letters of the Hotel Caliwood sign, but there's no silhouette of Beast.

"Beast, are you here? Do we need to talk?" Damn, I hope I haven't damaged things between us with my drunken shitiocy.

My sodden alcohol brain pounds so hard my vision narrows. When I close my eyes, searching for blessed relief, I'm thrown back into my dream. Mirrors flash before me with images of Beatrice and Beast. My heart skitters and I press both hands to my chest. I was dreaming of love, and in the dream, I saw two. One I loved, still love, if I'm honest, but it's the other that sends my skittering heart into a wild gallop.

Am I possibly falling for Beast?

17

SUCKER PUNCH

Gothel's uppercut to my outstretched hand is no more affecting than an annoying itch. He can strike over and over to build villainous muscles yet never damage his feathery servant, a personal punching bag. If there's one benefit to this harpy body, it's strength. I may look mostly bird, but I'm far from fragile.

Here in the Dark Vinyl Artist's lair, Sulaa lounges on the couch watching Gothel wail on me.

"You know you want to strike, Beast," she taunts. "Tell me. Do doormats always do as they're told?"

Gothel drops his fists and takes a step back. His inky gaze locks on mine as he raises a finger. It begins to glow, then a tiny flicker of flame dances across his fingertip. "I don't advise alterations to our workout."

Our workout. As if I choose to share anything with the bastard.

Sulaa slides off the couch with fluid grace. She saunters up behind Gothel. The sea witch tiptoes her fingers across the tight black T-shirt hugging his shoulders and continues to his biceps, giving them a squeeze.

I was surprised the first time Gothel insisted I be his sparring partner. I expected a soft, deskbound body without a lot to look at. I was wrong. He's cut and contoured in a way I would admire if he wasn't such a bottom-feeding vandal. Those black suits he lives in disguise what lies beneath. His punches also pack more than I bargained for. In our first session, he landed blows to my body with those freaky fire fists that singed feathers. I've been on guard since then.

Sulaa's lips press against Gothel's ear. "Such vigorous activity. One would think you are anticipating a fight, darling."

Gothel captures her wandering hands and leans his head to face her. A puff of steam rises from the contact as fire meets water. "Anticipating and preparing are two sides of the same coin, my dear sea witch."

Sulaa frees her hands and drapes them over his shoulders, molding her body against the muscles of his back. As her palms dance across his chest, Gothel allows his eyes to fall shut for a beat, clearly reveling in her touch. With a swift motion, he bends forward, balancing Sulaa on his back. Despite her impressive height and Amazonian build, her feet leave the ground. The sea witch chuckles her throaty laugh as Gothel spins her in a circle before setting her down.

Sulaa pours herself around his side until they're face to face. Her arms wrap around his middle. She trails fingers beneath the waistband of his track pants, heading in the direction of his ass. Gothel seizes her hair, tugging it until he's able to nip at her throat before he extricates himself from Sulaa.

"Let's finalize business in my room after I'm finished here," he says, rocking his hips into hers before guiding her away from his sweaty bod.

Heat warmer than Gothel's finger flames surges through my chest. I hate these two. They parade their foreplay in front of me like I'm a non-entity, which to this pair I am. I'm a prop, a thing to be used as they see fit. I don't give triple fucks if these two share sheets, and they give zero fucks if I know.

In my soul, Gothel, Sulaa, Rubata, and Tressa are as

inconsequential to me as I am to them. At best they are fleeting cankers on my transient existence as Beast. Beatrice will forget them. The difference being, I am at their mercy. Oh, how I wish they were at mine.

I hate myself for the jealousy nipping at me as these two tease one another. I'm not envious of who they are, but rather what they seem to have. Will I ever be in Benedict's arms again as Beatrice?

While Gothel and Sulaa send sex waves through the air at one another, I think of Benedict. He hasn't shown himself since my ghost friends did their number on him. They're mute on specifics, but effusive on encouragement I shouldn't give up. Encouragement that feels suspiciously like ghostly sunshine being blown up my ass.

The hard truth is Ben fled after his encounter with the spirits. I know my transparent friends care, possibly too much to level with me. Did they glimpse the place in Benedict's heart with proof he could never love a beast? Should I give up even though they egg me on to keep hoping? I don't want to abandon hope and concede one fight of regrettable words will seal my eternity.

I startle when Sulaa tugs at my wing feathers.

"Maybe I'll have a go at you later, Beast. Follow Grant's delectable lead to keep in shape." Her eyes linger on his ass while she slinks down the hallway toward the bedrooms.

Sulaa turns back to us. "By the way, Ms. Beast, ask your ghosts to lower the volume next time they hold a soiree to influence your former lover." She laughs. "It's quite charming you believe those watered-down spirits have a shot at brokering a reunion between you two." She clucks her tongue. "So naïve of you, harpy."

These damned Dark Vinyl Artists never miss a chance to chip away at my dream Benedict will be my curse-breaker. I can't allow their head games to weaken me.

Gothel catches me off-guard and lands a punch near my collarbone. I quickly pivot and block his next attempt. The tip of a claw digs into his skin.

He curses and sucks the drop of blood from the back of his hand where my talon kissed him.

"Sorry."

His coal black gaze assesses me. "I choose to believe that was in error instead of intent."

"Absolutely. I'd never..."

I definitely would, you rotting piece of sewer sucking shit.

Gothel shucks his shirt, and it strikes me how he's the antithesis of Ben, the only smokeshow on my fantasy score card. Coarse looking black hair covers Gothel's arms and pecs, drawing a dark line down to his waistband. His skin is olive, and I swear even his sweat absorbs the light.

My Ben is a runner, and a fan of weights. He'd never go in for this beating the shit out of someone for fun Gothel craves.

I'm pelted with a pair of punches to my gut. Thank you, harpy muscles. I raise my arms and focus on my attacker instead of Ben.

"Where the hell is your head at, Beast?" He drops his hands and tilts his head. "Have you stepped beyond my blows to the land of make-believe and Prince Benedict?"

I thrust my arms forward and stretch my claws, inviting his punches instead of his taunts. It was much easier to tune him out before Ben returned. I'm slowly going to mush. I must stop degenerating and stay tough if I've got a blended fuck's chance of finding my way back to Beatrice.

"Accept the life where you belong, Beast." Gothel rubs his knuckles.

"For now." I should keep quiet, but the tone of pronouncement in Gothel's tone pisses me off.

He shakes his head and clucks his tongue. "Life is nothing but a series of disappointments peppered with fleeting..." Gothel stares above my shoulder. "Not entirely soul-sucking moments." He levels his gaze at me. "People think they're happy." He shoves me. "Because we are all fools." He steps in. "Families are wiped out. Loves are lost." Gothel's glare constricts my stomach to the size of a pea. "Have I told you my name, Beast?"

I shake my head, afraid to speak and say the wrong thing as rage turns his skin ruddy.

His laugh is the char on burnt wood. "I'm not Grant Gothel. Grant was my brother. I'm Gregory Gothel. A weak name. A name to make the jaw move like clay."

His next shove is so hard, I stumble backward, and he pins me against the closed bookshelf door. "I stole my brother's name after they were dead, my entire family, shot down in the street. That was an entirely soul-sucking moment."

I stare at his eyes for any sign of humanity. They are as unrelenting as newly forged obsidian.

"Grant Gothel," he growls. "A name to fear with teeth to bite." His forearm presses against my throat. "Say it. Say my name, Beast, with all the savagery you possess."

"Grant Gothel," I choke out beneath the pressure of his arm.

"No," he roars and releases me. "Again."

This time, I put the weight of my inhumanity behind the words. "Grant Gothel." The rumble of my beastly cry shakes the walls of the apartment.

"Yes," he cries. "Again."

I obey, and he turns away, raising fists to the ceiling. The corded muscles of his arms ripple with power as his hands begin to glow a deep blood red. Fear compresses my windpipe with more force than Gothel's stranglehold did. The maniac is going to burn the place down, starting with me.

He stills, rolls his shoulders once, and turns back to me.

"Life lesson, you idiot bird. One you should have learned by now, given your situation. Dreams are toxic. They shine under a façade of hope, but there is always a trail of destruction behind their fulfillment." Gothel runs a hand through his hair. "Yet, we keep chasing them." His eyes narrow. "Even knowing this, I still go after what I want. Spitting in the face of ruination is my glory." He stretches his arms wide. "Ah, this fabulous music industry is the perfect medium to play the game. It's the black core of an already rotting apple with its illusive fame and fickle consumers."

He laughs, the sound of humorless humor before zeroing in on my face. "I've shocked you. Take a bite of the ruined apple with me, Beast. We've both been forced into shadow." He stalks me, and I half expect a spear to materialize in his hands so he can plunge it into my breast.

"I pity you when I do not pity myself. I will enjoy revenge and step back into power, inciting the destruction of those who believe they've bested me." He jabs a finger at me. "You will not."

My voice comes out weak, not the bellow of his name that rocked the walls of the Caliwood. "I don't crave revenge against you or the others. All I want is to reclaim Beatrice."

"There's the pity, Beast." He lays a hand on my wing as if comforting me. "Have you not figured it out?" His voice is a swarm of insects infecting my blood. "This is your reality."

"Until the curse is broken." The insects sting and bite.

"Does one ever grasp when their dreams end? Dark Vinyl Artists enlisted you in our army. There is no release. Maisie's tears answer to you. My erstwhile daughter is the sole conduit of your existence and your future." He steps away to retrieve his shirt from a chair and pulls it over his head.

I want to call him a liar. This can't be true. The words of the curse are etched on my spirit. My dreams have not ended.

"Do not deny that chance does dwell,
Despite sweet torments hope hides well.
Until the day when words reveal,
Broken oaths with truth may heal."

After Maisie is safe, and it will not matter if Beatrice forgets her and this horrid time with the Dark Vinyl Artists, Benedict will tell me he loves me. He will break the curse.

As Gothel slides the bookcase aside to dismiss me, the library alcove flashes with light. I surge past him to the songbook. The pile of pages now rises to obscure the bottom edge of the binding.

I glance around to see Gothel staring truth into my soul. In his twisted narrative of life's cruelty, the vandal believed he was doing me a favor, schooling the idiot creature to turn her back on hope.

Hope has a beautiful way of rising when people like Gothel attempt to snuff it out. He's right. I am a conduit to a child's tears and the connection to ignite his failure.

Tressa may toy with time and fate to defeat me, but I will not allow the Dark Vinyl Artists to do the same to Maisie.

18

WILL YOU EVER BE READY?

I DON'T PLAN ON RUNNING INTO ANYONE IN THE HALLWAY BETWEEN MY apartment and the library this late. It's nearly 2:00 A.M. and *Ben and the Boulevard Bunch* finally have a free night. Considering the pace we've been thrust into since we returned from the tour with the Haunted Hollywood crawl, the engagement party shitstorm, and rehearsing the album, it's the first total crash opportunity for my bandbros that's presented itself. At rehearsal this afternoon, even Claude, who I can barely look at without feeling sick, admitted he's out of gas.

Claude. Fuck. I'm totally torn about what to do there. I don't know how, but my gut tells me I'm missing a crucial piece in the demolition of Santino and Hero that has Claude's fingerprints all over it. I want to duct tape him to the iron railing of my balcony until he comes clean. With the album deadline nipping at my heels, the best move for the band is to swallow my suspicions and play nice until we lay our tracks. I've planted a juicy smack on Leonato's ass in the form of Beast's completed set of album lyrics. Instead of the delay Leo feared, we're slotted to start a few days earlier in the studio than the original schedule.

The tension seeping into my muscles intensifies as I consider the album. It's our first since Bea left. Will the fans buy the sound or hit reject because the heat of Beatrice and Benedict together on vocals is no more? Once Beatrice walked out—bolted—rocket jetted from my life and the band, we had to retool every vocal duet to fit Claude and me for the tour. We don't sing gazing into each other's eyes. The band's ballads take on the character of two dudes who can't catch a break in the game of love. It's too risky to fly the idea of a replacement singer for the album. I've barely escaped Leonato's guillotine as it is. If we're a band of bros from here on out, the album needs to reflect that.

I wish Beast could sing. Sadly, her voice is cringeworthy even though every word she sings drips with truth and depth.

For a few moments, I try to imagine the songs with my voice alone if I confront Claude now and discover my worst inklings of his fucknuttery are dead on. Musically, losing him kills the breadth of our harmonies. I pop my lips. It's too bold a move when I've already put the band's future on shaky ground with the boss.

Ah, Beast. She makes no bones about suspecting Claude of something grim. I half expect her to request I rip Claude's heart from his chest. Part of me wants very much to do just that if he did have a hand in orchestrating Santino's tragic meltdown.

I straighten my short-sleeve button down with its pattern of guitars and music notes, topping off a new pair of jeans. I'm going for the musical motif here, a metaphor for my partnership with Beast. There's no way I'll sleep tonight until I talk to her. I still don't know what my drunk-ass self said or did to cause her disappearing act after I passed out on her sofa. My current plan is to grovel for any misstep.

Liar, Ben.

My real intention tonight is to explore if our partnership has a shot of swerving in a more personal direction. I scrub a hand across my newly shaven chin. I'm nervous even toying with something between Beast and me. I don't know if that's because she's a harpy or I'm afraid she's not in the same place as I am. Her internal beauty calls to me, and it's music I can't ignore any longer.

That mind-fuck of a dream with the ghosts and the mirrors may have messed with my head, but it slapped my ass with the fact Beatrice truly is past tense. I've been in a pathetic wallow. No, it's worse. I've been running in place, refusing to move forward with my life. It's time to hit the gas and leave my emo-slump behind.

Snake bite of reality—am I using Beast as training wheels for my awakening heart? Letting someone in emotionally is a tiny first step to opening up. If I don't follow through, I could hurt her. I pull my apartment door open and pause. Could Beast and I be as much a fantasy as Beatrice walking through my door?

Still, I feel a pull toward Beast I'm not going to talk my way out of. To keep spending time with her will help me understand and define exactly how said pull is supposed to fit into my life. If she's only into being a treasured creative partner and lyricist that reads the soul of my music, well hell, a guy could do worse.

I rest my head against the door. Curse me. Despite our vast differences, I want more.

"What's with the *impress a lady* duds, Ben?"

I nearly shut my hand in the apartment door as Alfie sidles over to me from the shadows of the hallway.

"Jeez, Alfie. Isn't it past your bedtime?"

He rakes a finger up and down my body. "Lookin' good. You are long overdue for a raucous rendezvous, my dude. I was afraid your balls would explode soon if you didn't offer them a treat."

Alfie's chortle confirms I'm red faced. He slaps me on the shoulder before traipsing off in the direction of his room. "Enjoy the ride, man."

An uncomfortable thought zips through me. "Hey, were you on the roof?"

"Nah, I was watching sucky reality TV, old *Kickin' it with Midas* episodes, with Hero." He presses his lips together. "She's in a bad way. You should clock time with her tomorrow."

I nod. "Totally."

Alfie raises a hand, fanning his fingers in farewell. "Later."

I'm half tempted to knock on Hero's door and check on her. Maybe subtly dig around to see if Beast has said anything about me that hints at her feelings. Alfie's door clicks shut. He would stay in a brotherly way if he thought Hero couldn't handle the night solo. I make a mental note to visit in the morning.

After giving the hallway a chance to stay chill and vacant so nobody knows where I'm headed for my middle of the night rendezvous, I work my way to the library steps. It's the giddy feel of being back in junior high, passing my first note to a girl I crushed on. What if Beast doesn't let me in? What if she's asleep and pissed I'm wrecking her privacy?

Beast has a heart as big as her ridiculously large feet. Her lyrics tell me who she is, and Heaven help my soft egg yolk of a brain, I'm into who she is. What should it matter if the person knocking on my heart's door is fair or beastly? Beatrice was gorgeous and our relationship in the end was like throwing myself onto a grenade.

I'm damned edgy. My stomach grumbles as if I haven't eaten in a week while my nerves ping-pong.

"You are a big ass man, Benedict. Take the risk."

If Beast rejects me, I will deal. The dream mirrors flash through my brain, setting a parade of prickles down my spine.

God, I hope she opens the door.

I knock and wait. Twice. Not a sound from inside. No thud of her feet against the carpet or now familiar scratch of claws against the heavy wooden floor. A horrible thought strangles me. Has Beast left the library for good? Did I do or say something reprehensible and painful in my drunken haze to cause her to fly off?

It's a colossal breach of trust, but I brace a foot against the door frame and wrestle with the doorknob at the angles I know will free it from its setting. As I did the first night when I was desperate to get to the rooftop, I jimmy the mechanism until the door opens. Slowly, I ease into the library. This time, I hold on to the knob and click it back in place before I close the door. I'm afraid to turn and find Beast giving me stink eye, or worse, refusing to speak to me altogether.

The library is cloaked in near darkness. Three of the four statue torches and the fireplace glow as if they've been dialed down to their lowest setting. Shadows flicker along the bookcases and over the table in a sinister warning.

Stay away.

Across the library in the alcove, despite curtains drawn haphazardly at the edges of the arch, I spot the songbook in its dome. If it's here, then so is Beast. After a throat-cleansing swallow, I whisper. "Beast?" My volume is low enough that I barely hear my inquiry. A glance at her nest confirms Beast is not here. My gaze falls to the stairwell door. I'll hit the rooftop and pray she's hanging out on the Hotel Caliwood sign.

When I take a step into the room, I hear her voice. At first, I wonder if it's in my head or if the ghosts of the Caliwood are screwing with me. I still and listen.

Beast is singing, but the sound is faraway, like club music streaming from blocks away. I turn toward the barely there sound and startle. There's an opening in one of the bookcases that shares a wall with the door. It looks as if one section slid behind another. After a quick check that I'm alone in the library, I move to the altered bookcase. Carefully, I test it. The wall slides open even wider. I gape at what greets me beyond the books.

A very fancy apartment lies on the other side. Is this where Beast actually lives? Is her habitation in the library a front? A low burning fire in the secret grand salon provides the only light apart from a strange blue-green glow from a deep nook in the opposite wall.

Beast's grainy voice is louder as I step inside. Listening for any sound besides hers and hearing none, I move near the aquatic glow and nearly cry out. The walls of the space are filled with massive tanks holding truly creepy doll-sized versions of nasty sharks and other creatures with teeth I can't unsee. Is Beast curating a miniature sea freak collection the way people do with Bonsai trees? I don't know what to think about Beast's bizarre menagerie. It screams of a very dark interior. When a particularly evil-ass looking, torpedo-shaped thing with an underbite charges at me, I let out an involuntary yelp.

The singing stops to reveal the quiet snuffling of someone crying previously hidden beneath Beast's rough melody.

She's not alone.

Backing out of here and quizzing Beast later would be the wise choice, but her shadow immediately flows across the carpet. She emerges from the hallway drawn up to her full height, claws extended. A strange vibrating growl pours from her beak.

"Beast, it's me. Benedict."

She's in front of me in a single hop, pushing me toward the opening in the bookcase.

"Leave now. You can't be here."

I'll probably pay for the way my shoulders bow as I brace against the opening and refuse to let her shove me through.

"Look, I don't know what I said to you after Hero's nightmare, but I was drunk, and pretty sure I was hallucinating. Please, give me a shot to fix my cock up."

Beast pauses, momentarily flummoxed by my words. She stops giving me the bum's rush and drops her hands. Beast's shoulders slump as she shakes her head. "You didn't break anything." Her wide mouth twists into a smirk. "And I don't recall your cock being up."

I grab for her hands, wary of the claws. "Let me chill here in your place, and we'll talk."

Beast's eyes flash red, and she shudders. "This is not my place, and I'm serious. You can't be in here. Not even for a minute. Please go and wait for me on the roof."

Her hands tremble. She's afraid. Her fear makes my blood run cold, and I don't budge. "Who lives here in Creepyland?"

Instead of answering me, Beast calls, "Monty."

A frigid blast of air encircles me, whisking me back through the opening to the library. Holy mother of all that is otherworldly, I recognize this chill. It's a ghost void.

Beast summoned a ghost.

"I live here," says a high-pitched, sniffly voice.

Standing behind Beast is a little golden-haired kid who should be playing hopscotch on a grade school playground instead of lurking in a dark Goth-vibe apartment on the top floor of a hotel.

Beast whips around and tries to shield the child from my view.

Through chattering teeth from my ghost dip, I manage, "Hi, I'm Ben."

A cutie in a sparkle-pink nightgown peers around Beast. "I'm Maisie." She curtseys. It's damn adorable.

When I step forward and reach out a hand for her to shake, she looks to Beast for permission. Instantly, the icy coating sloughs off my body, and I stop shivering.

Maisie wraps teeny fingers around mine and pumps like she's bringing up water from a well. The motion jostles a small glowing pink bottle she holds in her other hand.

"I couldn't fill it up, Beast. Papa will be angry."

Beast takes the bottle from the kiddo and lays a gentle hand on her head. "We'll try again later, Maisie. Let me talk to Ben first. Go back to bed."

Maisie takes us in for a beat, then giggles. "Is he your boyfriend?"

Beast points at the kid's bedroom door, and the little princess dutifully skips from the room. Beast holds it together until we hear the click of Maisie's door closing. As soon as we're alone, or as alone as you can be with ghosts flitting around, she turns to me with the saddest freakin' expression I've ever seen.

My heart cracks. There's a tragedy here. I read it in Beast's eyes.

Tamping down the urge to demand the story of a secret kid, weird-ass fish tanks, and this behind the bookcase world, I focus on the flickering bottle between Beast's claws.

"What's in your hand?"

Beast's feathers fluff and then smooth as she takes a huge belly breath. She chooses her words slowly and carefully, speaking in a stilted cadence. "How much do you know about Zeli's history?"

"Do you mean her music?"

Beast shakes her head. "Her life."

"Do you mean her history with the Gothel shit?" I do not like where this may be headed. Mere mention of that dark freak nearly starts my teeth chattering again. Maisie's words creep across my skin. She said, "*Papa will be angry.*"

"Hold on a sec. I know Zeli called Gothel Papa, same as the kid."

Beast nods.

"There were stories about Gothel siphoning off Zeli's tears to feed his freaky fire hand magic?"

Beast's stuttering breath blows across my face.

"No fucking way," I say, stabbing a finger at the pink bottle.

Beast charges to a wall cabinet and slides it open. Inside are shelves with rows of pink bottles alight with golden liquid. "Yes, fucking way."

She grabs my hand and pours a single golden drop onto my fingertip. I stare at the perfect little bead, marveling at the way it appears to shine from within. It warms my skin. I dab the tip of my tongue to the single tear, and it feels like I tossed back an entire shot of Fireball whisky.

"Un-freakin'-believable." It takes me a few swallows to chase away the electric sensation.

Beast watches me silently.

I rub my throat, tracing the path of the tear. "This righteous kick comes out of that tiny person."

She starts to set the half-filled bottle on the shelf and then eyes its skimpy contents. As soon as she meets my gaze, my magnificent Beast collapses into a feathery ball, body convulsing with sobs. I rush to her, throwing an arm across her broad back, crouching next to her to catch the pink bottle before it spills.

Through hiccups and tears, she tries to talk. I can tell she's straining to find words, as if the wrong ones will set off an explosion. "Not alone." She thumps her chest. "Powerless."

"Who's here with the kid?" I glance around as if danger waits to spring from the walls.

Beast makes several disturbing sounds before a single word escapes. "Zeli."

"Zeli's here?" For a sec, I wonder if the kid is Zeli's. Hell, she could be a mini clone of the pop diva.

Beast shakes her head, feathers tangling.

My gut freezes. If she doesn't mean Zeli—

"Are you saying Gothel is here?"

Beast nods and attempts to get out a word that sounds like *ka urz*, but it won't fully form so she changes tack. "Must frighten Mmmmaz...Can't. Need tears. Scared, Ben. Scared for Mmmmaz... Scared for me. Scared for you."

"For me? Why?"

Beast emits a series of birdy clicks and then chokes. When she can't push intelligible words out, her sobs deepen.

I position myself and pull Beast's head against my collarbone, cradling her bulk as best I can in my arms. Beast needs my help and something's blocking her from asking for it. Is this the work of the ghosts?

"Let me try to piece everything together." I look around the room and understand Beast's fear of me being in here if Gothel is the creeper in residence. "Gothel is doing to the Maisie kid what he did to Zeli? The tear harvesting story about Zeli is true?" I admit, I always wondered if Justin Time and Zeli were making shit up to permanently put Gothel away.

Her feathers fan upright for a moment before they settle, but she can't speak. I stroke the soft russet down on her head.

"I take that as a yes. You're stuck here with the kid." Again, she attempts to nod, but it's like there's a steel rod in her neck, holding it still. I have a zillion questions, but clearly she can't clarify. Instead, she points at the rows of glowing vials.

"Are you screwed if the kid doesn't cry and fill the bottle?"

Beast stretches her three claws.

"Three bottles." Gothel always had a rep for being a hardass. Once Justin Time and Zeli whistle blew on him, the press trumpeted proof he's a monster. A monster that's supposed to be dead after the fire at the prison facility holding him. Clearly, the dude is alive and back to his same old shit. Add another two zillion questions. I stand and hold out a hand to help Beast to her feet.

Pacing in front of the entrance to the hallway and the little girl's bedroom, I run hands through my hair. "So, the kid has to cry." Damn, this is ten ways of ugly. "What scares her? How did you make her cry to fill the other bottles?"

Beast lays hands on either side of her beak. She begins to speak slowly and then speeds up when nothing blocks her. "Darkness. Awful things. Threats. Until she saw me in the light. Not afraid now. I asked the ghosts—"

I stop and stare. "Hold up." I point to the opening in the bookcase. "I'm not nuts. That Monty you sicced on me is a ghost, and you can talk to him?"

She waves me off. "Details later." Beast deeply concentrates before speaking every word. This is one screwy communication puzzle. "Ghosts worked once. Too sad, they said. Won't do it again. Spirits hate sadness. Their flimsy existence needs joy."

I lean against the wall. Beast talks to the Caliwood ghosts. I clench my fists, remembering the night Tressa Divine manipulated those resident spirits. There's an event I choose not to repeat in this lifetime or any other.

"You were singing when I came in."

"A sad song."

I straighten up. "It worked on the kid?"

Beast tests her neck and is barely able to nod, so she glances up and down, her eyes doing the nodding. We must be skirting forbidden territory.

"Go back in. Fire it up." I cringe at my poor choice of words given the invisible presence of Gothel and his handsy firepower.

"I'll try." She retrieves the partially full bottle from my hand. "Go to the roof. I'll meet you there—after." Beast grips my shoulder a little too hard. I get talon action through the shirt.

"Let me wait here for you. We'll go together."

Panic fills her large, curvy eyes. "Treh—Treh..." Her groan cuts off and she regroups. "You can't be caught in here. They—"

I lay a hand on hers to loosen the claw clamp. "They?" The ghosts? Gothel plus someone else?

Beast closes her eyes for a moment as if preparing to be hit by lightning. When nothing happens, she stares at me. "The rooftop. Go. Fast. Trust me, Ben." Without another word, she disappears down the hallway and into one of the rooms.

What in the hell and back is going on here? Beast is clearly in trouble, and it looks like the kid is too. Who are *they*? I stare at the aquarium nook. Can't those freak show critters scare the kid? Gothel and what other assholes curating sea monsters live hidden in Leonato's walls?

When I take a step toward the library, Beast starts her song. It's the last step I take.

Once upon a time
Starts a story with my rhymes.
About a girl and boy we'll meet
One was sour and one was sweet.
She sang her songs all day
But he turned the other way.
Until words she wrote shone bright

In his heart they sparked a light.

Will you ever be ready to love me?
Can the depth of your heart finally see,
That together we'd paint skies with beauty.
If two spirits embrace destiny.

Their music found a match
And the joy of love did catch.
Day and night they joined their hands,
Making music with a band.
Everyone who heard
Their words and notes concurred.
Magic came to dance
At the couple's fine romance.

There is joy that you truly do love me,
And the depth of your heart finally sees,
When together we paint skies with beauty.
We two spirits embrace destiny.

For treasured time they found
Love and music spinning round.
But one sad summer's eve
The girl shouted she might leave.
The boy felt low and spurned
And the spark between them turned.
Where love had touched their hearts
Was now cold and torn apart.

It's the day all is lost, you don't love me
And the depth of your heart cannot see,
Skies above won't be painted with beauty.
Now that sadly we've spurned destiny.

And so, the time was gone
When their voices joined in song.
Under weeping stars and moon
Both abandoned love too soon.

First one tear then another meander down my cheek. Hot drops of sorrow to echo the child weeping in her room as Beast sings a story I know too well. Why did she write the ballad of Beatrice and Benedict? Was it to torment or pity me?

Not to torment because I'm not supposed to be listening. Beast told me to leave. Was my story of lost love so profound she was moved to immortalize it in song? Was she ever going to tell me? My pity for Beast is ridiculous when her pity for me is infinitely more profound. My tender heart sloshes in my chest.

Beatrice and I were a real love song, and now we're nothing more than a tune to summon the tears of a child.

Treading as softly as possible, I leave this strange place, cross the library, and make my way to the rooftop. I can't sit on the familiar couch and not because of the very pleasant Beatrice memories imprinted on its natty cushions. I can't sit at all, I'm too amped. Gothel is here in the Caliwood, not dead, and keeping a Zeli Jr. locked away. Damn, the snake has a definite M.O.

I don't wait long. Beast flies at me from the stairwell door. I meet her halfway and grab her forearms. "Did Gothel come back?"

"No. Dawn."

I tug her toward the stairwell. "We've gotta spring the kid. Let's grab the cheese while King Rat Bastard is away."

Beast overpowers me and drags me to the couch. Since there's no way I'm going to win a wrestling match with a buff harpy, I sit.

"Tonight. Not safe. Need a plan quick."

I flap my arms as if I have wings. "What's with the choppy talk tonight? Spit it out."

She grabs her throat, then points to her beak and shakes her head. "Can't..."

I pull her hands away. "Did fire boy make you drink the tears? Is your throat screwed up?"

I recall what Justin Time said in an interview about Gothel making his singers drink an evil tea to squeeze their vocal cords producing the Rampion Records signature pop screech.

"No." She stamps her foot hard enough to set off car alarms in the parking structure attached to the Caliwood. Beast windmills her claws, encouraging me to keep going.

"Okay, you haven't downed tears or nasty Gothel tea."

Beast points to her mouth, nodding her head until her headdress dances. "Ka urz—Magic."

No clue what ka urz is. It sounds like a sound effect on a cartoon, but magic—Shit—Magic. That I get. My encounter with magic knocks into me. Tressa's ice wall. Trapped ghosts. Strange words Beatrice and I joked were a curse. My eyes stretch to the point of pain while my brain catches up.

Ka urz—curse

"A curse has you tongue tied?" I see the yes in her eyes. I'm afraid to ask my next question because I can't deal if the answer is what I think it is, but when it comes to curses, I have a singular point of reference. "Beast, is Tressa Divine with Gothel? Is she the they you mentioned?"

Beast squeezes her eyes closed so tightly, they drip tears. Oh, damn, this is bad. A horrible thought singes my brain. "Is Leonato part of this? Is he letting Gothel live in the Caliwood?" Leonato is a crusty biz dude, but a criminal? I can't fathom the boss being in bed with Gothel. They were intense rivals for years.

There's stink in the air having nothing to do with the exhaust and weed aroma below on Hollywood Boulevard.

This time Beast shakes her head and wiggles talons near her temples. "Leonato."

I copy her gesture with my fingers. "Leonato what? He's lost his mind?"

Beast grumbles. "Not *lost* his mind." She repeats the gesture, and then scoops me under a wing to drag me to the far corner of the rooftop on the back side of the Hotel Caliwood sign. Beast stops in the center of a makeshift circle of big chunks of granite. At their center is the coffee table missing from our bro cave on the Hollywood Boulevard side of the rooftop. It's littered with crystals, candles, matches, and women's cosmetics. Homeless folks, the unseen, the true ghosts of Hollywood have found their way to many a rooftop as temporary shelter, but this is no fire in an oilcan. I hung with Pagans in Ireland one summer night when we did a festival gig at an old castle. The arrangement feels reminiscent of a ritual ground they showed me.

"Is this—"

Beast feather's ruffle in the breeze as she huffs and tries a new communication strategy. "Rich, switch, kitch—Fill in the blank, Ben."

I stare into the shadows, making sure nothing is ready to jump out and sink its teeth into me. I can't believe I'm stepping into this weirdscape. "Witch? Witches?"

Beast repeats the *woo woo* finger wiggle at her temples. "Leonato."

"Dude's been zapped by a witch?" I swallow hard. "Is her name Tressa?"

Beast stares at me unblinking, like she's trying to send her confirmation psychically from brain to brain.

"Crapping damn," I growl. Old fears about Tressa Divine and her particular *woo woo* potential light up my barely banked fear.

Beast deflates, which I translate as me hitting the mark. I wish I'd been wrong. She stumbles. "One wrong word, Ben and—and— bad."

"Then I'll talk." I check the rooftop and pull her deeper into the shadows. I press fingers to my eyes as if that will bring this swirling mess into focus. "Okay, we can't remove the kid tonight, but we've got to get her away from Gothel ASAP."

"Figure out a safe plan. No screw ups."

"Got it." I smile.

Exhaustion clouds her eyes.

"I'm going to assume you got her tears tonight."

"Yep-i-dee-doo-dah."

The nonsense phrase doesn't choke her. I throw her thumbs up. "Whatever works."

She taps her throat. "I'm trying."

I take her hand, getting better at knowing how to slide my fingers between her claws and lead her across the rooftop to the sofa. She perches on the left cushion. I plant myself in the center. Our sides touch. "You're doing great. Beast, we're on the same team. One that means a lot to me." From this angle, I can see the lights of the Hollywood Sign and if I lean closer, the stars reflecting in her big, sweet eyes.

Beast settles closer, leaning against me lightly so she doesn't bowl me over. "Me too, Ben."

I shift to face her and lay a hand over my heart. "I give you my word I'll do whatever it takes to yank the kid from Gothel, but before we unlock the door to the war room, let's take a breath." I move my hand from my chest to her cheek. "There's something I need to say to you."

Beast bobs up and down, knocking my hand away. "No time, Ben. Let's plan."

I take her face in both hands with a firmer grip. Feathers soft against my palms. "We will. Let me get this out first." Beast stills, allowing my hands to warm her soft skin. "I heard your song."

"I told you to leave." She jerks her head from my grasp so fast, the hook of her beak scratches across my knuckles. Beast's hands fly to her beak. "Oh no. Didn't mean to hurt you, Benedict. Here—" She nods at the cut in my skin and then pauses. "Or here." Her fist presses against my heart.

"It's fine." I wipe the bead of blood on my jeans. "Just one of the things we'll work on in our partnership."

"Partnership?"

Suddenly the term sounds cold. "Friendship, alliance, creative coupling."

I don't know who flushes brighter red at my last choice of words, Beast, or me. I play it safer and grasp her shoulders. "Your song told the story that's been gnawing at my guts for the past year. I screwed up with Beatrice, and then I rolled into a ball of misery instead of accepting the truth and learning to face life without her."

Beast stares at me with such intensity, if I didn't know her for the gentle softy she can be, I'd think she planned to have me for her next meal.

"I never shared with Beatrice the depth of presence she had in my life and how vital it was not only to my creative existence, but my soul. I assumed she felt what I felt, and we communicated our deep emotions every time we sang together, but it was never voiced as passionately once we left the stage. That is a mistake I will not repeat."

Beast's breathing is loud enough to break the stillness of the night.

"People who are important to me will know it. I'm going to be transparent AF." I suck in oxygen to stoke my nerve. "You are one of those people. You are important to me, Beast. My life is richer for what you bring to it." I rise high enough to rest my forehead against hers. Feathers brush my skin. We pause in silence. The contact fills me with a peace, a liquid joy I haven't experienced since I lost Beatrice.

I pull away first to study Beast's face. Her expression shifts into many colors, each gone before I can read it. She's intense, then soft. I see longing and then fear. Joy, then disappointment. What did I nudge inside this dear creature she isn't sharing with me?

"Talk to me, Bea."

Beatrice's nickname shatters the moment. Beast hops off the couch. I go after her as she clomps to the edge of the roof, desperation rising around me like an unforgiving high tide.

"Wait, please. I meant Bea for Beast. I swear. I was not conflating you with Beatrice."

Beast flaps her wings. "Bravo, you've decided to become a transparently better person. Thanks for the compliment, but that's not our priority."

I am a certifiable royal fuck up. Instead of baring my soul to Beast, I've alienated her. Once again, I didn't jump in the pool. Here I am stroking my own desires when she's losing her shit over the kid.

Damage control.

Think, Benedict.

How can I keep things from going farther south? The answer is right in front of me. Before I attempt to get real with Beast again, the first step to prove to her I'm legit with my feelings is to go all-in to save the little person in Gothel's apartment.

I do what I do best: backpedal. "You're right. Priorities. You believe the kid is in danger? Does the kid even want to be away from Gothel? She did call him *Papa*." I hold up a finger. "Wait, is this kid his, as in daughter?"

Beast looks at me like I'm the biggest idiot she's ever seen. She chirps loudly enough to compete with a siren on Hollywood Boulevard.

"Okay, okay. Let's slow down," I say. "We'll take a few days and figure some foolproof moves."

Her irises enlarge. "No time. Moving soon. No Caliwood."

"He's leaving with her?"

Beast trills.

"How soon?"

She holds up the three claws of her left hand and then shrugs. "What can we do, Ben?"

"No clue...yet."

The narrowing of her eyes telegraphs the crushing disappointment I am to her. What the hell? I've just learned another kid is bound to Gothel, heard Beast sing the tragedy of

Beatrice and Benedict, and basically been rejected by someone I thought there might be a chance to be important in my life. A guy can only deal with so much.

"No time," she caws. The sound of her panic splits the air.

Tension spasms my back muscles. I grit my teeth to keep from whining. The night is so far afield from what I envisioned while I dressed nice for Beast, I may grow a spontaneous ulcer.

"Give me a frickin' second to think." Her head recoils at the anger in my tone. I'm such a jumble of emotional mess right now, it's best I leave before I make things worse. This harpy expects me to be her knight for hire when I'm simply a fool desperate to lick his wounds after her none too subtle rejection.

"It's late. I'll come to the library tomorrow, and we'll continue this." I refrain from storming across the roof to the stairwell door and plaster a pleasant look on my face. "Have a good night, Beast."

"Benedict, wait."

It's ridiculous how fast my heart fills with hope. Am I forgiven? Can we soften our torn edges?

"I need more from you?"

Great. Please don't let her ask for another thing I can't deliver. "Yeah?"

Our gaze locks when I turn back, and neither of us speak for a handful of beats. I feel the invisible strand still connecting us spark and pulse. I want to grasp it in my hands and pull Beast toward me. There must be a way to rewind to the moment right before I stupidly blurted Bea's name.

She slowly approaches me. "Hero is in pain. Can you help her?"

This I can do. Help Hero heal the nasty gash Santino dealt her. Hell, if Beast asked me to jump from the rooftop of the Caliwood to the moon, I'd at least try.

"I'm heading to Santino's place tomorrow to fire his ass as our media dude." I run a hand through my carefully coiffed hair, intended to impress Beast. It doesn't matter now if it sticks up like dry brush on the Hollywood Hills. "I don't want him to impose on Hero's reality for another second."

Beast gives me a smile sad enough to ruin Christmas. "The situation is a bigger rolling shit ball than you know. Go easy on him. He doesn't understand."

I squint at her. "Go easy? I thought you'd want me to feed him to the vandals."

"He's a victim of deception. Tell him." She lets out a strangled sound as if her throat has squeezed and coughs.

My head starts to pound. Too much weird infiltrates my world tonight. "The dude's an open wound. You want me to waltz up to him and say he's a victim of deception? Whose? His? Hero's?" Based on Hero's current state of unravel, I can't imagine her in the role of deceiver.

Beast fists her clawed hands and presses them to her eyes. She's trembling. What the hell will happen if she says the wrong thing? My stomach lurches. With Gothel and Tressa in the mix, it can't be anything less than epically fucked.

She drops her hands, and her mouth forms a word, testing it. Her gaze locks on mine. "Claude's deception. Not Hero with him. Not Hero with him." Each time she repeats the phrase, she puts more oomph behind it until she's screeching it to the night. "Trust me, Ben. Not Hero." She jabs a claw into the couch cushion.

Heights never bothered me, but as Beast's meaning sinks in, I'm smacked with the mother of all vertigo. Stars smear across the black sky. I reach for the couch to steady myself and miss, landing hard on the rooftop.

Beast chirps a note of concern and lurches toward me. I use the couch to climb to my feet. "Are you telling me Claude was not with Hero?"

Her cry of relief mingled with outrage makes my eardrums ache.

I drape my torso over the back of the couch. Holy, holy, damn. All I've been trying to do is get an album on the books and take the first steps away from my life with Beatrice and possibly toward Beast. I never bargained for playing rescuer to a kid, dipping a toe into potentially toxic magic with Gothel and Tressa, or getting caught up in the Santino/Hero shitshow. Yet here I am because I walked into Beast's life.

I should find a nice mound of sand, stick my head into it, and wait for this mess to fade away. The problem is, I'm not going to walk away from Beast. Despite her kiss off, she's part of my life now.

Straightening, I meet Beast's anxious expression. "I don't suppose you can elaborate?"

"Claude is the villain."

I wish I could defend Claude, but Beast's words ring true in my gut.

A subtle tremor vibrates beneath our feet. Her skin pales to the shade of the milky moon.

I pat her arm. "As quakes go, that was an afterthought." I want to stroke her feathers, rewind the night, and finish telling her I'm into her. Or do I? Beast is clearly not into me, or she would have let me finish. My bruised ego shifts into casual. "Or maybe it's your ghosts whoopin' it up."

Shockingly, I get a smile from her.

"I'll give Tino your message." God help me make sense of it. I snort and squeeze her upper arm that puts mine to shame. "We'll figure it out, Beast, the kid, Hero. I'm with you."

"Thank you, Benedict."

I wish I had more to offer than a tight smile, but my insides turn to mush like a cake in a rainstorm as my stare locks onto Beast's. "We're going to get you away from Gothel too." Turning from the stunned look on Beast's face, I slip through the door, down the stairwell, through the library, and into my apartment. Leaning against my closed door, I knock my head to the wood, hoping the blows will jar an idea loose. I don't want to be Benedict of the empty promises to Beast, but committing to spring a kid and Beast from a seriously dangerous felon in less than three days when I have no frickin' clue how to do that is not a jolly good start.

A gust from the notorious Santa Ana winds blasts through my kitchen window, causing a stack of lyric sheets to flutter to the floor.

Was I right about Beast's ghosts whoopin' it up?

I stoop to gather the paper and clutch them so tight in my hand they crinkle.

Beast's ghosts.

Crazy thought—Can Beast ask the ghosts of Hotel Caliwood to join our rescue party?

19

ONE LAST NIGHT

THE MOON AND THE THREE OS OF THE HOLLYWOOD SIGN STARE AT me, accusation pouring out of them.

I wail at them. "What have I done?" There was Ben, practically blabbering the opening lines of a love poem, and I silenced him. It wasn't because he's shit at lyrics. This is on me. Knowing he heard the song I wrote about us to make Maisie weep, then hearing him call me *Bea* knocked me sideways. Like the harpy I am, I turned screechy and cold.

Charging to the stairwell door, I fling it open. I'll go after Ben and apologize for ruining his sweet attempt at telling me he cares about me.

From far across the library, I hear the door to the hallway close. Ben is gone, and with him more of my shallow reservoir of hope drips down the stucco sides of the Caliwood like rare Hollywood rain.

Stop. Stop. Stop.

I can't reach out to him before Maisie is safely away. Beatrice must wait a little longer to come home.

I lay a hand to my breast and feel the pounding heart beneath. Was Gothel telling the truth or toying with me when he all but admitted my belief the curse is breakable may be nothing more than a naïve wish?

"Does one ever grasp when their dreams end? There is no release."

Did the black-hearted enchantress ever truly entertain any intention for Beatrice to return? Playing with my life is a familiar arrow from Tressa's quiver.

Benedict said he wants to save Beast.

Saving Beast and loving Beast are two disparate realities. I broke his heart as Beatrice. Did Beast do the same by shutting him down tonight?

I squeeze into the library. As I suspected, the slight tremor we felt on the roof came from the songbook. So few pages are left. I remove the dome and stack the fallen sheets, leaning them against the edge of the book's cover.

If the pages could speak, would they tell me not to give up? I release a bitter trill. I can't help but think any words they may speak are nothing more than shadings of Tressa's lies. They do not speak, and I replace the dome.

I must appreciate the victory within this defeat. If I'd allowed Benedict to declare his love for me, and Beatrice returned, where does that leave Maisie? Dim light flickers deep in my black mood. A flicker for a little girl who cries golden tears. A restored Beatrice would forget Gothel, Tressa, Rubata, and Sulaa, but she'd also forget Maisie.

I don't know how long I linger in the alcove with the decaying songbook. When I look up, four sets of translucent eyes study me.

"Our Beast suffers a definite case of melancholia," says Monty. "Did the child not weep?" He tears at his perfectly coiffed hair, which doesn't move under his touch. "I blame myself. She is far too adaptable and curious."

Audra lets out a long-labored sigh. "If only I could pinch the tyke." She wiggles her fingers. "Kidding of course."

"Oh, she wept." I confess my shame. "Four bottles worth."

Graham shakes his head. "Those fiends are a coven of spiders, playing with that poor girl like food before they consume her completely."

"I hate spiders," squeaks Sassy, ducking behind Graham.

"Graham doesn't mean actual spiders, dear one," says Monty, patting her head.

I'll never get used to the way his hand disappears into her.

"If you managed your tear quota, why so blue, Beast?" Audra gasps and puts both hands over her mouth. "It's him, your Benedict." She swoops to the library door and lays her palm against in. "He rejected you." In a blinding streak, she dashes to the alcove. "Oh, thank every Hollywood star on land and sky. You've still got pages."

"Benedict didn't reject me. In fact, I believe he was ready to admit he has feelings for me."

"That's wonderful, Beast," says Audra.

Monty lifts his arms to the ceiling. "Marvelous."

Graham's smile outdoes a fully lit statue torch for brightness. "Justice at last."

"I discouraged him."

A quartet of ghostly gapes surround me.

Audra is first to jostle her astonishment. "Oh, doll, you can't be serious."

Sassy starts to cry and buries her face against the side of Graham's suit pants and halfway through his form.

Their disappointment is a fraction of what I saw in Ben. My ridiculous bird throat wobbles and gurgling chirps pour from my lips.

"Gothel basically warned me I can't break the curse. He insinuated that Tressa has been lying to me this whole time. She can't let go of her sick revenge game." I drop onto the sofa and dig my pointy chin into its cushions. "If I could go back to the audition, I'd step away and give her the damn female singer spot in the band. If we were truly meant to be, Ben and I would have found some other way to be together. I craved the security of being in a band and curse me—" I let loose an ironic squawk. "I wanted a taste of fame. Once I had my taste, I realized it wasn't my end game. Joining my words with Benedict's music was the real passion."

There's nothing more depressing than ghostly pity faces. The way they waver and reset is like seeing your own sorrow on the surface of a wind-blown pond. Each time the image comes into focus, it's deeper and more painful.

Audra's face hovers inches from my beak. "But Benedict does love Beast. We saw it in the dance of the mirrors."

My precious ghosts' heads bob in unison.

"He also loves Beatrice." My wound from his use of my true name aches. "He called me Bea."

"Darling, you are Beatrice."

I jump to my feet, and then flap until I'm a few feet above the couch. "A truth I can never tell him. The Dark Vinyl Artists silenced every word either spoken against them or hinting at the curse."

Monty sweeps an arm at the lair behind the bookcase. "But he saw the child and those vile aquatic abominations Sulaa keeps. What did the fellow make of that?"

Audra stares at Monty. "And you didn't tell me any of this?"

Monty shrugs his blue tinted shoulders.

She whips her gaze to me. "Spill, doll."

My feathers quiver, making a quiet rustling sound as I settle on the carpet. "In a very circuitous way with the curse squeezing my wind, I attempted to tell him about Maisie and Gothel." My heart skitters. The beautiful shorthand Ben and I always shared was still there. Another painful reminder of what I may never have again. "He agreed to help me sneak her out of here."

Monty applauds. "You are a rare talent, my dear Beast."

Graham strokes his chin. "Were you able to convey the truth of Claude and Rubata's charade as well for Benedict?"

I sink onto the sofa, guilt making my feathers feel as if they were made of stone. "I did ask him to go easy on Santino when he fires him."

"This is quite the damnable mess," says Monty.

I purse my lips. They disappear beneath the shadow of my beak. "No kidding."

Monty raises an invisible glass. "This is why I celebrate the power of drink."

The last of my energy evaporates. I crave the comfort of my nest. I fly to the top of the bookcase and plant my head under a wing. Beatrice Sharpe would defy Gothel's doomsday prediction, create a plan to free Maisie, then test the curse by marching up to Benedict and let him try to love her, but Beast is not Beatrice.

Beast with memories intact is the sole person with a shot at changing Maisie's future.

And Benedict—Oh, Benedict, I can't allow you to love only to be ripped in half again. I wish I could explain and tell him his love is a precious treasure to both Beatrice and Beast. Ben's attempt to share his feelings with Beast proves he's trying to move on from Beatrice, but there is still an ache in his heart for my true self. I yearn to offer him the closure of a goodbye to replace my cruel vanishing act incited by Tressa's curse.

"Beast?"

Graham's voice below shakes me out of my introspection.

"What can we do to lessen your sorrow, dear friend?"

I hang my head over the top edge of the bookcase. "Go back into Ben's dreams and say goodbye for me—for Beatrice?"

Audra rises, one toe pointing behind a foot in a balletic pose until we're face to face. "We can do better, my lovely."

I cock my head to the side.

She strokes my feathers. All I feel is a chill. "If you dream you are once again Beatrice, we will take that vision into the dreams of your Benedict and gift you one last night together."

I sit too fast and nearly knock my head on the ceiling. "That's possible?"

Graham leans on the table with straight arms. "With the power of we four, a connection can be made between two spirits on a single night for an hour. Are you sure you're ready to use this single chance?"

Squeezing free of my nest, I drop to the carpet. "You were holding out on me!"

Monty claps Graham on the back and his hand slides through his friend's lapel. "We didn't want to tempt you prematurely, but I believe we're at the eleventh hour."

I jump onto the library table, my heart pounding. "Will dream me be able to talk to Ben?"

Audra joins me on the tabletop. "Of course. Your dream selves may speak to one another."

"Then I can tell him about the curse. Let him know his wait for Beatrice will be over once Maisie is free." My flattened hope revives. "Damn, if you'd waited much longer, I would have blown my only shot."

Sassy busts out crying again. I study the trio of ghostly adult faces. Now who's gripped with melancholia?

Graham, the least dramatic of the ghosts, delivers the blow. "The parameters of your curse can't be altered even in a dream visitation."

"Darling, we never would have kept you from Benedict's dreams if you were allowed to tell him how to break the curse. If only Tressa's power didn't bind us to the same silence, we would have helped you claim your love," says Audra with dewy eyes. I wonder how many heartbreaks she endured in her life.

"Let me get this straight. You can take dream Beatrice to say goodbye to dream Benedict."

"One time, one night, one hour," says Graham.

Has Ben dreamed of my goodbye before? I pray I can shift any bitter dreams of Beatrice he's suffered into sweet ones. This may be his one chance to see his Beatrice again. If the last page of the songbook falls before we liberate Maisie...— A shudder runs through me, and I wipe the desperate thought aside.

"I need to do it tonight. Now."

"Then sleep, sweet Beatrice, sleep," the ghosts chant in unison. The four begin to slowly circle me, one blending into the other. They increase speed until the deep blue blur curls into a sphere. My body floats in its center, chilled but not to the point of shivers. The library recedes into the distance as I fall from wakefulness into sleep. My body lightens, shedding the bulk of Beast, until I reclaim the feather-free, thin, slightly bony frame of Beatrice. Oh, how I've missed the feel of her.

I twist in my cerulean womb. Beatrice is back. Oh, glorious day. I run fingers, not claws over the skin of my arms and my neck. So smooth.

My ghostly transport allows us to drift through walls to the door of Benedict's apartment. Our apartment. With a gentle nudge, I'm propelled through the door, and basically dumped onto the braided rug I found at a West Hollywood garage sale—completely naked.

It's not quite how I pictured our reunion, but a girl's gotta work with what she has. I grab the aqua and chartreuse crocheted blanket off the couch and wrap it sarong style around my bod. Flo and Edie called the throw an acid trip in yarn. It took a lot of persuasion and more cash than I'd usually part with to convince them to relinquish the psychedelic gem. They had plans to drape it around the 1960s display in their vintage clothing store on Hollywood Boulevard. I love this flippin' blanket.

I thought I'd be transparent and filmy like the ghosts, but I'm not. I'm well—me. Dream me has substance. Benedict's snores remind me I'm on the clock for the heart slicing job ahead of me. Tiptoeing to not wake him, I skirt the love seat that serves as our couch and the forest green leather recliner I rescued after tenants who lived in the apartments behind the Caliwood abandoned it in the alley. Lowering myself onto the edge of the bed, I watch my love sleep.

Benedict is a noisy and restless sleeper. His blanket twisting dance is the sign of a dreaming mind racing with new melodies, counterpoints, and rhythms. Unlike the variety of laid-back rockers, Ben is a hamster wheel of creativity, both awake and asleep. I loved waking to the sound of him humming the seeds of a new song. There are journals stashed all over our apartment. He never had to walk more than five paces before grabbing pen and paper to capture notes before they floated out the window.

"Do you always watch me sleep?"

I whip my head from Benedict at rest to Benedict walking in from our skinny balcony. A slight breeze blows the pair of baby pink chenille bedspreads with ballet dancers in the middle I fashioned into drapes as he steps into the room. He's as bare ass naked as I am under the blanket.

I stand and face him, taking in the beauty of his corded muscles, sculpted from early morning runs and hauling band equipment for months on end. Moonlight radiates off his white-blond hair.

"Is that what you call your nocturnal bed flopping?"

His smile sends a river of pure joy coursing through my body.

"You're late, Beatrice. I've been waiting."

I take slow steps toward him, afraid if I go too quickly, he'll dissipate into mist. "I'm sorry, my love. I wanted to come sooner."

Benedict opens his arms, inviting me in. There's no more holding back. I must touch him. Either our dream selves will come together, or he'll disappear. I fall into his arms, and I feel his warmth, his solid chest against my cheek. My tears are immediate, filling every gap left behind by our separation. Ben wraps me in a forever hug. This time, we won't let go. I will not give him an ultimatum. I will love. Just love.

"Oh, Ben, I'm so sorry. I said horrid things to you during the fight. I didn't mean them. If I'd known—"

Benedict's chin rests on top of my head. He's once again taller than me instead of the other way around when I'm Beast.

"I would not have you weep, dearest Beatrice."

"Benedict, you are owed my tears of remorse."

He tilts my chin, bringing my lips a pinkie width from his. "Shh. Peace, I will stop your mouth with a kiss."

Ben presses his beautiful mouth to mine with enough pressure to part both our lips as if we are sharing one single note of a song. We begin to move together, relearning how to speak with kisses. His hot breath flowing across my tongue melts the bitterness of our last night together into a molten memory, burning away pain. I return the favor, and he sighs, sending another rush of sweet Benedict breeze across my lips.

Instead of deepening the kiss, Benedict pulls back and touches his forehead to mine. "Oh, Bea. I was the worst kind of shitiot for not jumping into the pool with you." His breath hitches and his chest rumbles against my hand pressing to his skin. "I didn't know." His sob reaches deep to my core, and I sense the true depth of pain my disappearing act raked across his soul. "I had no idea it would end us."

It's my turn to stop his words. Screw the tentative get reacquainted pace, I dive in deep and pour every second of my longing and loneliness from the last year into a fierce kiss. Ben answers, and we ignite with the passion that blazes between us in every duet we've ever sung. He paints my tongue with his to leave his mark, and I return the favor. Fingers run up my neck into my hair. He pulls my head back to plunge into renewed clashes of teeth, lips, and tongues. I dig fingers into the muscles of his shoulder while still holding the blanket with my other hand as he tightens the arm around me, yanking my body flush against his.

He kisses his way across my jaw and up my neck until words set fire to the shell of my ear. "I love you, Beatrice Sharpe. I loved you from our first dance the night of Leonato's Christmas party. When I left on tour the next morning, I loved you every day until you showed a year later for the audition and reinvented my band. I've loved you every moment since even after you left me. It is impossible to ever stop loving you."

I nuzzle the underside of his jaw with my nose. "I didn't leave you, Benedict. It was—" The fucking curse-clench wrings my throat into a soggy rope, and I can't speak. For one beautiful moment, I forgot how Tressa destroyed us. My main task tonight is to requite Benedict Boyd's love for me.

"From our first night on the rooftop until Beatrice Sharpe ceases to be, my love has been and will be yours, Benedict. Every word I write, every song I sing, and every wish I make on the stars, will always be about you, my precious love."

His warm tears dribble off his chin onto my face.

"I would not have you weep, my Benedict." I grab his chin. "Love me tonight, and then we will say a goodbye allowing us both to love again instead of petrifying our hearts for the rest of our lives."

Benedict clutches my body. "No. Not goodbye."

"Yes, Ben. A gentle goodbye, so you will see the beauty inside the monster I became to you the night of our break-up fight."

He rubs his face in my hair, inhaling deeply. "You were never or could never be a monster, my sweet Beatrice."

My fingers trail along the soft hair of his chest. "You have no clue what it means to hear you say that, Ben. Do love me forever, but not only me. Learn to open your heart, my love."

He exhales and hair tickles my ears. "It is easier to reason with love than to conquer it. Can we change the subject?" Ben dips his head to kiss the top of my shoulder. He works his way down my upper arm in a series of gentle nips.

I've delivered my message, given him permission to move on. Short of slapping him across the face and telling him to get over me, it's the best I can do. Right now, I want to be with my Benedict one last time as his Beatrice. Our single precious hour is something neither Gothel, Tressa, or their pet witches can take away from us.

Bless the ghosts of Hotel Caliwood.

Benedict slips one finger under the front of my crocheted wrap and slides it between my breasts, reaching low enough to tease the buds of my nipples. His touch, his warm and deliciously familiar caress, chases away the reality of my doomed future as Beast. All that matters is this man, this night.

One by one, he pries my fingers from the blanket, allowing it to fall to my waist before he grabs it, turning my shift into a skirt. "Perfect. So perfect. I wish I wasn't shit at lyrics, Bea, so I could tell you how beautiful your breasts are."

"Your moves are good enough, Ben. Don't spoil it with your lame ass attempts at rhymes."

We both laugh. Damn, our laughter feels right.

"Show me more, Benedict. Show me your poetry."

He wraps an arm around my ass and lifts me high enough to set me on our love seat, still holding the fabric around my waist. Dropping to his knees, he leans in to run his tongue from my navel along one breast, stopping shy of my nipple. I ache for him to take me in his mouth and suck until I scream. His naughty smile tells me he knows exactly what I'm thinking.

Keeping eye contact, he forges a rough and glorious trail with his tongue over the swell of my other breast and then winks at me.

"Having trouble breathing, Bea?"

Panting, I wrap my legs around his hips and scissor squeeze until he grunts. "If you don't get down to business, Bene*dick*, I'm going to take care of myself."

"Don't rush me, boss," he grins, slowly advancing pinching fingers toward my chest. Oh, how I've missed our sexual combat. Offenses, defenses, taunts, and teases.

I palm my nipple and begin to rub, dropping my head back in an exaggerated moan to prove I can rustle up my own pleasure.

He playfully swats my hand away to tease my rising peak with the tip of his tongue.

"Ummm, thanks for handling the preliminaries, Bea." Without another word, he takes me deep into his mouth, savoring the taste of me, the flat of his tongue stroking until he slowly pulls his lips away, stretching his dark pink treat to the point where I gasp from the sexy tingle of pain.

As he gives equal time to each breast, I moan in earnest not even attempting words. My hands rub the soft, moon-kissed hair on his chest and then tug, returning the favor of an ouch for an ouch. He loves this. He always did. I slide my hands to his skinny hips and back up his ribs, laughing when he twitches from the tickle. My fingers memorize every contour, then jerk his chest flush to mine, stealing another hot and naughty kiss.

The sneaky bastard uses the distraction to slip one hand beneath the blanket, sweeping along the inside of my thigh to cup the heat between my legs.

"Damn, Beatrice, a man could drown in this raging stream. See if I'm wrong."

Benedict grabs my hand and presses it to my pulsing wet core. I try to pull away, but he presses harder, circling our combined touch over my screaming nerves. "You, Ben. You."

"Us, Bea. Us." He guides my hand and together we stroke until I'm on the brink of imminent destruction. It's then he replaces my hand with his and pinches the exact place to make my star explode. I come against his palm with such force and vocal volume, he dissolves into laughter. "Missed me that much?"

"Fuck yes."

He slides up my body, pressing me into the love seat. "I missed you too. Help me forget the past year."

The root of his arousal strains against my still fluttering lady parts as the tip reaches across my lower belly. I've missed his impressive length and how well he uses it.

"Ease up, Bene*dick*, so I can lose the blanket." I buck my hips to create enough distance to slip the blanket out from between us. Ben stands in front of me. I free my body of all things yarn. His gaze roams from my eyes, down my chest, to the damp dark brown curls between my legs, and then to my calves, which he wraps his fingers around.

"I've always loved these. So strong." He flips me to drop kisses and bites on my calves. "And this..." His fingers knead and caress my ass.

He yips when I twist to face him. With him on his feet and me still seated comfy on the loveseat, I'm at the perfect height for——

Benedict's quarter notes turn into melodious moans as I appreciate his length and girth with my tongue. He pulses with an alluring rhythm that has me aching for another star explosion. I hold off to make this last until the last second of the last minute I'm allowed to be with him. There will be no kaboom then an exhausted roll over for a recovery snooze tonight.

After savoring the salty taste of his readiness, I take him in my mouth with a luxurious slide. His babbling and fragmented words are so hot, I continue to work him just to encourage the sexy nonsense. The flavor of his cock is pure Benedict, sweet with a tongue-tingling tang. When Benedict begins to tremble, I lay a hand on his chest and push him away. "Don't you dare finish until I tell you to." He's surprised when I jump into his arms, wrapping my legs around him. Our balance fails, and we fall to the rag rug. I bury my head against his collarbone and laugh. There is always laughter with our sex. It's the language of love and lust we're fluent in.

"My Beatrice," whispers Benedict as he untangles our snarled arms and legs to lay me on my back. With a loving touch, he slides my feet toward my body until he can press my bent knees apart. He bends to deliver one of his long, slow licks across my ripe opening. When his tongue plunges inside, I gasp. He repeats the movement, delving deeper each time, a prelude to what he plans to repeat with a more substantial part of his anatomy. I press against him.

"My Benedict," I answer. "Now, my love. All of you."

He pulls away. The love in his eyes destroys me. It's the last time I'll feel his kiss. The last time his body will know my love. I'm ready to dissolve into a weeping mass, but I force the sorrow deep. Our final night will be filled with joy alone.

I grab his hands to pull him closer and rest my legs across his strong shoulders, opening to him completely.

"I'm yours, Bea. All of me." He yanks me closer and dips his cock inside just far enough to scramble my thoughts. "All of me." Ben travels a few more precious inches.

I lock gazes with him as I groan in delight. "All of you."

This time, he travels deeper and deeper until he disappears inside me. We are two entities fused into one. We pause, exalting in our exquisite joining. I don't want to lose this gift. If I beg, will the ghosts take our lives and allow this to be the rapturous end of our souls?

I grip Benedict tighter, both inside and out. Dreams must end. Dreams must die. Let my dream die within the glory of love.

I rock my hips against Ben's, and our moment of stillness ends. He breathes my name over and over as if the saying completes our connection as he thrusts into me. His hands slide around to my ass as he attempts to bond himself closer to me. With each approach he cries a new note, faster and faster until he hits the place inside me that's waited so long for him to visit. I cry out with my own harmony as he ends our song with a final prolonged note of joy.

We shiver and flutter together for the length of a refrain as the fragments of our stars are pulled together once again by gravity. Benedict sits and pulls me to straddle him. Holding me, rocking me, loving me. Desperation in his grasp. From across the room, sleeping Benedict mumbles my name, and dream Benedict fades.

I sneak to the closet and from the top shelf where it still rests, free the top hat I wore the night of the audition that brought us back together. To my delight, I can grasp it with my spirity fingers.

Gently, I lay it on the bed next to the only man who will ever lay claim to my heart.

"Love on, Benedict. Love on," I whisper into his ear.

I startle awake. The hearth fire in the library and not Benedict's hot, salty skin warms me.

Our hour is over.

20

TEAM BUILDING

I WAKE WITH A HARD-ON THE SIZE OF A BASEBALL BAT AS I STARE AT the top hat on the pillow next to me. My Louisville Slugger deflates as I remember Beatrice's words from my dream.

"*Do love me forever, but not only me. Learn to open your heart, my love.*"

It's not the first time I've fallen asleep staring at Bea's top hat, the remnant of my own personal ghost, or had a vivid sex dream about the woman I'll never sing with or touch again. The quality was wildly different in this one. It was too fucking real, and the edges of my heart are singed with dream Beatrice's farewell.

Damned if I remember grabbing the top hat from the closet last night. I glance at the kitchen counter, but there's no telltale bottle of whiskey to explain my lack of post-dawn clarity.

Last night...

I stuff the closest pillow over my face as if I can smother the memory of Beast's dismissal of my feelings. Dismissal, hell. It's as if I offended her by even hinting at them. Rolling over, I run a finger along the soft felt of Beatrice's hat. On a whim, I pull a blood red feather from her collection in the nightstand's drawer and reunite it with the beloved piece of Bea's signature costume.

A ridiculous urge to drop a kiss on the brim and bid the hat farewell surprises me. Is my growing affection for Beast the sign I'm finally moving on?

Blast my dream for reminding me of the sense of completion I always felt with Beatrice. "What do you think, hat? Should I go one last round of trying to find Bea?"

I know the answer in my tender spirit. Beatrice is gone. She does not want to be found. The dream confirmed I know it in my soul, and I must stop second guessing myself. I may dream of Beatrice, but she is not my future, only my past. I hoped there was some chance Beast might be my future, but any fleeting thoughts I had of her continuing in my life were smashed last night by her disinterest in my feeble overture.

Beast needs my help, but she doesn't want a Benedict in her life.

When I needed help, Beast was there for me with her extraordinary lyrics. She saved the album. It's quid pro quo I return the favor. Although, circumventing Gothel and Tressa Divine feels more like a suicide mission than an even trade.

I sling my legs off the side of the bed and drop my head onto my hands. "How in the seven rings of hell can I help Beast when we're up against legit frickin' evil?"

Scratching fingers through my hair, I stand. I've got nothing, but she's got ghosts. After I break Santino into even smaller bite-sized pieces by firing him, I'll swallow my bruised ego and face Beast.

I pray her ghosts will be on board for a potential reunion with Tressa.

After a shower and the stale protein bar I find wedged in the back of the pantry, I hit Hollywood Boulevard. It's the time I usually take a run, but the sense of a ticking clock behind my ribs makes me forego the activity this morning. Ticking clock, hell, ticking time bomb. I feel horribly alone. I can't talk to Leonato because of Beast's magic finger-wiggle warning. Claude is off the list since Beast's convinced he's pulled dark dealings with the whole Hero mess. D.G. is too tight with Claude, and Alfie avoids discussing any and all band shenanigans.

A crunch underfoot reveals a pile of smashed CD cases. Looks like some poor fool hawking his music had a run in with vandals. I retrieve an insert from one of the destroyed cases. The CD is called *Take me on the Hollywood Ride*. The playlist is filled with optimistic titles like, "The Moon Smiles on the Boulevard," and "One More Step to Fame." I'm tempted to pocket a CD to see if the singer has any chops that might gel with *Benedict and the Boulevard Bunch*. One problem solved if the dude is a better Claude than Claude on vocals.

There's some damn fine magical thinking for an early morning.

I toss the liner into the nearest trash can and smile at the dude opening the side panel of his van to sell maps to movie star homes. Even if Claude is a true villain instead of a textbook asshole, stripping my band down to the studs and rebuilding is one headache I can't face today.

On the next corner, I nearly plow into the Edie half of Flo and Edie, carrying two cups of coffee from Perky Sue's Brew and Snacks. The flock of red and orange bird tats on her bald head give the gloomy morning much needed color.

She nods at my jeans and T-shirt. "Not running? No sexy man tights and basketball shorts?"

"Nah, gotta talk to Tino." I jerk my chin toward Fedele Costumes, a block away. "Walk with me." Edie joins my boulevard stroll since her vintage clothing store is across the street near Santino's place.

Her expression is grim. "What the hell got into the man? I could eviscerate him for what he pulled on Hero."

"Agree, but don't you think it was bizarrely out of character?"

She chews on her lip. "For Tino pre-accident—Truth. He's different, Ben. I hope someday he's able to heal from his metaphysical fire the way he did Gothel's literal flames." Edie bobs a coffee cup in my direction. "Are you off to take your shot at him for the engagement party shitstorm?"

I wince, dreading to come clean. "I'm going to fire him."

Edie stops and stares at me. "Harsh. Is Leonato making you do his dirty work?"

"My call."

She huffs. "At least you have the balls to do it in person."

"No objection? You're not going to school me on unfairness? I know how tight you are with Santino's Boulevard family."

"How can I? I love the dude, but he pulled an extreme diss on someone else I love. Even Rand Diggs gave Tino a verbal bitch slap over what he did to Hero, and our resident grampa thinks of him as a son."

Rand Diggs is basically the tribe elder of this crazy collection of Hollywood Boulevard locals. He's plucked more than one lost soul out of the gutter, including a young Santino Fedele. If Rand is taking Santino to task, things are as grim in Fedele land as they are in Hero's world.

Not Hero. Not Hero.

Beast's mantra unnerves me. If Hero is innocent, why is Santino dead sure she's guilty?

Edie leans in to kiss my cheek. "I've gotta get Flo her caffeine before she starts belching smoke," says Edie. Her gaze falls on Fedele Costumes. "Maybe we've been babying Tino too much since his accident. I think we need to call him out more on the anger shit. Sucks it falls to you to deliver this wake-up call."

I give her a wave and head down the block past Leeni's Hair for Days, Tino's sister's salon. The security gate is rolled up at Fedele Costumes, but the front door is locked, and the lights aren't on. I rap on the glass, hoping Santino is in the store behind the vampire capes and mummy onesies out for Halloween season and not upstairs in his apartment.

A version of a freakin' ninety-year-old Santino shuffles to the door.

When he sees it's me, his chest caves as if his bones refuse to fill out his frame. Damn, Hero's a peppy morning talk show host compared to Tino. As if it pains him, he unlocks the door. I shove it open.

"You look like shit, man," I say in greeting. "And I've seen you at death's door."

"Good morning to you too, Ben." He waits for me to clear the door and then locks it behind me. "How the hell do you expect me to look?"

I intend to be businesslike, but here person-to-person, anger roils in my center. "You deserve to look like shit."

Santino hangs his head. "Yeah, I do."

"You're a bastard for rejecting Hero and accusing her of disloyalty at your own damn engagement party."

Dude acts as if I backhanded him.

"I spent days on a flippin' sailboat, trying to find a way to live with what she's done. I tried, Ben. I truly did and even convinced myself I could deal until I walked into the room with everyone celebrating the love story of Hero and Santino. I lost it."

"No shit. Ever hear of talking to her first? How could you do that to Hero?"

His eyes blaze. "How could *I*? Did I fuck Claude on the rooftop?" With surprising strength for someone who looks like they're ready to blow away in the morning breeze, Santino attacks a rack of fairy wings and knocks it to the ground. "You want to talk disloyalty? It's too mild a word for what she pulled."

I raise my hands in defense. "Let's agree to fizz down."

Panting, Santino drops hands to knees and hangs his head.

Beast's insistence at Hero's innocence washes over me in a wave of certainty. Hero would never betray Santino. How could anyone ever buy into that, most of all, him? I'm ashamed I doubted Hero at all. Beast's belief in Hero tugs at my heart, and the whole purpose of this visit takes a drastic shift. "I came here with every intention of firing you."

He lifts his gaze to me. "So do it and get the hell out of my shop."

I take his arm and drag him to the chair behind the checkout counter. "Sit." Pacing in front of him, I dive into the opening act of my new material. "You're wrong about Hero."

Santino drills the toe of his superhero high top into the linoleum. "I saw what I saw, Ben."

I drop my hands onto his shoulders so I can look him straight in the eyes. "What do you think you saw?"

He shoves me away. "You know what I saw. Skin."

"What if I take you to someone who can prove you wrong?" As soon as the words are out of my mouth, I start to panic. Will Beast talk to Santino, or will she shred him with her talons first and ask questions later? No, she seemed concerned about him last night. I'm sure Beast wants Santino to hurt over what he put Hero through, but she doesn't want him to hang for it. She knows what really happened on the rooftop. Whatever forces her to swallow words is keeping the truth from coming out.

Santino releases a bitter laugh. "You're dreaming, Ben."

I hop up to sit on the counter and look down at him, mimicking Beast's intimidating angle. "Did you believe Justin Time and Zeli when they told you the truth of Gothel and his—" I wiggle my fingers and make a sizzle sound.

Santino sits back in the chair and stares at me. "What does that have to do with Hero?"

"Did you?"

He runs a hand through his dust brown curls. "Yeah. It was mega-bizarre, but they convinced me."

"Strap in, dude. I've got another dose of weird for you."

Old man Santino takes a very loud breath. "I think I'd prefer it if you fired me."

"Gothel's back in town."

His skin loses every bit of pink, making the scars on his face stand out in stark relief. "Absolutely no way. That bastard returned to the fires of hell where he belongs."

I shake my head. "Nope."

He makes a strangling sound and then starts to cough. When I pop down to slap him between the shoulder blades, he shrugs me off.

"Gets worse."

Santino drops his head. "Go away, Ben."

"Still nope." Slowly he raises his head, so I barrel on. He is one of the key players who brought about Gothel's downfall in the first place. Santino should have popped into the forefront of my mind when I first learned Gothel's new tear machine needed help. I've been so pissed off at him for shaming Hero, I didn't think clearly. Beast and I need him and whatever Boulevard family resources he's willing to muster to pull off another miracle. Santino Fedele is the connective tissue for this whole Hollywood Boulevard community. I pray he can summon enough vengeance in his heart for Gothel to get onboard.

"He's milking another kid for tears, the way he used to do with Zeli."

Santino pops out of his seat. "No. No. Not me. Call Zeli and Justin. I'm not going near that poison well again." He spins on his heel and powers toward the back of the store.

"Do you still love Hero?"

My question kills his escape plan. He raises his arms to plant both palms on a wall under a line of freakish rubber masks. "God help me, I do."

"Will you consider helping me and the, ah, person I'm working with to rip the kid away from Gothel, if I prove what you think you saw is wrong?"

He drops his arms and turns to face me. "What are you doing to me, Ben?"

Guilt surges through my bloodstream. Santino should be allowed to live his life Gothel-free, but hell, we need him. I close my eyes to gather my thoughts. "Come with me to meet my friend. You'll want to hear what she has to say about Hero. The value of your experience with Gothel is key to help us get the kid away from the bastard. What do you say?"

"Will Hero be there?"

"Tino, she's falling apart too."

He grasps his hands in prayer. "I don't think I can face her, Ben. I won't survive it."

I walk up to Santino and clasp his upper arms. "Listen to me. I deserved to lose Beatrice because of my assumption I gave her everything she needed. Claude deserved to lose Hero because he never valued the treasure he had in her. Don't be us. Believe there is still a chance for you and Hero. Find the frayed end of your trust, and let's see if truth can mend it."

It sputters out quickly, but for a beat I see the tiniest glimmer of hope in Santino's eyes.

"I don't know, Ben. A guy can only get beaten to near death so many times." He snorts. "I should know."

"It's not going to happen again, Tino." I lay a hand to my heart. "Swear. I'll arrange the meeting. All you need to do is show up."

A rush of *what the hell am I doing* heats my skin. There's no plan. I haven't even broached the subject of Beast meeting Santino and spilling what she knows about whatever actually happened with Claude on the rooftop. If this goes south, I'm adding to the list of people I let down.

"Tomorrow night. I'll call you with specifics." One night to plan before Beast and I convince Santino to go into battle even tangentially against the devil that nearly stole his life. Before doubt or the certainty I'm insane stops me, I wave and head for the front door. Keys sail over my head and hit the glass. I let myself out and slide the ring back across the floor to avoid eye contact. I can't unsee the speck of hope I planted in Santino Fedele's heart.

21

MOONLIGHT TRUTHS

THE RED NEON OF THE HOTEL CALIWOOD SIGN REFLECTS OFF THE slashes my claws etched in the faux wood covering of the rooftop, making them look like bloody trails. At one point, Leonato renovated the top of the Caliwood to rent for A-lister parties until one drunken middle-management studio type went over the edge and added his name to the roster of hotel ghosts. I've never met the poor fool. He's not one of the spirits flitting through the library to grab Monty, Audra, or Graham for whatever is on the ghostly agenda for the evening.

Now the rooftop is the domain of *Ben and the Boulevard Bunch's* man cave and Rubata Lear's ritual circle. If tonight goes well, it will also be the site of a grand reconciliation between Hero and Santino.

I'm more than a little nervous about keeping my cool when I come face-to-face with Santino. I appreciate that he bested Gothel twice before, plucking both Zeli and Justin Time out of the fiend's clutches, but I'm still tempted to introduce Santino to the business end of my talons after what he did to Hero.

Despite a new layer of awkwardness between Benedict and me after I trounced on his attempts to confess his feelings, we've managed to sketch out a few ideas to free Maisie. Today, each time I caught a flash of hurt or longing in his eyes when he looked at me across the library table, I broke a little more. I'm desperate to return his feelings, but I can't risk becoming Beatrice and forgetting all that's happened since I was cursed before Maisie is safe from Gothel. Beast's knowledge is essential to our success.

At least Benedict and I have always been able to find our way together through collaboration. Maybe he sensed the same thing so he hung in there while we plotted to help the people we care for. If only there were a way not to lose our partnership. It's an empty wish, but I still ache for Gothel to be wrong. If Benedict says he loves me before the last page of the songbook falls, could there be a chance for Beatrice?

I scold myself with an angry trill.

"Stop thinking that way, Beast. It'll make failure tear your heart into more ragged bits." I discouraged Benedict. I forfeited my right to hope when I shredded his overture for something more with Beast. The focus here is on Maisie and her future.

Wind blows the stairwell door open. I duck behind an AC unit, but no one comes out. I look at the position of the moon. Hero will be here any time and phase one of the plans Ben and I made to blow Claude and Rubata's nasty charade wide open will commence, as long as Santino shows. Ben swears he'll come, but the man has become a wild card.

I'm gambling that if I stick to pointing a claw at Claude instead of Rubata tonight, the curse won't shackle my words. It took convincing and the promises of multiple story-reading sessions, but Sassy finally agreed to play a part in priming Claude to confess.

Once Santino and Hero join Benedict and me to broker a peace, we can move on to phase two: Getting Maisie the hell out of Hollywood. Monty, Graham, and Audra are working on ghost recruitment for our caper tomorrow night. Understandably, none of the transparent Caliwood residents are keen to tangle with Tressa again after she encased them in an ice wall. If things go as planned, their part will be over before the enchantress even knows they were involved.

It's a clear night. Technically, birds can't see in the dark, but my enhanced harpy vision is like having built-in binoculars. Stars spill across the Hollywood sky. I taught Benedict the name of some, and during the year before we reconciled that wonderful Christmas Eve, he'd learned so many more. Now Ben can name the stars below on the Hollywood Walk of Fame as well as the ones above the boulevard. It's one of the thousand quirky talents I love about him.

"Beast?" Hero's sweet voice dances across the rooftop. I move from shadow into red neon glow. "There you are." Her smile encourages the stars to twinkle. "I saw your note in the library."

"I'm glad you came." I gulp so hard I'm surprised the muscles of my throat don't clack like maracas.

She looks at the sky. "Me too. It is a beautiful night. I'm glad to see you out of the library."

"You might not be glad after I tell you why I wanted you to meet me."

Hero tilts her head. "What do you mean?"

I gesture at the couch cushions while I perch on the arm. "Promise you'll hear me out before you take off running?"

"You're making me nervous." She sits on the very edge of the cushion in a *poised to flee* position.

"Santino is on his way up."

She's on her feet, hands covering her mouth. "No. Why? I can't do this. He hates me for committing a horrible act I didn't do." Hero's voice wavers as her eyes fill with tears. "Beast, I can't face that terrible look in his eyes again." She streaks around the couch toward the stairwell door, but I flap up and over her to block the way.

"Please, Hero. Benedict and I figured a way to prove you never betrayed him."

The poor thing is shaking. "If Santino didn't believe me, why should he believe you?"

"Because Claude is going to confess he duped Santino." I rest my hand on her shoulder, making sure my claws don't snag her clothing. "If he finally accepts the truth, do you think you can ever forgive him for his shameful accusation at the engagement party?"

Hero trudges to the couch and drops onto a cushion, burying her head in her hands. I give her all the space I can afford since Santino is already on his way.

"Look, Hero, I wanted to fling Santino off the Hollywood Sign for what he did until I forced myself inside his head. I see now he may be forever battered from Gothel's electric fence at Rampion Ranch."

I pause for a moment, waiting to see if speaking Gothel's name squeezes my throat. When there's no clench, I continue.

"All those surgeries he had to endure. It does reduce a person to a ball of raw emotion. His resiliency is shot to hell. In his shoes, I'd be in self-protection mode too."

"I know," she whispers. "I thought he believed in my love enough to trust me, not in lies he assumes are truth."

"If you swore you saw him banging someone on the couch, would you stop and chat before you flipped out?"

Hero chews on a thumbnail. "No, but I would talk in private before bashing him in public."

"That is where he fucked up." I put my hands behind my head, putting my wings on display. "If you don't want to give him a shot at fixing this, I'm on your side. Benedict and I thought you might want to try."

The gusher hits, and Hero becomes a blubbery mess. "I do want to try. I still love him, Beast, but he must swear to believe what I say is true from now on, or I walk."

"Agree." I crook a talon around the drawer pull in the chest next to the couch and yank it open so she can grab a handful of tissues.

"And there is the matter of him not having a coronary when he meets me."

She looks distressed. "Why does he need to see you?"

I hang my head for a moment. "Forgive me, Hero, but I was here on the rooftop when the whole nasty charade went down. I knew it wasn't you with Claude."

"Beast! Why didn't you tell me? Who was it?"

Hero's disappointment in me shatters my bones. Some friend I am. "I'm dead sorry, Hero. I didn't want to hurt you even more. Until Benedict helped me concoct a way to tell Santino the truth with Claude's admission, I couldn't share what I know."

Footsteps across the plank board connecting the Caliwood to the next building send me back into hiding.

"Tell Santino what truth?" Santino takes a single step onto the roof. He and Hero lock gazes. Even in the dim light, I see the torn fragments of love between them. There is pain, but it's a thin coating over the surface of what they both yearn for.

He steps closer to the hangout. "Well, Hero." His voice is soft. None of the accusation from the night of the engagement party tinges his words. My heart beats faster under my layers of flesh and feathers. We're halfway home. Santino Fedele wants to believe Hero.

Hero looks in the direction of my hiding place.

"I was there that night," I say from the shadows.

Santino's gaze locks onto my position. "Who the hell are you?"

I stay hidden. "I am called Beast. You will know me as what people call a harpy. I am a friend to Hero and mean you no harm."

He looks between Hero and the metal box shielding me from view. "Is this for real?"

Hero walks over to me and holds out her hand. Slowly, to let Santino get used to me, I lay my hand in hers and let her lead me one step at a time from the darkness.

He stumbles backward and raises both hands as if to protect himself. "Hero, get away from it."

"Fizz down, Santino. Beast is not an *it*. She's my friend and a damn loyal one."

Santino lowers his hands, but still looks wound tight enough to spring to the top of the Hotel Caliwood sign.

"I'd like to shake your hand, Santino, but watch the claws."

He stares, and I fear he's forgotten how to breathe. Finally, he leans forward a little to study my hand.

"It's okay, Santino. Beast won't hurt you."

His expression is skeptical.

Hero stands straighter. "If you want to continue the conversation, then I insist you accept Beast as my friend. If not, then this is the end of us."

Santino's eyes go buggy. He blinks rapidly, but then settles. He takes a first tentative step, and when I don't attack, he closes the distance between us.

I reach for him. "You can grab a claw or slide your fingers between them. Your call."

He opts for a full hand grasp, which I respect.

"Happy to meet you, Santino. Hero's told me all about you." I want to shout I've known him as a friend and not just from Beast's conversations with Hero. I burn to reveal I'm Beatrice.

They may never get a chance to discover the truth.

We shake, then he reclaims his digits.

"Feel free to sit now that you've seen I'm not going to hunt you for dinner."

"Beast!" says Hero, mortified.

I shrug. "Thought I'd break the ice with some harpy humor." No one's laughing. Hero stays close to my side as Santino lowers himself onto the couch without taking his gaze off us.

"Listen up, Santino. What you saw that night was Claude and a Hero look-a-like." No throat clamp. "He set you up because the bastard wants Hero for himself." It worked. The curse didn't come out to play.

Focus on Claude.

Santino gives his head a quick shake. "She was one hell of a perfect look-a-like. Hero, I'd swear on my life it was you. I saw your body. I heard your voice."

Hero balls her hands into fists and lunges at Santino. She punches his shoulders hard enough to send him bouncing off the back of the couch. "And I swear on my life it wasn't me. Do you know me at all? How could you ever believe I'd be faithless? I love you, Santino. I don't betray the people I love."

I see Santino's mask of disbelief start to crumble. "I, I..."

"Is it gone, Ben? Is it gone?" Claude scrambles on all fours out of the stairwell door. He tries to stand and fails, racing on hands and knees away from the stairs. I smile. Sassy and her signature haunting did us proud.

My smile grows as I picture Ben waiting behind the library door, listening as Claude strolls along the hallway to meet him. Sassy with her ringlets and bright blue dress would huddle with her back to our villain, crying, "Who will read me a story?" Claude, as any adult, even a rat bastard, kneels next to her and asks the right questions to help an upset little child. "Where are your parents?" Blah, blah. That's when Sassy slowly turns to look at him. Instead of tears, Claude sees dark and sinister liquid oozing in streams from her eyes. She growls, "I don't want a bad man like you to read me a story."

My chest rumbles with a laugh as I picture Claude stumbling away from my tiniest ghost buddy. Sassy follows him with unnaturally long strides for a child, and overly loud footsteps, her stare locks on him. With each step, her form becomes more transparent until she vanishes before his eyes. The only thing left would be her voice echoing off the flocked wallpaper. "Bad man. Bad man. I won't leave you alone."

Now Ben joins the party to escort a completely terrified Claude away from Sassy's voice, through the library, and onto the rooftop. Where now he sits in a quivering heap between the stairwell door and couch.

Benedict grins, enjoying every moment. "Claude, I believe you know everyone except my good friend, Beast."

I try to avoid looming over people since I know I'm intimidating, and I value the few companions I have. Tonight, I loom.

"Holy shit," screams Claude and tries to retreat toward the stairwell. Ben blocks his way and closes the door. There's deep satisfaction in terrorizing the asshat.

Claude finds his feet and attempts to run to the wobbly board walkway between buildings. It's my turn to fly and block his escape route.

He picks out the only potentially friendly face in our group. "Hero, what the fuck is going on here? What is that?" A shaky finger points my way.

My brave little warrior walks right up to Claude and smacks him across the face. "What the fuck was going on the night you and D.G. staged a show for Santino on this rooftop?"

Claude's mouth hangs open, and I step next to Hero. "Answer her question or..." I clack my beak.

Claude attempts to muster bravado. "The thing better not touch me."

To my surprise, Santino charges Claude and grabs his shirt front. "*She* won't if you tell the truth."

I'm damn proud of him and grateful he's so accepting of me. Friends of friends are friends. That's the Santino Fedele I know.

Claude attempts to push Santino away, but our mild-mannered PR media genius shows excellent oomph and doesn't let him pass.

"Fine," barks Claude and twists out of Santino's grasp. "D.G. and me were just pranking you, Tino."

"Pranking," yells Hero. "You liar."

Claude shoots me a wary look I answer with a harpy glare. The red of the Hotel Caliwood sign enhances the unnatural color of my eyes. I can tell he's ready to freak again. Good.

"Okay, okay. I wasn't here with Hero. It was a babe that looked like her freakin' twin." He shifts his focus to Santino. "I hate your ass for stealing her from me. If you dumped Hero, I thought I might get another chance."

In the second shocker of the evening, Benedict strides up to Claude and pops him one in the jaw. "Find yourself another band, vandal."

Claude grabs his face and then turns in a frenzy. He jabs a finger at Benedict. "Fuck you." Santino is his next target. "And fuck you." When he turns to me, I take a menacing step in his direction. Claude doesn't wait around to test my patience. He tears across the rooftop to the fire escape and disappears.

"Should we go after him?" asks Benedict. "What if he tells someone about Beast?"

I screech a laugh. "Who's going to believe him?"

Santino rushes to Hero and drops to his knees in front of her. He grabs her around the waist and buries his head against her. "Oh God, Hero. What have I done to you? I'm the biggest shitiot in the world. I'm massively sorry for ever doubting you, sweet Hero." He lifts his gaze to hers. "What can I do to earn your forgiveness, even though I don't deserve it? Anything. Name it."

"Love me, Santino, and never doubt again." She drops to her knees, and they fall into each other's arms.

"I never stopped loving you, Hero, not for a red ass second. I will never stop loving you."

Their kiss is sloppy, sobby, and wonderful. I know they have a lot to work through, but damn my insides are on fire with joy at the sight of their reunion. Smiling, I turn to Benedict to find him staring at me the way I've dreamed of. There is love in his eyes, and I never want to look away. If he would say the words——

No. I can't encourage him to speak of his feelings for me. Not until Maisie is free, and it won't matter that Beatrice reborn forgets the nightmare of tear harvests, Gothel, and his evil female backup band.

Santino and Hero are on their feet, arms locked around one another.

"Benedict, Beast, thank you for helping a fool see reason and find my way back to my heart," says Santino. "I'm ashamed and grateful and amazed and...How can I ever show you how much what you've done means to me?"

Benedict's mushy love face shifts into conspirator mode. "Well, actually, if you're willing to step back into battle with Gothel, there might be a way."

22

FOUND AND LOST

HERO WAS GOBSMACKED AS THE FOUR OF US HUDDLED ON THE rooftop. Santino practically had smoke coming out of his ears as I recounted the deets to Hero of Gothel's tear harvesting gig with Maisie. Bottom line, they're both on board as well as Beast's ghost friends.

The reunited couple left for what I hope is spectacular make-up sex. After Beast, her ghosts, and I pull off our end at Hotel Caliwood, we've got to design an untraceable escape route for Maisie. That's where Santino comes in. It took convincing to get him to believe Beast's ghost buddies are viable co-conspirators to guide us through the first leg of the rescue. I wish there were a way for Beast to coax her invisible friends into showing themselves to instill more confidence in the team. Since she's adamant they will play their part, Hero, Santino, and I made a pact to accept Beast at her word.

It's a relief to have an energized Santino again. He's confident with his Hollywood Boulevard connections and backup from Justin Time and Zeli's Rampion Records resources, he'll be able to set up way stations Gothel and Tressa will never able to second guess. A path to lead the kid as far from Hollywood as possible.

Beast perches on the table, and I sit in the lone chair. It's the first moment of quiet we've enjoyed after the rooftop drama with Claude. How many more moments will we have? I want more. I don't want Beast out of my life.

She taps her claws on the library table. "I'm feather-clenching scared our adversary..."

I notice Beast avoids using Gothel's name. My brilliant lyricist found the way to obfuscate her words and keep them flowing.

"...Is so thirsty to get his revenge on Santino, Zeli, and Justin Time, one whiff of their involvement will scramble his judgement and work to our advantage."

I gesture in the direction of the apartment. "We could dump his tear supply to douse his flames."

Beast shakes her head. "It won't make a difference. According to what I've heard him tell the others, he's downed enough volume of Maisie fuel to render the daily doses unnecessary. He keeps the bottles as insurance his powers will perpetually stay on full."

Gothel can go off like a firework at any time, even without being primed. Dangerous news.

Beast stares at my swollen knuckles. "How's your hand?"

My chest fills with warmth at her concern. I crave Beast's attention. If only she cared more. I shake out my fingers. "Sore and satisfied."

"Will losing him hurt our album?"

I love that she includes herself. Beast is a major factor in the beating heart of the album. I'm glad she understands. "We laid down most of Claude's tracks first. I'll overdub any missing vocals or give Alfie a crash course in the harmonies. He's got a decent ear and voice."

We gaze at each other for a long moment. My heartbeat and breathing crank up to high. Beast made it clear she isn't interested in me other than a collaborator in music and escape plans, but I have to say what's in my gut. "Beast, you saved the album. I don't want this..." I fan a finger between Beast and me. "To end."

Beast gently lays her massive hand on mine.

"I'm happy for the band. It was a pleasure to write for you. The album is rich and lovely. Your music speaks to the soul."

I'm surprised at the affection in her voice. Oh, that Beast knows me so well in such a short time. She had me pegged from day one as both a floundering soul and a musician longing for the right words to bring his songs to life. This marvelous person spoke my language perfectly when she barely knew me. No one except for Beatrice has seen me so clearly. Losing this rediscovered synergy with Beast, a brand of joy I thought had slipped from my life forever, is unbearable.

I rest my other hand on top of hers. "Maybe we don't have to end, Beast. Once Maisie is away from Gothel, we can find our way back together. Santino will help us."

Beast hops down from the table to nuzzle her head in the groove between my neck and shoulder as best she can. I can't tell if she's doing it to be close or to avoid looking at me.

"Ben, I'd lost faith this beastly form would ever find a true heart to believe in me. I'm twice blessed. Once with Hero, and then with you."

I rub my head against her soft feathers. "Stop talking endings. If everything goes as planned. You'll be free of Gothel and Tressa. Trust Santino will help you lie low until we're sure those evil asses are out of the picture."

Her breath is so deep and long, it rattles my whole body. She tries to speak several times, but an odd strangling sound is all that flows from her. I wish I knew how to cut the invisible binding around her words.

She may doubt the future, but I won't lose faith. Once Beast escapes with Maisie, she'll find her way back to me.

Finally, Beast does find words. As soon as she speaks, I wish for her silence.

"I love your endless hope. Never lose it, but we are impossible, Benedict."

When I try to protest, she cuts me off.

"Impossible doesn't mean imperfect." She guides my hand over her heart. "You've carved a place here that will never be filled by another."

Beast scorned my attempts at voicing my affection, but here she is saying the things I yearned to hear from her. Yet, there is no hope in her tone, only sadness. Based on her resistance, I thought her spirit invincible against any assault of affection. I want to tell her I love her. Feathers, claws, muscles that put mine to shame, none of it matters. We speak the mutual language of creating art. Souls touching souls. What do outward appearances matter when such a connection has been made?

I can't believe I thought she was a brute the first night she flew at me in the library. I am a thick-headed and thick-hearted man. Beatrice discovered the truth of me, and she fled. What insurance is there that in time Beast wouldn't reach the same conclusion? Maybe she's already seen worthlessness in me. Her kindness is born of knowing a natural ending is upon us.

I wish I could promise yanking Maisie away from Gothel and Tressa is a lock. Our odds are not pretty. One shot is all we get, and heaven help us if that doesn't work. We'll wear flashing neon targets on our asses for Gothel to take shots at for God knows how long.

Am I insane to risk my life and livelihood for a kid who doesn't seem unhappy? Maybe, but I put my trust in Beast.

As if reading my mind, Beast clacks her beak. "Benedict, are you positive you want to go through with this? I'm having second thoughts about putting Hero and Santino in danger."

This woman won't take my heart, but I will give her my loyalty. "Listen to me, Beast." I'm careful to include the *st* every time I say her name. "I will deny you nothing, no matter what it may cost me."

We stare at one another for a long moment. Beast tilts her head back and to the side so the beak rises out of the way. For the first time, I see her entire mouth clearly, a very human mouth with lovely, full lips. She's offering me a chance to kiss her.

Carefully, I angle my head and ease in under the hook at the end of her beak. My lips meet hers in a gentle tap. I kiss Beast delicately and sweetly, appreciating how vulnerable she must feel. It's a kiss of mutual affection, not lust but a connection honoring that we've made something beautiful as a team, our songs. I'm filled with a longing for the kiss to be a beginning, not an ending. With my eyes closed, Beast does not have the challenges and limitations of a harpy. As our lips move together, I cherish this partner and her beloved spirit. I thought I'd never find such completion with anyone again.

I consider deepening the kiss, but given the emotional boundaries Beast made clear, I end it slow and tenderly. Our gazes meet in silence.

"I didn't know if that was possible," she whispers. "I'm glad we managed it at least once. Thank you, Benedict."

At least once.

There's a finality in her words I long to ignore. If she'd give me any sign we shouldn't separate, I'd chase it. I stare at her a few beats too long, waiting for Beast to say or do anything to encourage me. For a moment, I believe I see a spark of desire in her eyes to match my own. I hold my breath, readying myself for a sweet morsel of reciprocation, but the light in her crimson eyes fades too quickly to hang my hopes on.

Why does she hold back? Is it trust? Beatrice gave me her trust once, and I crushed it. Beast knows that. Am I not worth the risk that we might flourish beyond what Bea and I began?

Beast slides the two wine glasses I brought along with a bottle of Leonato's finest from the Ghost Lounge. "You pour."

I do and marvel at how deftly she manipulates the glass in her claw.

"To Mmmm," she says.

I finish for her. "Maisie." I raise one finger. "And your ghosts," I answer.

We clink glasses, but Beast discards her glass for the bottle that fits better beneath her beak. How I hate the underlying farewell in our toast.

Beast smacks her lips. "Offer Hero and Santino a chance to back out."

"I will," I say, positive Santino won't pass on any chance to make Gothel's life miserable.

"Goodnight, Benedict."

I'm being dismissed. It hurts like hell. "Shall I leave the wine?"

Beast laughs. "You better. I'll see you tomorrow at half past midnight."

I laugh with her and stand. "Goodnight, my lovely Beast."

There are far too many painful goodbyes in my life.

23

LAST PAGE

I PRESS THE BACK OF MY HAND AGAINST MY LIPS AND CLOSE MY EYES. Ben kissed Beast. My mouth still tingles a day later. It wasn't a kiss drowning in the wild passion Benedict and I always excelled at, but in many ways, it was dearer to me.

How I miss my love. I relive the ghost's gift of our shared dream, of holding him close, feeling his touch on my body. The memory is bliss and torture. It's what I yearn for and what I'll never have again.

Benedict infused last night's gentle kiss with the question of our future. One I can't respond to. I know my Ben. This was his attempt to risk a deeper partnership with Beast, one involving the heart. For a hot second, I feared his bravery of daring to kiss Beast might disrupt the curse and doom Maisie.

Hard truth—the contact of his kiss was not enough. Tressa's curse hinges on words.

Despite sweet torment hope hides well.
Until the day when words reveal,
Broken oaths with truth may heal.

Benedict must tell Beast he loves her for Beatrice to rise from the ether. I am eternally damned. Even though there was still boundless love in my heart for Benedict when I spoke those fateful words the night of our terrible fight, it wasn't enough armor against Tressa's curse. The enchantress uses the currency of words to damage and destroy.

I must make my peace with the reality that Benedict cannot tell Beast he loves her if Maisie is to have any chance at a life free of Gothel. Retaining my knowledge of the Dark Vinyl Artists and the child bound to them is essential for tonight's success.

I wish I could take those rancid pieces of filth down when we spring Maisie, but that's far too grand a scheme for our fragile team to tackle in addition to the escape. For now.

Once again, I've placed the songbook in the center of the library table. I lay my hands over its dome, dreading the fall of the final pages. The glass shudders beneath my fingers and light flashes from the songbook. A single page falls, its faint golden glow reflecting off the sides of the dome. There's no tremor this time. It's as if the songbook is drifting quietly to sleep. I tip the glass just enough to slide the page free, press it to my heart, and then settle the paper back inside.

One page left. I grasp my thick silver pen. When the last page falls, I'll be writing of my love for Benedict. Our last song. I hope he finds it after I've gone and knows it speaks my truth even when I couldn't. Will he hear Beatrice in the words of Beast? How lovely that would be.

I write my goodbye.

Can you hear my love?
My song is the night's sigh when all else is silent.
Can you see my love?
My words summon stars to dance across vast inky skies.
Can you touch my love?
My caress against your beating heart tells truth.

Can you scent my love?
My ambrosia of orange blossoms you often praise.
Can you taste my love?
My fevered kisses tell the story of my soul.
My song is yours alone.
My words are yours alone.
My caress is yours alone.
My ambrosia is yours alone.
My kisses are yours alone.
Embrace them within your soul.
For even though I no longer have these gifts to give.
They were always yours.
Love was always yours.
Always. Benedict. Always.

My tears drip and pool along the edge of the sheet. It's the last song I will ever write. Without Benedict, there is no joy in making music.

I hear faint murmuring in the Dark Vinyl Artists' lair. Quickly, I shove my lyrics between two books of poetry. I'll find a moment to tell Hero the hiding place. She can lead Benedict to these words after I've gone.

Sorrow leaves a bitter taste on my tongue as the bookcase slides open. Gothel is first through, followed by Rubata, chattering about a duet with her latest hunk. Sulaa glides past them, preening the multitude of blue strands in her hair as she speaks in low tones to Tressa Divine.

"Beast," says Gothel. "There are five empty slots left in the case for tear bottles. Fill every one tonight. We won't have time tomorrow with the move." He fans an arm around the library. "Say goodbye to your ghost buffoons and this cozy perch, Beast."

Tressa leaves Sulaa and marches to the songbook's dome. She taps a pearl painted fingernail against the glass and *tsks*. "Oopsie. There's only one page left." The enchantress lays a hand on my shoulder. "So close, Beastie. So close." Her false sincerity sickens me.

Rubata casts a disinterested gaze at the songbook. "I need duets, Beast. Whip me up a couple tonight. They need to be peppy, poppy, pretty..." She waggles her shoulders and then nudges Gothel. "...To convince this one to green light my future trail of hits as—" Rubata morphs into her new favorite persona. "Brandy Winter and her string of soon to be platinum tunes."

Duets? What unsuspecting fool has she roped into teaming with Brandy Winter?

"Excuse me," sniffs Tressa. "Jump back, witch. I will be Dark Vinyl Artist's first rising star." She aims a finger at me. "Solo hits first, Beastie, for Moi." Tressa lays both hands over her chest.

Gothel and Sulaa share a swift glance of superiority as the witch and the enchantress trade sophomoric sneers.

My heart feels as trapped as the songbook within its glassy prison. If we fail tonight, these horrible people are my future. If we succeed tonight, I may not have a future at all.

Oh, Benedict. My future should be with you.

"I'm afraid time for your goodbyes to Hero and Benedict has expired," says Gothel side-eyeing me. "Stay with the child until you've done your duty, and she falls asleep. Pack her things and stay with her in the apartment."

He waits until I've entered their salon. Gothel slides the bookcase closed behind me with a click.

This is new territory. He's never cared before what I did after collecting his precious Maisie tears as long as I went no farther than the library or the rooftop. Does he suspect something? Did I give him reason to think tonight is any different from the rest?

My heart pounds, and I suck air. I'm panicking for nothing. His head is on final preparations for the big move tomorrow night. Gothel wants as little movement in his machine as possible. The less motion, the fewer the chances for mishap.

Oh, I'd love to see the faces of the fetid foursome when they discover our surprise, but I'm sticking with Maisie as Santino's network whisks us out of Gothel's reach. After that, Beast will disappear. It's best for Benedict, and best for me since Beatrice will well and truly be gone once the last page of the songbook falls.

I listen at the sliding wall until I hear the quiet *thump* of the library door being shut and then slide the bookcase open. Moving with stealth, I peer through the keyhole into the hallway.

The swish of Tressa's silver dress is last through the secret door disguised as mahogany wainscoting and flocked fleur-de-lis wallpaper they disappear behind each night. The dead end of the hallway is bathed in shadows. I picture the fiends descending the hidden staircase, another of Hotel Caliwood's secrets, to blend into the Hollywood night.

It's the same route we hope to secret Maisie away to a few hours from now, once we're certain via ghostly confirmation the route is unfettered by a hot-handed Gothel and company.

"Should we start following them now?" asks Graham, sneaking up behind me.

"No," I hiss. "Tressa will sense you. We already know she can manipulate ghosts. Sulaa and Rubata may be able to see you too."

Monty, Audra, and Sassy melt out of their statues.

Audra wipes her arms as if she's ridding herself of a distasteful coating. "I do not want to get stuck in another ice wall, thank you very much."

"We'll go ready the troops," says Monty, throwing me a salute.

I shake the feathers of my headdress. "Let's all chill—"

Audra shrieks.

"Sorry, Audra, bad choice of words." I'm surprised how on edge the ghosts are. They truly are wary of the enchantress's power. I remember their horrorstricken faces from the ice wall. They never speak in detail of the torment they endured that night.

"Go hang at the pool. Make sure the gang is in place by 2:00 A.M." I force lightness into my tone. "We'll check the route then. If it's clear, off we go."

The ghosts hesitate, all four staring at me. "What?"

"There are things to say," said Graham.

My breath stutters. Shit, they've decided not to risk damage from Tressa to their eternal souls. I don't blame them. I understand their fear. Every day the enchantress is in my life, the probability of doom is a constant dread.

Monty clears his throat. "My dear. We—" He acknowledges the other three occupants of my library statues. "Owe you gratitude."

My throat vibrates with its version of a birdy laugh. "You owe *me*? That's nuts, Monty. I owe you." I adjust my tone to match his reverence. "The companionship and compassion you four have shown me made my situation bearable. You saw past a hideous shell to who I am beneath wicked beak and claws. You gave Beast and Beatrice hope when hopelessness was all I had."

"Oh, darling Beast," says Audra, spinning swiftly around me until the bluish tint of her spirit body washes over me. "Don't you see? You've done the same for us."

I snort. "I doubt it."

She shakes her head. "Let me explain. The ghosts of the Caliwood remain because this hotel shines with our most joyful memories."

Sassy attempts to grab the hem of my dress. Her hand flits through the fabric, never taking hold. "I won a shiny award here in the ballroom instead of the other grownups who thought they should win it. I was best at pretending to live in stories. I love stories."

Monty steps up next and holds his hand out to Audra. When she takes it, I marvel at this new brand of ghost-to-ghost contact where they're not passing through one another's form.

"How do you do that?" I say, nodding at their clasped hands.

Audra smile. "It uses a lot of juice, but being touched every so often is worth it."

"Can I touch you?" It would be lovely to experience the

embrace of my ethereal friends at least once instead of a tingling cold chill.

"Alas no," says Monty. "But how we wish it were so." He treats me to his dazzling smile for a moment before it fades. "As you know, friend Beast, Audra and I did not bid the world farewell in a haze of Hollywood stardust." They meet each other's gaze with sadness that wrenches my heart. "We were mired in the stench and fodder of gossip and speculation during our lives and after."

Audra lays her head on his shoulder. I see a beautiful portrait not of love or lust, but of a deep and abiding friendship. I ache for these two generous souls and the torturous scrutiny they had to endure in the Hollywood of their day. Happy endings were never destined for this pair of earthbound stars.

Audra lifts her head. "Here at Hotel Caliwood, we shined. We danced. We drank. We howled at the moon. People were kind, and life was always a party."

I think of Leonato's annual Christmas shindig where I first met Benedict, danced with Benedict, drank with Benedict, and indulged in our own version of howling at the stars above Hollywood. The hotel is not haunted, it's charmed.

Monty kisses her hair. "Hollywood used to be a place filled with magic, and we were part of it. Today, we're thin and fading memories of that magic to everyone but our fellow ghosts. We stay because wisps of wonder still exist here at the Caliwood."

Audra rubs Monty's sleeve. "But even though this hotel is our chosen eternity, we are merely skips in a vinyl record, each day too close to being an endless repetition of the one before."

Graham holds out his arms. "Boosting your spirits lifted us from the tedium. It gave us a purpose. We learned to dance and be electrifying once again."

Tears pool in my eyes. "Let's nix the fading talk. You're legends. Each generation just needs ramp up time to rediscover each of you but discover you they do."

Four faces shine brighter at my words. Have I given them

energy to appreciate they are still valuable to the insane history beneath the Hollywood Sign? I hope so.

"Please understand you've given me far more than I can repay. The dance of the mirrors showed me Benedict's heart. Even if we never reunite, I know he loves me. Combining our dreams gave us the last goodbye we never had. I'm at peace knowing Benedict can be sure Beatrice never stopped loving him. He and I may not get a happy ending, but our story will always end with love, thanks to you."

"Do you want me to scare the bad man for you again?" says Sassy, making her contribution to the convo. We all laugh.

Audra strokes Sassy's ringlets. "Our brave little ghost."

With a pout, the little girl stamps a foot. "I will do it tonight."

I squat on my bird legs to look into her eyes. "I don't think he'll be around anymore, Sass, but if he ever comes back, scare him anytime you want."

"I saw him," she insists. "I can find him again."

How do ghosts experience time? Graham, Monty, and Audra seem to understand its passage. Maybe Sassy's frozen young age makes it difficult for her to differentiate one day from another. Her last memory of Claude may feel more immediate than it actually was.

Graham takes a frustrated Sassy's hand to lead her past the sealed elevator doors. "I'm sure you could, Sass." He takes a final look back over his shoulder. "Guard that beautiful heart of yours, Beast."

"We'll return soon," says Audra. "To give Maisie her happy ending."

"My Beautiful Beast," says Monty. "Remember, the character you play must always be supremely confident in who they are."

I gasp and lay a hand against my breast. "Why Monty, am I finally worthy of your tips on method acting?"

He chuckles. "Life is a role, friend. We must play it with all the authenticity available to us. I admire the way you live your truth. I should be begging for tips from you." He blows me a kiss, and the ghosts fade through the library wall.

I'm alone, staring at four flameless statues. If anyone had told Beatrice a year ago her besties would be a quartet of filmy blue spirits, I'd tell them to cut their alcohol consumption. Even in my strange reality, I have been gifted with so much. Ghosts, Hero, Maisie, and my beloved Benedict color my life with love. Love is the gift that will sustain me through the rest of Beast's lonely existence.

I wish Ben or Hero were with me as time melts like ice on a summer-warmed Hollywood sidewalk. The last page of the songbook shudders, poised to fall. I trail a claw across the dome, then move around the room past the four cold, dark statues, and stare gratefully at the books of poetry and romance that nurtured and inspired me in the year before my Benedict returned. If I never write another word, I'm satisfied. The stack of love poems for Benedict will always be my greatest achievement, the language of my soul.

I circle the library table in an endless loop and then settle near the songbook as one hour slips into the next. Finally, it's time. Willing my heart to still, I listen for the sound of anyone near as I slip back into the Dark Vinyl Artist's salon.

Silence.

Pushing Maisie's bedroom door open, I marvel at the perfect, golden-haired cherub asleep in the bed. Excitement and apprehension mingle into an accelerant that steals my breath and sets my heart ablaze. We're doing this. Stealing Gothel's golden goose from his treasure vault.

I drop next to the bed. "Maisie."

She startles and her tiny pink lips quiver as she wakes. Wide eyes relax when she registers who's roused her from a peaceful sleep. Maisie rubs her eyes. "Are you going to sing me the sad song?"

I ease the tip of my claw through her curls. "Never again, Maisie. We're going on an adventure."

This perks her up. "Where are we going? Is Papa coming? Auntie Rubata?"

A twinge in my chest reminds me the Dark Vinyl Artists are the only family Maisie knows. She's not afraid of the villains. The wrongness of her sitch hasn't yet registered in her kid brain.

"We're all going to meet up," I lie. There will be time to explain once we've delivered her to safety and into the loving embrace of people who will treasure her for who she is instead of what she can do for them. That's what Santino promised. I begged him not to give me any specifics. If Gothel gets ahold of me, I'll know nothing he can use to track Maisie.

I nod at the end of the bed where I've laid the clothes Hero brought: tiny jeans, a navy hoodie, black slip-on tennies, and a slate gray beanie to hide her bright curls. "You even get to wear a special adventure outfit."

Maisie wrinkles her nose. "It's not pretty."

"It's pretty sneaky. We get to play hide and seek on our adventure. You want to be able to blend into the shadows, don't you?"

She brightens up. "Yes." In a hop, she's out of bed and changing into the getaway clothes.

I hear the telltale swish of ghosts from the library. Here we go. I lift Maisie into my arms. "Okay, sweetie. In the first part of our sneaky game, we must be absolutely silent. Can you do that?"

Maisie nods, gulps, and holds her breath.

I chuckle. She's totally buying in, thank goodness. "Just no talking. You can still breathe."

She allows her breath to leak out and pops a hand over her lips with a nod.

"We're going to meet new people, but they are friends."

Maisie lifts two pudgy thumbs up in front of my beak.

I step into the library with my slightly wriggling bundle. Monty is there to greet me. The network is ready. Maisie makes no sign of noticing him. He nods and gestures to the door. All clear. The first leg of our dangerous relay race has begun.

We pass through the door into the corridor where Audra, our next ghost scout, hovers. She points at Benedict's apartment. Still good to go.

Once inside, Graham takes over and gestures us toward the balcony and fire escape. I made a last-minute decision not to risk the Dark Vinyl Artist's secret stairway in case Tressa or the witches planted a magical alarm system on their secret path. The pool and ballroom ghosts are set to guide us down the exterior metal ladders to a floor with a different hidden passage leading us to the lower lobby of the Caliwood where Benedict will initiate the second half of our baton passing to Santino's team. Maisie being the baton.

I head for the sliding glass door. "Put your hands around my neck, Maisie, and hold tight."

A sudden blast of frigid wind knocks me away from the balcony. In a blur, I see Graham's face, frozen in a scream, swirling past us in the middle of a scattered blue haze. A distant howl that sounds like Monty resonates in my chest. As if reacting to my fear, Maisie buries her face against the feathers below my collarbone.

Three figures step through the balcony curtains into the darkened room. Two silhouettes I recognize immediately, Tressa and Rubata in her showy Brandy Winter persona. It takes me a beat to register the third.

"Claude?"

Rubata/Brandy tiptoes her fingers along Claude's shoulder and then kisses his cheek. "Meet Dark Vinyl Artist's newest costar for my fab duet album, Beastie." She links arms with him. "Claude and I are going to make beautiful music together."

Maisie trembles in my arms as Tressa circles us. "Claude here is not only a major asset with his talent, he's also a very good listener. Especially when it comes to the thin walls of an ex-girlfriend's apartment."

Claude deserves to be pitched into the most massive furnace in hell. My feathers droop. We were fatally careless to assume he'd left the Caliwood when Benedict booted him. Now Sassy's insistence she could find him falls into place. Damn it. Leo is in the thrall of the Dark Vinyl Artists whether he consciously realizes it or not so he wouldn't evict Claude, and of course Rubata would want her latest plaything close by.

I growl. "Claude, you useless sack of skin."

He grins. "It's my turn to play dirty, harpy."

"Claude doesn't get all the credit. Stupid Beastie, did you forget I speak ghost?" Tressa twirls a finger and a thin stream of vibrant blue blasts light into the apartment. I catch glimpses of Monty, Sassy, and Audra squeezed into long threads, tangling around one another. Their expressions locked in agony. "Every blue smear in the hotel is buzzing about your misguided mercy mission."

"Where's my papa?" Maisie whimpers.

"Time to go to dreamland, kiddo," says Tressa, waving a hand over Maisie's beanie. The little girl's body relaxes into enchanted sleep. "Take our sweet Maisie back to the apartment, you naughty bird," she says, bobbing her head at the door.

For half a heartbeat, I consider rushing to the balcony and flying Maisie free into the Hollywood night. Terror trumps the impulse. What if I hit the sky and Tressa zaps me down? Maisie could be hurt or killed. Hope dies right here in the middle of the home I shared with Benedict. I suppose there is poetic justice in that somewhere, but I don't sense any poetry or fairness in this utter disaster.

Failure makes for heavy footsteps. Maisie isn't free. Heaven or hell knows what Tressa will do to the ghosts of the Caliwood.

Ushered or rather guarded by a witch, an enchantress, and a traitor, we return to the shadows of the library. Rubata plucks the sleeping Maisie from my arms, and Team Evil leaves me behind in the library as the bookcase slides shut.

I begin to pant and rush to the hallway door. It doesn't matter who sees me. I've got to find Benedict, and he can warn the others.

It's dumb luck Tressa didn't turn me into a pile of feathers. The Dark Vinyl Artists must think I'm too stupid to be a threat or their control over me is so complete my attempt to flee with Maisie is nothing more than entertainment for them.

I begin to shiver. Or they have yet to pull the trigger on their retribution plans. The vandals relocate tomorrow. Perhaps the new place has a more hellish confinement waiting for Beast.

I grab for the doorknob. It's gone. A solid gold rectangle in the beveled wood is the only indication it was ever there.

"You truly are a Beast..."

I spin around to find Gothel standing in the shadows next to the fireplace, one glowing hand resting on the mantle. His back is to me. Darkness defines this man. Darkness of soul. Darkness of purpose.

"...A disloyal renegade who still after a year of trial has not learned her place." With painstaking slowness, Gothel half turns. Light from flickering flames illuminates a face more demonic than human. "And to my reckoning, never will."

"Fuck loyalty. Did your sludge for brains believe I'd ever accepted my nightmare? You and your pawns spent the year lying to me, using me." I take step after threatening step toward Gothel. If I can get close enough, one good swipe of my claws across his belly should end him. I never thought myself capable of murder, but everyone harbors a flash point.

Mine has arrived.

"Beatrice is gone forever, you said it yourself the last time you used me as punching bag. The four of you can rot for what you're doing to Maisie."

As I'm about to strike, Gothel twists, taking advantage of my clumsy advance to grab my throat and knee me in the gut, effectively thwarting my attack. "You are the pawn, Beast, and pawns are nothing more than disposable fodder."

His hand is hot enough to burn my skin. Feigning defeat, I let my body go slack from his choke hold. When a twinge of pressure releases around my windpipe, I strike fast and hard, driving my clawed foot into his abdomen, shoving him backward over the sofa and against the end of the cherry oak table.

I fly to the stairwell door. If I can make it to the roof, I will soar the hell out of here. When I grab for the knob, my hand meets smooth metal. A deep black scorch mark is all that remains. He's sealed every avenue of escape.

Gothel is on his feet, smoothing his tar black suit. "There will be no more starry nights for you, Beast."

I press back against the door and raise my claws, prepared to fight my way free.

Benedict. I must get to Benedict.

Gothel approaches steadily, his irises and pupils bleeding into black circles. His fists, poised to strike, glow red gold.

I will kill him before he kills me.

His first blow drives into the center of my outstretched palm. Instead of our familiar sparring moves, his fire hands are cranked to full. A scorch digs into my skin and then races up each talon, reducing each claw to ash that rains onto the carpet. The pain is instant and intense. My body shudders violently, rendering me momentarily helpless. Gothel uses the single beat to press his fist against my breast. Those fiery knuckles slowly sink into my flesh, burning, destroying. His pulsing heat surrounds and shackles me, holding me captive inches above the carpet. I lower my gaze to witness the horror of Gothel's hand vanishing inside my body.

In an excruciating burst of agony, I sense his fingers flair apart inside my chest cavity and tap almost playfully against my ribs. His flame intensifies as it takes hold and creeps at a mockingly glacial pace along bone.

Gothel is destroying me from the inside out.

This despicable imitation of a man extricates his hand, which still glows bright gold from his Maisie tear-fueled power. He turns it over, examining the results of his death blow. Not a single hint of my ruined flesh is left as an accusation on his skin. His smile is a disturbing blend of bleak humor and satisfaction as he relishes the encroaching death of Beast.

The Gothel generated heat shield suspending me in place dissipates. My legs buckle and I collapse to the floor, screeching in pain as an inferno blazes within me.

"And in the end, it is the folly of Beast that erases the life of Beatrice Sharpe." He lays his palm on my chest, guiding his heat to seal the hole where his fist plunged into my body, which hides his killing blow. Gothel hums with pleasure at his work before his gaze meets mine.

"Let me leave you with one final truth." Firelight turns his teeth a sickly orange color as he smiles. "As we sparred, I hinted you were deluded to believe Tressa's curse was unbreakable. You so easily believed and took the bait. Ah, Beast. If Benedict had professed his love before the last page of the songbook fell, the curse would indeed be null and void."

His laugh is a second flaming fist to my heart. "There's such gratification in quenching the hope of the hapless. As my touch turns your insides to ash, think of the Benedict you once again failed, believing my words instead of your heart." He stands tall, turning his back as if I'm already tomorrow's garbage.

His words burn hotter than the literal legion of minute flames consuming flesh and bone. As my heart begins to melt, pain at the harm I've done to my sweet Benedict's heart, outdoes my own agony.

The last thing I see above me as I writhe, dying on the carpet next to the library table is the songbook, my false redemption. Its last page dangles from the spine by one single corner.

24

FOUNTAINVISION

WHERE THE HELL ARE BEAST AND MAISIE? I TAKE ANOTHER LAP around the fountain in the lobby, sneaking a glance at the invisible panel in the far corner behind a towering palm that should have opened by now to reveal the pair of fugitives.

My phone buzzes with a text. Santino again, asking the same question squeezing my brain.

Where are they?

Instead of typing a response, I hit the thumbs down icon.

Trouble at your end?

Damn, he's persistent. I'm sure he's fielding texts from our rescue chain. Robo Robbie, Santino's bud and the tech wiz at Rampion Records, has Hotel Caliwood under surveillance. He'd sound the alarm if he saw any sign of Gothel and Tressa. I text five question marks.

Would it kill the Caliwood ghosts to reveal themselves to me for an update? According to Beast, they're still in perpetual fear of Tressa and the ice wall even though two years have passed without a repeat performance. It's a miracle they agreed to form the ghostly railroad to ferry Maisie and Beast out of the hotel.

Beast keeps pushing to hand Maisie off and return to the library to buy us time, but I won't let that happen. I insist she escapes with Maisie to Flo and Edie's. From there, Santino's sis, Leeni, will shuttle the pair in a van for a three-day nonsensical route ending at their folks place in Santa Barbara. Next, he and Hero will whisk them to Lalale Island under the protection the alleged benevolent sorcerer, Prospero Tempesta, and a coven of green witches living in the artist's commune. An unnamed team arranged by Justin Time and Zeli are scheduled to arrive on the island and fly the pair to a mystery location as secret as any witness protection program. Not even Santino and I know what happens once the plane takes off. If Gothel gets ahold of any of us, we dead end at the same piece of the escape puzzle, and he'll be screwed.

It rips my heart to imagine Beast disappearing from my life, but her freedom as well as Maisie's is key here. We've prepared everyone in the chain for Beast. Bless the open-minded lunacy of our team to accept a harpy woman and a magic tear-producing child on their journey out of hell.

I'm not supposed to draw attention to the terminus of a secret passage leading from the Ghost Lounge to the lobby of the Caliwood. Here in the time suspended between midnight and dawn, the graveyard shift manager of the hotel hunkers down behind the counter, playing a video game. Even the doorman dozes at his podium.

I slip behind the palm and scratch a finger against the gilded wallpaper until my nail feels a groove. Damn, there is a door here. I push lightly and then bash my hip into it. Nothing moves. Intellectually, I know the door opens from the inside, but a guy can hope.

They're already ten minutes late. If it gets to fifteen, I'll get Santino to send someone to cover my position, and I'll blast to the library. Patting my pocket to check my newly acquired knife is still there gives me a few drops of courage.

As I leave the dim corner, bubbles start to rise from the fountain. Shit. Did a teen prankster staying at the hotel with their folks dump dish soap into the water? It's happened before when troublemakers attempt to blame ghosts for such shenanigans. A foaming fountain draws attention we can't afford.

I sprint to the waterworks to see if I can perform any sort of damage control. Gripping the edge, I study the water and freeze. The cascade from the fountain's pinnacle down through a series of sculpted bowls stops flowing. In the bottom reservoir, bubbles agitate the surface, turning it neon blue.

Ghost blue.

The moment I touch a finger to the water, it calms shining like mirror glass. The sight beyond brings a rush of memories from the night Beatrice and I saw Tressa trap Caliwood ghosts in her enchantress prison of ice. A mob of horrified faces silently scream at me.

"What's wrong? Can you tell me where Beast and Maisie are?"

The faces swirl with bobbing mouths and desperate expressions. Beast is the one who speaks with them not me. Instead of a question, I blurt. "Show me Beast."

In an instant, the ghosts fade, leaving a single image in the fountain.

Beast.

She lays on the carpet next to the library table, one hand gripping the edge, the other clutched to her chest. Her face contorts with effort to pull herself up. She's suffering or harmed, or Heaven help me, something worse.

I don't wait to see more. Running like my ass is on fire, I charge into the elevator and press its highest stop. The trip can't be more than a minute, but it feels as slow as dragging my body through mud. Pushing through the barely open doors, I sprint down the hallway I swear doubled in length. My apartment hangs open. What the hell? I yank it closed.

I fly up the carpeted steps to the library and stop dead. There is no doorknob. Even the door itself has transformed to appear as just another panel in the wall. I kick at it again and again, ripping the edges of the wallpaper covering its upper half with my knife.

"Beast. Are you in there? Can you open the door?"

I press an ear to the door, hoping to hear her dear scratchy voice. Instead, a low guttural trill sounds inside the library. Panic chokes me. I'll break my damn leg if I keep kicking. Rushing to my apartment, I desperately search for anything to throw against the door. Nothing in the kitchen or living room fits the bill, and then I remember it. Beatrice's antique glass casement with the fire axe than used to adorn the hallways of the Caliwood.

I dash to the bed, praying she didn't take the treasure with her when she left me. Lying on my stomach I reach underneath and feel the metal corner of the case. Yanking it free, I raise the hammer and follow directions: *In case of fire break glass.* I turn my face away as I pulverize the case. The freakin' axe is hella heavy with a wicked blade on one side and a hook on the other.

Adrenaline is my friend as I bolt to the library door and start hacking. Ignoring the strains and pops in my back, I destroy the wood. Finally, I create a hole large enough to force my way through, throw the axe into the library, and burst in after it.

The room is dark as sin. Fireplace embers emit a near useless red glow, and every statue torch is cold and dead. The sign Beast told me that means the ghosts are elsewhere. Even in the scant light, I see the bookcase is thrown open, revealing Gothel and Tressa's apartment. Nothing moves or makes a sound within it. Even the low hum of the aquarium filter I once mistook for bad plumbing has ceased.

On the center of the library table, the tall glass dome holding Beast's songbook provides a meager glow to the room. The corner of a single page dangles from the binding. Within its weak radiance, I find her.

Beast's form curls on the floor. Her head tucks under a wing, knees pulled to chest. My dear one is the epitome of defeat.

"Beast," I cry and drop down next to her. When I touch her

wings, my hands spring back from searing heat. "Can you hear me, Beast?"

With brief, careful touches, I unfold her arms and hover over her face. "Oh, Beast. Please open your eyes. Tell me how to help you."

Cruel time skitters and pauses. I lay my palm against her cheek. It's much cooler than her body. Too cool. Lifeless.

I caress her beak with my thumb. "Oh, my darling Beast. What have they done to you?"

My eyes dart to the empty apartment, and I remember not only Maisie's tears but Zeli's . Tears that healed Justin Time's eyes after they were ruined in his escape from Gothel.

I dash to the cabinet where Beast stored the pink tear bottles. It hangs open and empty. At the end of the shelf is a single tiny sparkle. I dab a finger to it and feel the warmth of the magical tear.

Rushing to Beast, I search for any obvious wound to smear with the healing elixir. Testing the heat level, I rest my other hand over her heart. The skin and feathers are hot, but bearable. A sob escapes as I touch the roughness of puckered flesh. I smooth the tiny tear across her fresh scar. The shimmer evaporates, leaving no change at all.

Swallowing the horror of my imagination as to who or what inflicted this blight on Beast, I focus on her face as I replace my hand on her chest. I may be imagining it, but the faintest flutter of a heartbeat taps beneath my fingers.

"You possess a beautiful heart." I move my finger to gently stroke her lips. "You create beautiful words." My own hot tear sketches a path down my face. "The world doesn't understand what a treasure it has in you."

Words, as they often do, fail me. I'm shit at lyrics, so I use hers.

"Will you dare the climb at all,
If I swear, we'll never fall?
As one, we'll grasp sweet love divine,

When we dance together on the Hollywood Sign."

Taking this mysterious and wonderful creature in my arms despite the hot waves radiating off her body, I gently caress her lips with mine.

"Oh, my brave and magical friend. You may not want to hear the truth of my heart, but I'm going to tell you anyway."

I wish the challenge of my words will bring her back to me, but she's as still as the last exhale of daylight before the sun falls beneath the horizon.

"I love you, Beast. A heart I thought had forgotten its purpose, came alive when we made songs together. You took a Benedict Boyd who'd checked out on love and showed him how wrong he was."

I stroke her soft headdress of feather.

"I love nothing as much as you, my darling Beast."

As I rest my head against Beast's, the glow from the glass dome seems to brighten. A strange *pop* echoes within the songbook's casement. I watch as the last page tears loose from its binding and floats downward. As soon as it touches the wooden base, the whole damn dome explodes.

I shield my eyes against Beast's wing, but don't feel any shards of glass sprinkling around me. Instead, the library fills with near-blinding flecks of what could be golden stars. They swirl in a gentle whirlwind, searching until they find their way to Beast's body and encase her like a silken shroud. An invisible pressure eases me away from her.

I marvel at the delicacy of the light's movement. Am I witnessing the journey of a precious soul leaving the injustice of life behind to find a place willing to embrace all she is? I should hope that for my Beast, but I ache for her to stay with me. I want to love her and find a way for the world to accept and celebrate her the way I long to do.

A quiet voice rises from the corners of the room. I recognize Beast's warbly, scratchy screech. Oh, how I'll miss it.

As I scour her body for any sign the melodies are coming from this magnificent creature, the golden sheen surrounding her steadily collapses in on itself becoming smaller and smaller until it disappears, taking Beast with it.

"No." I reach for her, but it's too late. I whip my gaze around the library. Is this the work of the ghosts? "Bring her back, please." I fall to my knees, holding my hands out in supplication.

The only thing preventing despair, from making me crumble into a heap, is Beast's voice. I close my eyes and let the sound flow through my spirit. She sings the songs we wrote together, our mutual creations. I fling my arms to the side as if my action will allow her voice to run freely through me.

If I never open my eyes again, will I hear Beast's voice forever?

My body thrums with stuttering breaths, and sobs threaten to knock me off balance. I long to join Beast in her journey and not lose her.

The music and singer play on, but not as they began. The less than melodic tones of Beast soften and begin to change. I squeeze my eyes tighter and will the song not to fade away. A smooth, rich purr rushes through my bones, never missing a note of the song. Lyrics sung with a raw passion I've heard once in my life fill the room, reverberating off the polished wooden walls and floor.

I would know this voice from the space between the stars to the deepest depths of the sea.

Beatrice.

Fingers twine through mine and I clutch them. I know the shape of these hands, the contour of each palm.

Beatrice.

Still, I choose blindness. I will not open my eyes and break a spell of yearning fulfilled.

A woman's chest presses against mine. The vision wraps my arms around her. She runs fingers through my hair, then the echo of Beatrice takes my lips in a desperate kiss.

It's Beast's lips I taste. It's Beast I answer with my own urgent kiss. Beatrice, Beast, does it matter? I love both. I've lost both. This dream born of sorrow is a stark reminder of my failures. I end the kiss with a gentle parting.

Hands cup the sides of my face. "For heaven's sake, Bene*dick*, open your eyes."

The shock of Beatrice's voice shatters my will not to look. In my arms is a goddess in garage sale couture—a denim skirt covered in round multi-colored patches, topped off with an electric blue, short sleeved, button-down blouse with a *Betty's Bundts* logo splashed across a breast pocket, and the *fait acoompli*, a black felt top hat.

My voice is a strangled whisper. "Beatrice?"

Her smile is more beautiful than any single snapshot in my memory. Strands of short, cropped, crème brûlée-colored hair stick out from under the brim of her hat and catch light from the now blazing chandelier.

Beatrice strokes the sides of my face, never taking her gaze from mine. "Yes, Benedict. Yes." She drops a circle of kisses around my lips in the way she always loved to tease me.

A cry of joy mingled with disbelief, bursts from me as I clutch her and run my hands over her body to convince myself she's really here.

"Oh, Ben, I love you with so much of my heart, none is left to protest. I'm sorry I broke us."

I pull back to look at her. "Stop Beatrice. It's my fault. I should have jumped into the pool." I take her chin in my fingers. "I will always jump into the pool for you."

She jerks her chin from my grasp. "You stop and listen to me."

Her familiar bossiness snaps me out of any remnants of belief this is a dream. "It is you, isn't it?" I pinch her arm, and she yelps.

"What are you doing?"

"Pinching you to make sure this is real."

Beatrice grabs my fingers and forces me to deliver a wicked pinch to my biceps. "It's real. I'm real. You're real."

"When did you come back? How did you find me?" A wave of

guilt smacks into me. Did Beatrice see me with Beast, hear my vows of love?"

Beatrice captures my hands and kisses them. "You found me, my love." When I attempt to continue with my mountain of questions, she lays a finger on my lips. "You gave a devastated harpy the joy of making music with you again."

My mind reels. "Harpy?"

She smooths my hair and rests her forehead against mine. "You looked beyond Beast to the beating heart within the monstrous form. My monstrous form. You saved me, Ben." Beatrice pulls me to my feet and then gathers the pages of the songbook scattered across the cherry oak surface. "You dared to fall in love with Beast before the last page fell."

I ease in behind Bea and wrap my arms around her. "I fell in love with Beast long before that."

She turns in my arms to face me. "Beast's lyrics were always me, trying to find my way back to you."

"Beatrice, how did you become Beast?"

My love lowers her gaze. Her creamy skin flushes dark pink. "The night of the audition when you chose me over Tressa Divine. Do you remember what happened?"

I pull her closer as if I need to protect her. "As if I could forget the trapped ghosts and her freaky threat. We wrote it off as the mother of Caliwood hauntings and Tressa being insane."

"We were wrong. She's an enchantress, Ben, a real one. Her threat was a curse." Beatrice recites the exact lyrics of what Tressa Divine shouted at us on that fateful night.

"This dream you grasp with rising joy,
The pair of you will soon destroy.
What once shone bright as future charm,
Will sever bonds and spirits harm.
A curse I summon soon will rise,
When shattered hearts swear to despise.

May pain surround you fated pair,
For slights delivered, souls despair.
While one shall travel forth alone,
The other shackled tooth and bone.
Do not deny that chance does dwell,
Despite sweet torment hope hides well.
Until the day when words reveal,
Broken oaths with truth may heal."

Mind. Blown. Tressa's use of curse was literal not sour grapes metaphoric. Our fight, the harsh words we spoke to one another turned Beatrice into Beast.

Shackled tooth and bone

It wasn't until I said fuck all and told dying Beast I loved her, that my Beatrice returned. Curse me again for not manning up to tell Beast how I felt as soon as I realized it. I let the sting of her rejection mute my truth. New fear grabs me by the balls.

"Does Gothel know who Beast is, I mean that you're Beast?"

A look of utter bafflement crosses Beatrice's face? "Gothel? As in Grant Gothel? What on earth does he have to do with Beast?"

It's my turn to swallow a dose of confusion. "Gothel and Tressa hid in those apartments." I gesture to the opening in the bookcases.

Beatrice's eyes open wide. "Holy shit." She pulls free of my grasp and walks into Dark Vinyl Artists' HQ. "I had no clue this was here." Her gaze takes in the alcove where the bizarre evil fish aquarium used to be, and she fans the air in front of her nose. "Who cooked fish in a microwave?"

Reality hits like plowing into a stone wall. Beatrice doesn't share Beast's memories. Her only remaining clarity is Tressa turning her into the harpy, and my words yanking her free of the curse. Maisie, Gothel, her ghost friends, are wiped from her consciousness. Now I truly understand Beast's opposition to my advances. If I managed to profess my love, Maisie would cease to exist for her. This remarkable woman in the form of Beatrice or

Beast is a rare spirit. She gambled her existence for the sake of an innocent child.

Beatrice slides an arm around my waist. "Ben, what's wrong?"

I gather her close. "Nothing and everything, my perfect Beatrice." We stand for a long moment, reveling in the feel of one another. What was lost is found, but not without a price.

Maisie.

I will tell her everything. Never again will a thought in my head or a whim in my heart be kept from my love.

"Beatrice—"

"Benedict—"

We both smile as we take our first step back in sync.

"Beatrice, there is a lot to tell you. I'm not going to lie. It will break your heart, but I swear never to leave your side while you deal with everything."

A deep crease forms between her light brown brows. "Do I absolutely need to know?"

"You deserve to know." I smile gently.

"I did something awful didn't I?" She clasps her hands beneath her chin.

"Actually," I say, claiming her hands. "You're the hero of the story."

She trembles in my grasp. "Will it change anything if you don't tell me until the morning? I want to be with you tonight, Ben. I need to get lost in the joy of you and me."

Pulling her head to my chest, I kiss the soft skin behind her ear. There's nothing we can do to change the outcome of tonight's unbelievable events, the death of Beast, the rebirth of Beatrice, or the loss of Maisie. I'll text Santino and break the tragic news of our failure. He'll pass the terrible news along. Once the sun rises, Beatrice will join in our sadness, but I can give her tonight. I owe her one night of the happiness she seeks.

"Anything for you, Beatrice. Anything." I take her hand and lead her back into the library to the shredded door. "Let's go home."

Beatrice twirls into me and nuzzles my neck. "That's the sweetest thing you've ever said to me Bene*dick*."

"First of many, starting with I love you, Beatrice Sharpe." I crush my lips to hers. This time, I celebrate the mingled taste of Beast and Beatrice. Unlike Beast, Beatrice opens to me, and we lose ourselves in familiar, beloved kisses.

Beatrice grabs my ass and snugs her hips to mine. I lift her up off the floor as I deepen the kiss. It's strange once again being taller than the last woman I kissed.

With a pop, her lips leave mine, and she points to the edge of the library carpet. "Is that my axe?"

25

LOVE ALFRESCO

IT'S HARD TO LEAVE THE APARTMENT. THE TRUTH OF MY LIFE AS Beast is too overwhelming. Benedict and I collaborated on the cover story of how Beatrice Sharpe licked her wounds after the epic Battle of the Caliwood on a remote Scottish island writing a catalogue of new songs. Santino and Hero come by every day to fill in gaps. Their portions of this bizarre tale help me understand the strange part I've played over the last year. I'm heartbroken for Hero at the possibility her father, Leonato, still may be under Tressa's influence. When the boss visited to welcome me home, I made him nervous with my piercing looks and bizarre questions as I tried to sense any trace of Tressa. He didn't stay long.

Alfie and a much-chagrined D.G. made an appearance to gush over me, insisting I rejoin the band. D.G. offered to quit due to his part in nearly killing Hero and Santino's future. Ben was super pissed and nearly let our drummer go. Being the generous soul that he is, my man offered to reassess if D.G. did a stint in rehab for his relationship with oxy. The biggest surprise of my reintroduction of being Beatrice was learning Ben had finally kicked Claude to the curb. Surprise and satisfaction. That ass always was a sour note in the band. He never accepted me, but I played nice since he and Benedict had history.

Zeli was the brave soul who held my hand and told me about Maisie. Ben thought such a tragic chapter would be best coming from the woman who'd endured Gothel for most of her life, but in the end, helped to orchestrate her own freedom. Zeli's assurance that the worst part of the tear harvesting was a spacey kind of fatigue eased a tiny bit of my guilt for failing the kid. The pop diva and her husband, Justin Time, vowed to commit resources to continue the hunt for Gothel and Maisie.

If I'm truthful, fear is the biggest force keeping me wrapped in my color-clashy crocheted blanket. Grant Gothel is alive and made me do his dirty work with a kid who probably feels she's been abandoned by Beast. Tressa still on the prowl is equally disconcerting. On a gut level, I know everything Ben, Hero, and Santino told me is true. There's a constant buzz in my head like voices trying to bust free. I can't help but believe they hold missing pieces of Beast. Are they the ghost companions Benedict said I spoke of, trying to reconnect with me? He never met the ghosts, but swears they showed him Beast in the famed Caliwood fountain in time to save me.

While Ben slept last night, I left the apartment to visit the lobby and stare into the rippling water of the fountain, hoping to see any sign that might jar my memory loose. A relentless ache in my heart confirms these ghosts Benedict speaks of were dear to me. Some nights I dream of a handsome leading man, a perky blond pin-up girl, and a kindhearted chap in a tuxedo with a ringlet-headed girl attached to his hip. The dead giveaway these are my ghosts, pun intended, is their Hollywood Boulevard neon glow.

Benedict tells me of dreams he had while I was Beast, including dancing mirrors and sexy time between the two of us. He and I batted around hypnosis or visiting a psychic to hopefully draw lines between the dots of my memory to sketch a more complete picture.

There is a portion of my memory shining as clear as a crystal—

the lyrics Beast wrote. I remember creating every word because they were love letters. Beast and I are forever connected through expressions of our love for Benedict. I keep the pages from the enchanted songbook on the stand next to the bed. Every night, I read one of Beast's songs to Benedict before we make love and hold each other until we fall asleep.

A gust of warm evening Hollywood breeze invites itself into the apartment, reminding me I have a date. Benedict waits for me on the rooftop.

After dressing in ankle-high, zebra print boots, the turquoise vinyl shift dress Flo and Edie sent as a welcome home gift, and my signature top hat, I leave the apartment and head for the library. Leonato had a new door installed and granted the band permission to use the space as a rehearsal studio. He wanted to clear out the statues left behind, but we voted against him. They lend the room a cool, funky vibe I'm not willing to let go of. The apartment behind the bookcase is sealed off until Leo brings the place up to code. I suggested to Ben maybe we could take it over as our new digs, but he refused with such vehemence, I didn't press. It's a shame to waste a juicy hidden nest.

Crossing the room, I absorb the renewed energy of the library. The first time Ben dragged me through here, I was terrified, but now it feels like an extension of home. In an alcove near the fireplace, Ben fashioned a cozy writing nook for me to spin my lyrics.

The door at the bottom of the roof stairs is gone. I cross through the empty frame and climb to the top step. As Benedict requested, I knock loudly.

"Beatrice?" he calls from the other side of the door.

"Have you invited more than one woman to your rooftop boy's fort?"

"Not tonight," he quips back.

"Thank goodness. That could be awkward."

He cracks the door and his arm snakes inside. "Take my hand and close your eyes."

I slip my fingers through his and give my full trust to the love of my life. He leads me through the doorway onto the cheap imitation parquet flooring. Circling behind me, he pulls me against his chest and covers my eyes with one hand so I don't peek.

I was totally going to peek.

His lips graze my ear as he sings.

"Take my hand and come with me
To a place neither you nor I have seen.
Hillside magic we will find
When we dance together on the Hollywood Sign."

Ben slides his hand away from my eyes and wraps it around my waist. "Open."

The familiar rooftop where Benedict insists Beast looked down upon from the H in the Hotel Caliwood sign is transformed into a glittering fairyland. White gauzy fabric infused with bits of silver appear to float across the floor of the band's getaway. The ratty old couch has been replaced with a huge bed, sporting white iron head and footboards, and covered in a fluffy wine-colored duvet.

Benedict follows my astonished gaze. "The deep red color reminds me of Beast's gorgeous headdress feathers."

Strands of clear twinkle lights flow beneath the white gauzy floor covering and drape over the bed. The red neon of the Hotel Caliwood sign covers the scene in a rosy blush.

"Oh, Ben," I gasp as I discover the raised platform near the edge of the roof. Written in more twinkle lights on its face are the words: Hollywood. On the hillside behind, the letters of the real Hollywood Sign shine brighter than I've ever seen.

He scoops me into his arms and sets me onto the platform, leaping up to join me. Under the stars in the Hollywood sky, I slow dance atop our personal Hollywood Sign with my Benedict.

"My darling, Beatrice. I vow never to be casual about the value of our love. It is my joy and my reason for being."

"Ditto, Benedict. We may be a pair of flawed souls, but love will never be one of our shortcomings."

Benedict reaches into his pocket, and I hear a click. The letters of Hotel Caliwood wink out, and we truly dance between stars below and above. His lips trail down my neck and along the scoop neck of my dress. He grasps my hips and drops to one knee.

Guessing at the purpose of his travels, I tug up the sides of my dress to invite his kisses to a more personal destination. To my surprise, he pulls my skirt into place and takes my hands in his.

"Beatrice Sharpe, my heart never wants to be farther than a beat away from yours. Will you consider making music and love with me for the rest of your life?"

I stare down at my rockstar lover and smile. "Huh, for a moment I mistook you for Benedict Boyd." Even in our tender moment, my sharp tongue is part of the magic. "But that fool never even sent me flowers."

"Maybe not, but this Benedict brings you the stars." He points to the sky. "Shall I name them?"

This is the man who learned the names of stars to impress a one-night stand he might never see again. Neither of us realized at the time that one special night marked the beginning of our destiny. I shake my head, tipping a tear from the corner of my eye. "Benedict, you are every star in my sky."

"Make me a married man, Beatrice."

Taking in the sight of my dearest love, a fragment of memory flashes of seeing him at this angle from a different set of eyes, larger ones with a reddish tint. It gives me unexpected comfort to believe Beast is not lost, but happy within Beatrice. "If it will put you out of your misery, I will marry you, Benedict."

"I didn't dare choose a ring without you. Will this do for now?" Ben stands and from his pocket, pulls the bright turquoise feather that adorned my top hat the night we performed at the Band Beat

Awards before our legendary fight. He slips it into the slot on my top hat where it belongs. "I love you, Beatrice."

"Say it again."

"I love you, Beatrice." He kisses the edge of each eyelid. "I love you, Beatrice." His lips tap the corners of mine. "I love you, Beatrice."

I throw my arms around him and devour his mouth. I love the tip of his tongue tasting my skin. I love the rising level of heat in his kisses and the way he grazes teeth gently across my lips. I love the moaning breath he sends to meet mine, sweetening the air between us. I love the grip of his fingers behind my knee as he hitches my leg over his hip. I love the hard length of him imprinting into the vinyl of my dress through his tight jeans.

He catches me as I jump up into his arms and attempt to strangle him with my legs. I nip at the side of his neck, and he rocks his body against mine.

"Beatrice," he groans. "Give me a shot to knock that hat off your head."

With a flip of my wrist, I bat at the underside of the brim and send my top hat and its feather flying across the rooftop. "Beat you to it."

Benedict sets me on my feet and spins me. With those talented guitar-playing fingers, he slowly pulls down the body-length zipper of my dress until the naked skin of my back and everything below is exposed. As I gaze across the magical landscape of Hollywood Boulevard, he slides warm, calloused hands inside the vinyl around my sides to cup my breasts, pulling me back against his chest. I suppose my lack of bra and panties could be considered an engagement gift.

His fingers lightly stroke and tease as my breasts ache for him to be rougher. I press on his hands from the other side of turquoise vinyl to encourage him. Message received. His relentless attention ignites sparks that travel down a superheated pathway in my body to the very places that must have yearned for Benedict home when

Beast was my reality. As Beatrice, I pulse and burn to feel my lover's touch between my thighs.

Ben extends his arms forward, flipping the dress off my body. He walks his fingers along my sides to my ass where he delivers a gentle smack. "Someone came prepared to get lucky tonight."

I grab his hand and nibble kiss his knuckles. "This rooftop has never failed me yet."

"And it won't start now." Ben hops off the platform and holds out his arms to lift me down.

The moment I'm on equal footing with him, I grab the bottom of his T-shirt and tug it over his head. I run my hands across his pecs and twirl the soft hair of his chest around the tip of a finger. I'm feeling nice tonight, so I don't tug to give him the tiny burst of delicious pain that drives him to full power in an eye blink. I want to be tender and loving, sealing my promise of being his forever Beatrice.

My touch dances to every contour of his defined but not overdone abs. The man hums a note of satisfaction. He backs up, leading me to the bed as my hands travel lower and attempt to slip into the waistband of his jeans. The damn things are too tight. I fumble to undo the buttons of his fly but can't successfully maneuver that either. I rise on tiptoe to whisper in his ear as I rub him none too gently through his jeans. "You didn't come prepared to get lucky."

"Oh, I'm prepared." Benedict squirms away from my sexy torture to sit on the edge of the bed. He shimmies out of those skinny jeans in record time. When his happy cock springs free, I stand between his legs and offer him a much slower brand of attention, using my own talented guitar-playing fingers.

"You really are quite marvelous," I say, stroking him from root to tip as I lean in to drop whisper kisses across his shoulder.

He tilts his head to look at me, eyes sparkling with highlights from the strings of white twinkle lights. "What was that lovely Beatrice?"

"You heard me, Bene*dick*."

"Did I?" In a flash, he drops onto his back, pulling me on top of him. He nudges my shoulders, encouraging me to sit and position my slick and swollen parts against his marvelous self. I lock my knees on either side of his hips and slide along his length, the ready parts of me surging closer and closer to a yummy payoff.

"How marvelous am I, Beatrice?" groans Benedict as he adds his fingers to the party.

A whip-smart answer tingles on my lips, but for once it never makes it out. The primed coil inside me springs apart. I scream Benedict's name loud enough for all of Hollywood Boulevard to hear.

Turning wonderfully flimsy, I lay back, starfishing on top of Ben's legs, my core still positioned near his hard heat. While riding the luscious post-shimmies of my release, the refreshing breeze tickles my quivering nerves instantly initiating another wind up.

Benedict shifts beneath me, and I barely register the rip of the package as he dons his costume for our second set. Without disturbing the decadent relaxation of my position, Ben replaces the cool breeze soothing my lady parts with hot lips and a scorching tongue.

"I could get drunk off the ripe taste of you, lovely Beatrice." He works me so thoroughly I teeter on the edge of another plunge. "Fill my glass, love," he growls. His words blow me apart. Maybe he's not shit at lyrics after all.

Giving me no time to recover, he lifts me into his arms and thrusts his tongue past my lips, encouraging me to suck and take his kiss deeper. While kissing his way between my breasts, Benedict rests my head atop a soft pillow and covers my body with his.

"I love you, Beatrice." He opens me with gentle fingertips then pushes his cock inside. "I love you, Beatrice."

I raise my hips to take him in farther.

"I love you, Beatrice." His voice grows raspier with each

proclamation. His hands cover my ass, and he brings me harder against him. "I love you, Beatrice."

"I love you, Benedict. I love you, Benedict. Always. Always."

"Always," he answers. As he rocks into me, we turn the words of our love play into a duet. The passion of our harmony builds until we find the top of our range together in a screeching cry worthy of Beast.

After an encore or two, between sharing wishes for weddings and babies, we snuggle beneath the covers. Skin to skin. Heart to heart.

As the moon rises, a long shadow falls across the bed. I shiver and twist to see what has the gall to blot out our moonlight. In the distance, a huge cylindrical structure rises above the other building on Hollywood Boulevard. "What the hell am I looking at?"

A half-asleep Ben digs his chin into my shoulder to follow my eyeline. "Oh, the Emerald Spire," he says with a breathy voice and then turns on his side, pulling me against him.

I shake my head. "They actually built the thing." Faint memories of the monolith changing owners several times and delayed construction drift through my mind.

Benedict yawns. "It's touted to be an immersive destination experience with the usual hotels, over-priced retail, and full-blown amusement park to revitalize the boulevard. The new A-lister restaurant/nightclub Stalk is the cherry on top. Leo's already booked *Ben and the Boulevard Bunch* at the opening."

"Who?" I slap his shoulder. "I think you mean *B 'n B Plus Two*."

He slings his leg over mine and buries his lips in my hair. "Yes, my sweet Beatrice. That's exactly what I mean."

Despite the uneasy feeling of lying in the shadow of the Emerald Spire monstrosity, I manage to relax against the man of my dreams.

"Benedict?"

"Umm?"

"I've decided. We'll definitely take our kids on tour with us."

He smiles against my neck. "Anything you want."

"Benedict?"

"Umm?"

I reach back to tug his ear. "I know where I want to get married."

"Vegas?"

"No, no. I require a much bigger spectacle."

His lips move up to my ear. I can tell by his languid pace he'll need an intermission before we start another tune. With Benedict, I'm always ready to sing. "Anything you want, my high maintenance sweetheart."

"A wedding on the Hollywood Sign."

His laugh is a pleasant rumble as he sings.

"On H so high, we'll taste the sky.
Around the O our steps will glow.
A pair of Ls will kiss and tell.
Dear Y spins promises to fly.
W presents a view.
Where O and O brighten your soul.
Last, darling D frees dreams to be."

"Exactly," I say, leaning back to press a gentle kiss against my Benedict's soft puffy lips. As he starts to snore, I gaze up at the unlit letters of the Hotel Caliwood sign and try to remember what it was like to fly.

EPILOGUE

AURORA HERMAN PRESSED HANDS TO HER QUEASY STOMACH AS THE high-speed cylindrical elevator shot in express mode to the top of the Emerald Spire complex. They should install a Dramamine dispenser and airline sickness bags for the employees who had to travel like a bullet out of a gun to get to work.

She was what management referred to as a "cocktail magician" for Stalk, the premier restaurant and nightclub at the top of the Emerald Spire. Tonight is slotted for yet another brainstorming session to finalize themed cocktails for the drink menu.

Aurora had a list of proposals all paying tribute to Hollywood such as the *Hotel Caliwood Haunt*, a blackberry and lime infused vanilla whisky poured over a bed of tiny butterscotch beads that promise to fizz for the life of the cocktail, or the *Rampion Records Tower*, a frozen bed of champagne topped off with layers of pureed blood orange, strawberries, a peach/kiwi blend, and pulverized chilis to add a surprise kick.

Stalk hadn't even had its soft opening yet, and it was already sold out for a year and a half. It's the hottest ticket in town. Reservations for opening night were reselling on secondary ticket sites for upwards of five thousand dollars apiece. No surprise there, considering the talent line up for the big night. Justin Time and Zeli from Rampion Records, Chorda and Midas Lear from Golden Pipes, Rai Cloud from Cloudpath Music, The Mermaids, a sister group that rarely leaves their underwater concert hall, and *Benedict and the Boulevard Bunch* from Caliwood Inc.

No, wait. That band just rebranded back to B & B + 3 when Beatrice Sharpe reappeared from her celebrity vanishing act, a year after her legendary public fight with the other lead singer of the group, Benedict Boyd.

Aurora was more than willing to put up with nausea-inducing rocket ship elevators, spoiled celebrities, and management that never bothered to introduce themselves but sent lackeys to the Stalk meetings and trainings for one reason. Once a month, Stalk would audition amateurs to be the warmup act for Tuesday night's professional talent. The gimmick was an homage to the now defunct Summer Number One professional vs. amateur singing competition Rampion Records used to host every June.

Aurora planned to claim one of the first coveted open mic spots.

Finally, the elevator eased to a stop. Its curved glass wall slid in on itself to create a nearly three hundred and sixty degree opening. Instead of stepping onto the plush emerald carpet leading to Stalk's entrance, Aurora arrived at a dimly lit landscape of what could loosely be interpreted as a dark forest.

She must have mumbled the floor number to the elevator instead of speaking clearly, sending her to this funky destination. Aurora accepted voice command was status quo in the age of smart phones, smart watches, smart cars, smart homes, etc. Still, a good old fashioned elevator button got you where you wanted to go.

When she turned to step back into what the employees loving called the *turbo tube*, the glass door was already *whooshing* into place. This was not an elevator where you stuck your hand in to reopen the door unless you wanted to get that hand sliced off. With a *huff*, she faced the chrome post next to the elevator, and spoke.

"Pick up for Stalk."

A cheery automated voice answered her. *"Estimated arrival time nine minutes and twenty-eight seconds. Please stay behind the emerald glitter circle while you await your ride."*

Aurora groaned. The damn elevator must be heading down to gather other employees. Even on ear-bleeding speed, it took a good ten minutes to go back and forth between Stalk and street level. The central lift was the only one in use until opening. Once the Emerald Spire threw its doors open to the public, the ring of exterior elevators with killer views of Hollywood would go operational as well.

A flicker of light off the glass cylinder of the elevator shaft caught Aurora's eye and she whipped around to stare into the fake forest. Eight minutes of snooping would allow her to discover a little about the place and left plenty of time before she had to return to toe the emerald circle.

As soon as she stepped beneath the boughs of one of the trees, it began to glow a faint silver. Aurora pressed a tentative hand against the bark and twinkling pinpoints of golden light trickled up until they outlined every leaf.

"Wow." The tree was breathtaking. It looked sculpted from real gold and silver.

Off to her left, Aurora swore there was another flicker of light, but when she turned, it vanished .

At the edge of the brushed stainless-steel circle surrounding the elevator, several paths led into the trippy forest. Aurora braved a single step onto the path next to the shimmering tree she'd brought to life. The moment her toe touched the dark road, it flashed so brightly, she had to cover her eyes. The blaze settled quickly. Aurora sucked in a breath.

Before her, a meandering trail of diamonds twinkled beneath a sheet of thick glass. The undersides of still dark branches and leaves caught the path's shimmer, giving the illusion they swayed with elegant shivers. The diamond path's brightness beckoned to her as if to say, *"Take the next step."*

The foot Aurora rested atop the diamonds began to tingle, and she quickly yanked it off. As soon as she did, sounds that could be quiet giggles or merely the tinkling of bells erupted from several places deep in the trees.

Aurora took a few steps away from the unlikely woods toward the known quantity of the elevator. As soon as she was no longer within the arms of the forest, it returned to darkness. The tree she'd touched lost its light and the diamond path shifted back into a dark brown smear.

Not being the timid sort or easy to freak out, Aurora reapproached the tree and repeated her actions. Once again, it glowed with precious metal elegance. A tap on the path spilled diamonds across the darkness. This time she braved steps along the diamonds. Cup-shaped petals of aquamarine popped on like Christmas lights to line the pathway.

This place was delightful. Aurora grinned as she looked around at the shapes of other dark treasures waiting to be ignited by her touch. Just then, the warning chimes of the approaching elevator broke the silence.

"*Estimated arrival time thirty seconds. Please stay behind the emerald glitter circle while you await your ride.*"

Reluctantly, Aurora skipped out of the forest to catch the elevator. As expected, her lack of presence shut the light show down. She searched the chrome post next to the lift to note the floor number so she could return and explore further, but there was nothing to indicate where she was. Had they not finished marking all the floors? Maybe this one wasn't going into operation at the get-go. She'd ask her supervisor. It would be a blast to be one of the beta testers for such a fantastical attraction.

"*You will have twenty seconds to enter the lift, single rider.*"

Aurora had the urge to wave at the friendly sensor that calculated the passenger load. As promised, the elevator door slid away, and she stepped inside the car. A heartbeat before she was sealed within the cylinder, a flicker of light flitted from one tree to another. Instead of laughter, voices sang an unexpected melody.

"*We'll be waiting, Aurora.*"

Thank you for reading! Did you enjoy? Please add your review because nothing helps an author more and encourages readers to take a chance on a book than a review.

And don't miss EMERALD SPIRE, book five of the *Rockin' Fairy Tales* series, available now. Turn the page for a sneak peek!

You can also sign up for the City Owl Press newsletter to receive notice of all book releases!

SNEAK PEEK OF EMERALD SPIRE

Call me a "cocktail magician." Management wants us to use the kitschy, flirty title they've assigned to those of us designing fancy themed drinks for Stalk, the much buzzed about LA hotspot. The set-to-debut premier nightclub sits atop the Emerald Spire complex in the dead center of Hollywood. The only way to access the place at present is via the glitzy steel and frosted-glass elevator currently holding me prisoner.

What I'd give to possess even the tiniest bit of real magic to calm my queasy stomach as I white-knuckle it inside this ultra-high-speed cylinder of mayhem to clock in at work. Give me sky, clouds, the horizon, or anything natural besides the smear of floors screaming by.

Today is the final brainstorming session to finalize cocktails for Stalk's elite gala opening night drink menu. We have to lock it down so there's time to order the exotic ingredients we need from Europe and Asia.

I've prepped several new proposals for enticing sips that all pay tribute to Hollywood, such as the *Hotel Caliwood Haunt*, a blackberry and lime infused vanilla whisky poured over a bed of tiny butterscotch beads that promise to fizz for the life of the cocktail. The *Rampion Records Tower* boasts a frozen bed of champagne topped off with layers of pureed blood orange, strawberries, a peach/kiwi blend, and pulverized chilis to add a surprise kick.

I'm in major *impress the boss* mode. Stalk is my ticket to solid employment as long as I don't screw anything up during this final prep period leading to the club's whammo premier gala. One perk of the job is a front row seat for the big night's talent lineup. I'll be in the same room with Justin Time and Zeli from Rampion Records, Chorda and Midas Lear from Golden Pipes, and Rai Cloud and Azure Tempesta from Cloudpath Music. The real kicker is the hitmaking Benedict and the Boulevard Bunch from Caliwood Inc., who recently rebranded back to B & B +3 since vocalist Beatrice Sharpe reappeared after her year-long celebrity vanishing act.

Priceless inspiration for my own musical dreams.

I strum an invisible guitar to calm my nerves. I'm more than willing to tolerate nausea-inducing rocket ship elevators and spoiled celebrity clientele for an even bigger reason than a steady, well-paying job. Once a month, Stalk will audition amateurs to perform as warmup acts for the high-octane talent booked on Tuesday nights. Their professional vs. ammie gimmick is an homage to the now defunct Summer Number One annual singing competition Rampion Records used to host every June.

I'm determined to see my name, *Aurora Herman*, or maybe simply *Aurora* to come off more mysterious, on the club marquis as one of the first warmup singers. It's time to start taking musical risks and jettison the specters of my past that have constantly made me question my self-worth. A buzzing bee of anxiety flits through my chest, asking...

Do you have the courage?

I've always been better at building up others instead of myself. Before I have a chance to contemplate anxiety's question, the gut-twisting elevator eases to a stop. The frosted tint of its walls becomes transparent as the curved door swishes open.

My step falters at the sight beyond the elevator. When I step out, instead of the plush emerald carpet leading to Stalk's entrance, a shadowy forest greets me.

I turn back, but the damn turbo tube's glass door *whooshes* into place. This elevator is not one to stick your hand in to stop it from closing unless you're willing to bid your fingers farewell. With a *huff*, I growl an over-enunciated voice command into the chrome post next to the elevator.

"Pick up for Stalk."

A cheery automated voice answers. *"Estimated arrival time approximately fifteen minutes. Please stay behind the emerald glitter circle while you await your ride."*

Ugh. I shouldn't have been so hasty to leave the elevator. This central lift is the only one currently in use to reach the nightclub and other attractions with soft openings in progress. Any day now, the ring of exterior glass elevators with killer views of Hollywood will go operational, leaving this one as an exclusive and much quicker non-stop ride to Stalk.

A flicker of light off the glass cylinder catches my eye. I whip around to stare into the fake forest. Since I'm stuck here, why not snoop for a few minutes?

As soon as I step beneath the outstretched boughs of the closest tree, it begins to glow a faint silver. I press a tentative hand against the bark to sample its strange glittery texture. Twinkling lights like shiny flecks of metal trickle up its trunk until every leaf is outlined in dazzle.

"Wow." The tree looks sculpted from actual silver. It's breathtaking.

Off to my left, a second flicker of light draws my attention, but when I turn, it vanishes.

Strange.

I brave a single step onto the path that leads into the trippy forest next to the shimmering tree. The moment my toe touches the dark road, the ground flashes so brightly, I have to cover my eyes. In seconds, the blaze settles into a lovely, illuminated path.

Is this place ten ways of weird or wonderful?

Underfoot, a meandering trail of diamonds twinkles beneath a sheet of thick glass. The undersides of unlit branches and leaves beyond the tree I brought to life, catch the path's glimmer, giving the illusion they're bobbing in an invisible breeze. The diamond path's brilliance beckons as if saying, "*Take the next step.*"

Curiosity prompts me to oblige. As soon as I step fully onto the diamonds, my skin begins to tingle. When shivers bubble along my spine, I quickly yank my foot off the path. Sounds that could be quiet giggles or merely the tinkling of bells erupt from several places deep in the trees.

I rush away from the unlikely woods to the known quantity of the elevator. As soon as I'm no longer within the arms of the forest, the woods fade back into shadows. The tree I touched loses its light, and the diamond path degrades to a grayish blur.

A heaviness in my chest accompanies the dimness. I reapproach the tree and touch it again. Its glow of precious metal elegance returns. I brave a few steps along the path of trapped diamonds. The tingling resumes as before. This time it's more akin to a gentle tickle than a painful zap. As I venture farther, cup-shaped petals of shimmery teal pop on like a string of holiday lights to line the pathway.

This place is delightful. I make out outlines of other dark treasures that could be flowers or willowy trees. Pleasant sensations simmer in my chest, tempting me to awaken more of the forest with my simple touch.

"*Estimated arrival time thirty seconds. Please stay behind the emerald glitter circle while awaiting your ride.*"

Curse the elevator's timing. I'm powerfully drawn to linger in this discovery of mine.

Reluctantly, I skip out of the forest. My departure shuts down the woodsy light show. I search the chrome post next to the lift to note the floor so I can return and explore further, but there's no number listed. Odd they haven't finished marking the floors so close to the Emerald Spire complex's official opening. Maybe this attraction isn't going into operation at the get-go. I'll ask my boss, Mr. Cinnabar, about the forest. It would be a blast to be one of the beta testers for such a fantastical attraction especially if its managers are paying for the effort.

"*Rider, you will have twenty seconds to enter the lift.*"

As promised, the elevator door slides open. A heartbeat before I'm sealed inside, a tiny dancing light jumps from tree to tree like a manic firefly. Instead of giggly bells, voices sing in a quirky melody.

"*We'll be waiting, Aurora.*"

Don't stop now. Keep reading with your copy of EMERALD SPIRE, available now.

Don't miss EMERALD SPIRE, book five of the *Rockin' Fairy Tales* series, available now, and find more from Leslie O'Sullivan at www.leslieosullivanwrites.com

One last shot at stardom. One irresistible romance. One impossible choice.

In the spellbinding conclusion to the *Rockin' Fairy Tales* series, sassy pop singer, Aurora, has worked her way up from living on the streets to finally earning a chance at her big break. Working as a cocktail designer at Stalk, Hollywood's hottest new nightclub, she lands a shot to audition as a warm-up act for the club's glittering grand opening.

But Stalk hides more than velvet ropes and VIP lists.

Tek Goodfellow, her quirky co-worker, is no ordinary bartender— he's a mischievous fairy prince from a hidden realm that coexists alongside humans in the Emerald Spire entertainment complex. Drawn to Aurora's voice and fire, Tek offers to help as her vocal coach... and maybe something more.

As their partnership progresses and feelings deepen, Aurora's interaction with Tek and his world court dangers she never imagined. When Tek devises a risky magical plan to protect her, a golden career making opportunity may be lost.

And Aurora must make an impossible choice: **Follow her musical dream... or trust her heart to a fairy.**

Please sign up for the City Owl Press newsletter for chances to win special subscriber-only contests and giveaways as well as receiving information on upcoming releases and special excerpts.

All reviews are **welcome** and **appreciated.** Please consider leaving one on your favorite social media and book buying sites.

Escape Your World. Get Lost in Ours! City Owl Press at www.cityowlpress.com.

ACKNOWLEDGMENTS

I'm always happy to welcome new members to my Advanced Reading Team. Get a first peek at upcoming stories. Join the party HERE.

Thank you to my readers who share my never-ending love of fairy tales and happily ever after. Your reviews, messages, and social media posts make my heart do the happy dance. Love-love-love you to bits.

Lisa, oh, Lisa my amazing editor. Thank you for making my stories sing without hitting any sharps or flats.

I'm a forever fangirl of the wonderful works of S.C. Grayson, Megan Van Dyke, and Sarah Skilton who've generously contributed touching blurbs to the stories in this Rockin' Fairy Tales series.

So-much-gratitude to the hotbed of creativity and dream makers at City Owl Press. Tina, Yelena, Heather, Lisa, owl-eyed copy editors, the cover artists at miblart, and all the wildly talented fellow owl authors who continue to set the bar higher and higher, I'm so thankful for all your support and inspiration.

I'm the luckiest person in the world to have lovely friends and family that never cease to be enthusiastic about the products of my crazy imagination even if they skip the spicy parts so they can still look me in the eye without blushing. Hugs to Rich, John, Cameron, Melissa, Elizabeth, Stanley, Sidney, Chuck, Heidi, Karen, Bobby, Jon, Jane, Lizzy, Julie, Sarah, Katharyn, Shona, Diane, Laurie, Flo, Rob, Tiffany, Gwynneth, Trillian, Shannon, the Plum Canyon Book Club, and all my brilliant, witty, colleagues at Emblem Academy.

ABOUT THE AUTHOR

LESLIE O'SULLIVAN is the award-winning author of *Fae Destiny*, a romantasy series that explores the collision between the real world and the Irish Faerie realm. Her *Rockin' Fairy Tales* romantasy stories shine a new spotlight on favorite fairy tales set against the backdrop of a fictional Hollywood music scene. The completed *Behind the Scenes* contemporary romcom series peeks into the off-camera sizzle of a wildly popular Irish television drama. She's a UCLA Bruin with a BA and MFA from their Department of Theater where she also taught for years on the design faculty. Her tenure in the world of television was mainly as the assistant art director on "It's Garry Shandling's Show." Leslie is a voracious reader who loves to connect with other book lovers and indulge her fangirl side at cons.

www.leslieosullivanwrites.com

f facebook.com/leslie.osullivanauthor
○ instagram.com/leslieosullivanwrites
♪ tiktok.com/@leslieosullivanwrites

ABOUT THE PUBLISHER

City Owl Press is a cutting edge indie publishing company, bringing the world of romance and speculative fiction to discerning readers.

Escape Your World. Get Lost in Ours!

www.cityowlpress.com

facebook.com/YourCityOwlPress
x.com/cityowlpress
instagram.com/cityowlbooks
pinterest.com/cityowlpress

www.ingramcontent.com/pod-product-compliance
Lightning Source LLC
Chambersburg PA
CBHW051334020726
47501CB00007B/2078